Angel of Blades

By

M.G. Digby

Paperback ISBN: 978-1-61929-565-0
Hard Cover ISBN: 978-1-61929-567-4

Flashpoint Publications First Edition: February, 2025

Printed in the United States of America.

Cover design by TreeHouse Studio

www.flashpointpublications.com

Chapter One

Harlowe sat in her car and stared at the list in her hand. Blank. She sighed and rested her forehead on the steering wheel. She never thought working for a newspaper meant she'd start out selling subscriptions. Who even bought anything from door-to-door salespeople anymore? Harlowe scowled. For a fleeting second, she considered ripping the paper up and tossing it out the window, then calling Ronald Buckminster, aka "Bucky" aka "chief editor of the *Maritime Gazette*" aka Harlowe's boss and telling him where he could shove his subscription list plus all those stupid sample newspapers that were basically toilet paper with more steps.

Harlowe straightened her posture, shook her head, and took a calming breath. No, she had to try at least. Bucky had said as much in that annoyingly old-school chuckling way he had. He said it was to give her the chance to understand the newspaper "from the roots up." Whatever the fuck that meant. Even though she thought the whole subscription thing was bullshit, she wouldn't give up now. Harlowe hadn't spent all that time in journalism classes, plus busting her ass at the college paper to just up and quit on her first day at a real paper, and the *Maritime Gazette* fit in with her goals admirably.

The reason why she chose that paper was they had a great remote work policy, allowing her to live in the cottage she'd inherited from her unmarried and childless great-uncle. Instead of dying, he was off gallivanting around the world with his lifelong male companion who, strangely, never married either. The cottage was located just outside the small town of Brooksville, New Brunswick. It was the textbook definition of smack in the middle of nowhere, and Harlowe loved it. She'd only been there for three days. It would suck to start job hunting all over again, especially from such a remote location, so she decided to try her best.

That day Harlowe pretty much exhausted the small

population of Brooksville. She went around to the bowling alley, hit up the library, the diner, and the three antique shops—basically she visited every business in town plus knocked on a bunch of doors, and even chased after a few people wandering around the main drag. The most she got for her efforts was a free can of ginger ale from Nelly Gallant at the drugstore, which she suspected was out of pity. Harlowe balled her hands into fists, crumpling the list. She wasn't going to give up. Not yet. She had two options. One was to drive a few hours to Moncton, the other was…looming up in front of her.

Surrounded by forest, the tall concrete bunker peeked through the trees, almost hidden by the sky-seeking branches. She'd seen the bunker from her cottage. Technically it was her closest neighbor, and she was curious about who lived there. While the outside walls were weather-streaked and ancient, she'd seen lights from the windows. It was worth a shot. It wasn't like Harlowe had a lot of other places near her.

Case in point—in the time she'd been parked there, not a single car had passed by. The area was dead quiet. Harlowe peered at the sky. It was well into November, and the days were noticeably shorter. The first snowfall had yet to come, although that day the sky was low and heavy, which probably meant rain. She didn't have much time before the pale disc of sun vanished below the horizon. Harlowe didn't want to be on the road all night, especially if it rained, so the second option it was. With her luck, she'd probably end up walking into a sex dungeon that wouldn't even result in a story the "family oriented" *Maritime Gazette* would agree to publish.

Harlowe twisted the rear-view mirror to check she didn't have any smears of ketchup from the supermarket hotdog she had for lunch on her face and that her long hair wasn't a windblown mess. Once platinum like her namesake, over the course of her twenty-one years it darkened to a golden blonde with a hint of red in certain lights. She brushed back her bangs and clipped the straight lengths back more securely. After a moment of inner debate, she pulled out her lip gloss. She applied a shiny pink layer and made a kissy face at her reflection, then pulled a fierce scowl that dissolved into snickering at herself. She never really got into makeup. Harlowe considered herself more able to pull off cute than pretty. Slathering heavy colors on her face would make her look more like a clown than a cover girl. Definitely cute, though. Harlowe was small and slim, with deep green eyes and a slightly upturned nose. She got carded every single time she even went near the liquor store and she probably would for a long time to come. She grabbed one of the newspaper's free samples and stuffed it, along with the subscription list, into her backpack-style purse, which she slung over her shoulder.

Harlowe checked her outfit. She was in a work-appropriate light blue skirt and jacket over her blouse, with low-heeled pumps which weren't the best for forest walking but they'd have to do. Her destination wasn't too far from the road, and Harlowe was determined to at least leave her business card with the occupant of the mysterious bunker. She got out of the car and squared her slim shoulders, as if walking into a bar fight. She found the path and started on her way up the hill. Soon, the tall old-growth trees closed over her head and threw the forest floor into shadow. The path was overgrown and rocky, but she powered on. The brisk pace helped to offset the chill wind that cut through her jacket as if it wasn't there. Harlowe made good time until a rock caught her heel and she pitched into the bushes.

"Welcome to Earth Harlowe, ever heard of gravity?" Harlowe said aloud. She'd always talked to herself, a habit her parents called charming and everyone else "a lack of brain-mouth filter." She floundered around until she got her footing and waded out of the brush. She muttered not-polite words to herself as she brushed leaves and orange pine needles from her clothing. Luckily, Harlowe's butt took the brunt of the impact, and the forest floor was soft, so ultimately the only casualty of her fall was her dignity.

"They better get *two* subscriptions," Harlowe said. Her dream of following in the footsteps of Lois Lane and becoming an intrepid investigative reporter seemed very far away. The path came to an end. She stopped in her tracks and looked up.

"Oh wow."

From a distance, the bunker looked somewhat ominous; up close, the faceless, towering building gave off evil-lair vibes like a miasma. The path led directly to the front gate, rusted iron bars set into a high concrete wall that circled the bunker. A sturdy chain and padlock held them closed, only adding to the "keep out" aura. A metal door was set into the wall, a meter or so off the ground which seemed to be the mail-slot. The main building was a tall tower-like structure, with lower wings on either side that looked like they sank deep into the hill. There were a few windows, long, narrow slits like suspicious eyes.

No doorbell or welcome mat greeted her. There was no attempt at decoration or even identification. The only indication of life was a cardboard box sitting on the other side of the wall, just under the mail-slot. It bore the logo of a popular internet shopping site and was crisply clean, as if it hadn't been sitting there long. Harlowe peeked through the bars to try to get a name, but the angle and distance stopped her.

Harlowe frowned. She hadn't come that far to just give up and go home. There had to be a way to get in. She peered through the bars at the grounds. In stark contrast to the weathered concrete walls, the narrow garden was pristine and held a whimsical air of wonder. Cobbled paths meandered over the moss-covered land, which was surrounded by sculpted bushes. Some of them were cut into geometric shapes, others into what looked like complex molecules Harlowe only vaguely recognized from her school days. She grimaced, thinking of the overgrown and unkempt garden behind her cottage which was choked with brambles.

The grounds surrounding the bunker were dead silent. No birds roosted in the carefully maintained trees, no squirrels scampered over the soft moss. That, combined with the blank concrete walls, lent an inhospitable and cheerless aura to the place.

More than just being unwelcome, a feeling of intense sadness permeated the air. The silence around her added to the desolate feeling. Even the normal forest sounds seemed muted. Harlowe felt it like a weight on her, pressing her into the ground. There was somebody there who needed her. Nobody could live in that lonely place all alone forever. The intricate, scientific beauty of the garden spoke of a similarly complex soul. Harlowe ached with the need to know who had made such a unique landscape in such an inhospitable place.

First, she had to figure out a way to get in.

"Nothing to it but to do it," Harlowe said. She stood on her tiptoes and waved a hand, feeling like a dork but willing to try anything. "Hello, is anybody home?" Harlowe called out. No answer. She harrumphed to herself and called out again. Again, nothing. Stymied, she sat down on a boulder a few paces from the path. She pulled out her cell phone and stared at the screen, hoping for inspiration. A droplet of water hitting the screen startled her and she looked up. In the time she'd been there, the sky clouded completely over and it looked like it could pour at any moment.

"Shit, their box is gonna get ruined."

She jumped to her feet and pattered up and down in front of the wall a few meters in either direction. Once more, she tried the gate. The chain holding it closed had enough leeway that she thought she could squeeze through. By that time, fat raindrops were falling, making splashing sounds as they pelted through the trees on their way down. Muttering, Harlowe took off her backpack and squeezed through the bars sideways. She only had enough time to grab the box, which was surprisingly heavy and clanked a bit, and make a mad dash for the front door before the rain started in earnest.

Harlowe edged as far as she could into the overhang and knocked at the iron door.

The rain beat against her back. Harlowe twisted the doorknob. To her surprise, it turned in her hand. The door swung open and she stumbled into the bunker. She blinked into the dimness. The door closed behind her and cut off the wan grey triangle of light. The room was vast and cloaked in shadows. A few scattered lights on the faraway ceiling provided some illumination, but most of the room was in darkness. She carefully set the box down beside the door and took a cautious step inside.

"*Maritime Gazette,*" she called out. Her voice echoed in the cavernous room. She shivered and rubbed her arms. In a couple more weeks, that rain would be snow.

"Hello," Harlowe called out. She shrugged into her backpack and patted down her hair, which was hanging damply over her shoulders. "Is anybody home?"

The tapping of her shoes sounded very loud in the large room. On either side of her, massive steel shelves towered, filled with half-assembled machines and components. Banks of tools and welding equipment squatted between them. A few sheet-covered mounds lurked ominously. Whoever lived here, it seemed they were really into mechanics. Her journalistic mind whirled. What could they be making? It didn't seem like a drug lab or counterfeiting operation. In fact, the few recognizable pieces seemed to be streamlined body armor. There was something elegant, almost beautiful in the pieces. One of them caused Harlowe to stop and catch her breath. It was a breastplate, powerful and graceful and most definitely made for a person with feminine curves. She was so entranced with the piece that she didn't notice the dark figure until it solidified from the shadows only a few feet from her. Harlowe squeaked and whirled.

The figure was tall and lithe, all in black. An electric shimmer brought the figure to life, blue glowing patches illuminated the bodysuit that encased him? No, *her*—she was most definitely female-bodied. The bodysuit had the same elegant line of the body armor, but conformed to her curves instead of compressing them. More analogue than the other pieces, the material was leather-like, uncountable buckles and studs crisscrossed the surface. They wrapped around her powerful torso and thighs, as if desperately trying to reign in some destructive force. Long black hair hung over her shoulders like a cape, bangs fell across her face and obscured one eye. The visible one was a piercing silver-blue.

Harlowe couldn't breathe.

The stranger was as stunning as she was scary, possibly the most beautiful person Harlowe had ever seen. She was magnificent, with chiseled features and olive skin. Oddly,

Harlowe felt as if she knew this woman, but that was impossible. There was no way they'd ever met before. Harlowe was certain she would remember someone like that.

At any rate, she was not happy to see Harlowe. Her lips, full and a natural deep pink, were twisted into a snarl.

The figure clenched her fists and thrust out her arms. Three blades shot out from each forearm, clear like quartz crystals, slightly curved and deadly-looking. A blue glow streamed from between her clenched fingers and snaked over the blades, illuminating the cutting edges like a laser. A hum rose, building in volume along with the light. Fingerless gloves pulsed with blue, as if the light was blood running through her veins. She flexed her fingers and the blades moved in synch with them as if...Harlowe drew in a shocked breath.

"Those are your fucking hands?" Harlowe squeaked. For the first time, the armored woman looked directly at her. It seemed like that silver-blue gaze saw straight into her soul. She took a step toward Harlowe.

"No trespassing." The words were a low growl, quietly menacing.

"Okay, yeah, I'm totally on board with that. You know what? How about I just show myself out," Harlowe babbled while frantically backing away, hands held out in front of herself. She manufactured a laugh which sounded more like a hacking gargle. The woman matched every backwards step with a forward one. The light continued to grow brighter. Harlowe couldn't stop her mouth from talking. "I didn't mean to bother you, I can see you're quite busy with...whatever you're doing here. So yeah, I'm just going to—eep!" Harlowe's heel collided with the corner of a heavily laden shelving unit and she went down in a clatter. Above her, the shelf swayed and clanked. With a tired, metallic groan, the shelf tipped past the point of no return and began to fall.

Harlowe screamed in panic and covered her head with her arms. Heavy mechanical components crashed down around her, pieces smashed onto the floor, bolts and shards of glass exploded everywhere. She waited for the inevitable crash of the shelving unit on her.

Nothing happened. In the sudden silence, Harlowe uncurled and looked around. The floor was littered with stuff, but she was miraculously unhurt. Maybe not so miraculously. The shelf rested on the shoulders of the battle-suited woman. Her luminous eyes were squeezed shut. With a groan, she straightened and eased the heavy metal unit up. Once it was secure against the wall again, she staggered forward a step. With a gasp, she clawed at the wall and sagged against it, struggling to keep her balance. One hand was pressed to her forehead.

"Are you okay?" Harlowe asked. Her voice came out squeaky.

"Fine." The word was breathy and hoarse, as if she wasn't used to speaking aloud.

"You're not fine," Harlowe said. She placed her hands on her hips. "You're obviously in pain. You look like you could fall over at any moment now. I bet you've got a concussion. You need to go to the hospital."

Long black hair swirled as she shook her head. The woman groaned and grabbed at her head, cradling it in both hands. The long, wicked-looking blades gleamed.

"No hospital."

Harlowe huffed out a sigh. Of course. "Is there anybody else here who can take care of you?"

"No. I am alone."

The words brought such sadness to Harlowe's heart that her eyes welled up with tears. That confirmed her theory about the isolation of the occupant. She couldn't imagine how lonely it must be, living there away from everyone else in that drafty, cold bunker. Add to that being injured and helpless. Harlowe had to do something.

"That decides it," Harlowe said. "You're coming home with me."

The woman shook her head again. This time the movement sent her crumpling to her knees, where she stayed.

"I can't leave you here all by yourself," Harlowe said. She paused, then spoke in the softest, gentlest voice she could. "You're injured and unless you get comfortable and warm, you'll end up with bronchitis too. I feel responsible. It's my fault you were hurt. Let me take care of you.

Please?"

A long silence stretched out.

"Agreed." The word was barely above a whisper, but it lit a flame in Harlowe's chest.

"Don't worry about a thing," Harlowe said. She moved a half-step closer. "I'm as harmless as cherry pie. And you are, oh..."

Harlowe's face went warm when she ran her gaze over the woman's body. She was long-limbed and athletic. Even under the body armor, her curves were subtle but unmistakable. Harlowe mentally scolded herself and focused on watching the mysterious stranger stagger to her feet. She wondered if she should risk those blades by ducking under the woman's arm to support her. The woman solved the problem by straightening up by herself. Slowly, haltingly, they made their way to the door.

"I'm Harlowe Tremaine, by the way." Harlowe grinned. She was elated the mysterious woman actually let her help. It felt good to be trusted. She wanted the responsibility. Harlowe said, "Nice to meet you. I'd offer to shake hands, but..."

Maybe it was her imagination, but the woman's lips curved up the slightest at that.

"Edwyn," she said. "Tatum Edwyn."

Harlowe glowed. "That's such a cool and nice name. Tatum sounds so butch, it really suits you. Do people call you Tate? How about Ed? You can call me Harlowe, I don't really have any nicknames except sometimes my dad calls me 'punkin' for some reason. They named me after this actress who—"

"Harlowe," she said in a strained voice. "Please be quiet."

"Absolutely, not a peep. I can do that," Harlowe gushed. In the woman's—in Tatum's— husky voice, her own name sounded sexy. Like her tongue was caressing it. What would it feel like to be pressed against that tight body, to be held in those strong arms? What was she like under that suit? Harlowe stopped in her tracks and shook her head to clear the unwanted, but very hot, thoughts. Harlowe glanced guiltily at Tatum before she scampered on ahead.

Chapter Two

"We're home," Harlowe said, ushering Tatum into the living room. She got a burst of nerves. Had she accidentally left something embarrassing lying around? A quick glance revealed the room was free of random panties and she distinctly remembered her one little toy was safely stashed in its case in her room. Harlowe's great-uncle Florian had cleared out all of his (and his "friend" Rockwell's) personal items before they left on their grand adventure three months previously. The room was tidy and furnished simply with a solid oak coffee table and long, brown velvet-upholstered sofa. The carpet was worn in places, but it, and the wood-paneled walls, were clean and tasteful, if lacking in amenities and decoration. Harlowe's new TV had been delivered and installed just that morning, but besides that, the walls were bare. She hadn't even gotten around to unpacking her small collection of family photos yet.

Tatum collapsed onto the sofa and lay there, unmoving. During the short car ride back to Harlowe's cottage, she hadn't spoken. She seemed naturally withdrawn, almost feral. How long had she been alone in that cold, lonely bunker? Harlowe ached for her. She wanted to warm Tatum and feed her nourishing meals, talk to her, maybe even see that tiny, elusive smile bloom for real across her austere features. The silent woman fascinated her. Fascinated and attracted her. Not that Harlowe would do anything about that. Tatum was probably straight; this wasn't college anymore where you couldn't swing a cat without hitting a lesbian.

Even in college in the bustling metropolis of Toronto, Harlowe hadn't swung much of anything. She was too driven to finish her studies to explore the delights of Church and Wellesley and she didn't give off strong enough gay vibes to stop guys from continually trying to hit on her. Their ham-fisted and often aggressive approaches took away most of Harlowe's desire to interact romantically with other people, and her toy took care of the rest.

Now, she had an injured guest to take care of. That had to take priority over her own childishly infatuated musings.

"Let me get you some acetaminophen," Harlowe said. She was halfway across the room when she stopped in her tracks. "Wait, is it okay to give that to people with a concussion? I can't remember," Harlowe fretted aloud. She raced into the spare bedroom where she'd put most of her stuff and frantically dug through one of the boxes with one hand while her thumb scrolled her phone's screen.

"Gotta make her comfortable," Harlowe muttered while scrolling more. It seemed the main treatment was rest and time, but not too much rest. Harlowe sat back on her heels and chewed on her lower lip. She wondered how long her houseguest would need before her condition improved. She'd need fluids, some pain meds, and somewhere to lie undisturbed for a long time. Maybe a water bed would be good for her. Harlowe slapped herself on the forehead. Brilliant idea, dumbass! Until they got her out of that suit, a waterbed was the last place she should be. Harlowe managed to put together a care package with headache medicine, cold compresses, and some bottled water before she barreled back out to the living room.

Tatum hadn't moved. She looked extremely out of place in the cozy living room, in her stark black battle suit and glowing blades. But she was in pain and Harlowe wanted to take care of that.

"Can you stand?" Harlowe asked.

Tatum nodded, then groaned and pressed a hand to her forehead.

"Don't nod, use your words." Harlowe crossed her arms over her chest and glared at the battle-suited figure.

"Sorry," she said. She levered herself up, supporting her weight by grabbing onto the sofa. Harlowe reached out automatically to help. Tatum flinched, holding her arms close to her body. The blades jutted out for a moment, before she forcibly relaxed.

"Um, how about I get you something to sleep in?" Harlowe offered. "You might want to take off that suit thing, you know, to relax a bit?"

"No. Not yet."

"Okay," Harlowe kept her tone light. "First things first, let me show you to your room."

She trotted ahead of Tatum, glancing over her shoulder from time to time, to make sure she hadn't collapsed or run off or anything. The master bedroom was on the first floor, separated from her own by a walk-in linen closet and a small washroom adjacent to the spare room. It was decorated in the same simple but tasteful style as the living room, with a stately Queen-sized bed and a stained oak dresser. A comfy armchair sat in front of the window, which looked out over the backyard. On a clear day, you could see all the way to Tatum's concrete bunker. In the lingering drizzle and fading light, nothing was visible beyond the large hedges that surrounded the garden, which looked worse than usual, choked with weeds and overgrown. Her great-uncle told her it was their lack of ability to keep up with the grounds that was one of the deciding factors in giving up the cottage.

Harlowe put the things she'd gathered down on the bedside table. She turned on the small lamp by the bed before she drew the curtains.

With trembling hands, Harlowe fluffed the pillows and pulled back the comforter. Tatum edged into the room and stood with her back to the wall. She looked pale and drained. Harlowe had never had a concussion, but she imagined it wasn't fun. Tatum being on high-alert wasn't helping either.

"Welcome to your room at the Tremaine mansion," Harlowe said blithely. "The mattress and bedding are all new, courtesy of my parents. There's a private bathroom through that door, help yourself to a toothbrush and towels and whatever else. If there's anything you need, just give me a holler."

Tatum remained standing, unmoving. The multiple buckles on her suit gleamed in the warm lamplight.

"Anyway, I'm down the hall, right next to the linen closet," Harlowe said. "Um, so that's it. Do you think you could eat something?"

Tatum turned her head sharply to one side, groaned

and staggered.

"Words." Harlowe planted her hands on her hips.

"I just need to rest."

"All right, but don't hesitate to let me know if you need anything." Harlowe swept into a curtsey in her slightly scruffy work suit. "I aim to please."

This time, Tatum looked directly at her and one side of her lips twitched up. Harlowe drew in a breath. One small victory. With her heart singing, Harlowe gently backed out of the room and went into the tiny kitchen cubby off the living room. Her thoughts were full of the stunning, mysterious, and probably extremely dangerous person camping out in her cottage.

Humming a cheerful tune, Harlowe chopped up a bunch of veggies and grilled them up in her trusty frying pan.

In her final year of college, Harlowe was so tired of cafeteria food and the lack of privacy in the dorms, she rented a tiny self-catered room in an old estate that had been converted to student housing. With the help of her Korean landlady, Mrs. Che, Harlowe had learned to cook fairly well, if simply.

The cottage's kitchen was too small for a table, but it had a wooden breakfast bar equipped with two tall, wooden chairs. Harlowe had always wanted to have her own home, and to that end, she'd accumulated a collection of dishes over the years. The cupboard was filled with handmade bowls, souvenir and joke mugs for every occasion, colorful plates of every size, and even a vintage Willow Ware platter she found at a flea-market.

Once the veggies were done, she threw in some noodles and added a dash of sesame oil. Harlowe wondered if she should set some aside for her guest, but judging by the pallor of Tatum's face, she had to be feeling pretty bad. If she wanted something later, Harlowe had lots of stuff in the freezer that for a quick meal.

In the way that she had since she was younger, Harlowe took her bowl of food and curled up on the sofa with it. She propped her phone up on the coffee table and selected a video to watch. It was one of her favorite channels, where a lesbian couple did home repairs. Harlowe drooled into her noodles as the two buff, flannel-wearing women installed drywall. As much as she loved Dena and Blaize, Harlowe's attention soon drifted. She couldn't stop thinking about Tatum, wondering what the story was behind the battle-suit—and the person herself,

Harlowe finished her dinner and cleaned up absently. She itched to go check on Tatum, but wondered if her presence would be unwelcome. Harlowe settled on tiptoeing by the door to Tatum's room. It was slightly ajar and she peeked in. Tatum was sitting in the corner with her knees pulled up to her chest and her head down. She appeared to be asleep, even though her blades were out, as if expecting an attack.

Harlowe wanted to earn Tatum's trust. More than that, she wanted to know Tatum and be close to her—in a purely platonic way of course. With time, maybe, Harlowe would know what lay under that armor and why she was so defensive. She had to be careful not to drive Tatum away. And if that meant hiding certain aspects of herself, then she would do it.

With a heavy heart, Harlowe went back to her room. She changed into her favorite pajama set, wide-legged mermaid pants that sat low on her hips and a cute teal camisole trimmed with stretch-lace. Over that, she tossed a pink and white robe that had bunny ears on the hood, and settled down with an eBook on her phone. Just as the story was getting good, a heavy thud filtered through the sturdy walls. Book forgotten, Harlowe jumped up. Tatum needed her. She skidded to a halt in front of Tatum's room and cautiously knocked.

"Are you okay? Mind if I come in?"

No answer. Worried, Harlowe eased the door open and stepped into the room. Tatum was nowhere in sight. Sick with the feeling she might have escaped, Harlowe rushed to the window and pulled back the drapes. Outside was completely black, none of the motion-activated lights had been triggered. Harlowe breathed again.

"Looking for me?"

The words made Harlowe whirl. Tatum was in the doorway of the bathroom, still in the battle-suit, but the blades were stowed. She had a large towel wrapped around her head. The fluffy, pink mass looked unbelievably funny paired with the buckled, belted battle-suit. Before she could stop herself, Harlowe burst into giggles.

Tatum cocked a brow. She looked stern, but the feral rage was gone from her expression.

Harlowe swallowed her laughter. "Sorry, I heard a sound, like you fell or something."

"I knocked over the bottle of shampoo," Tatum said. She looked sheepish. The expression, plus the towel gave Tatum an air of humanity she didn't have before. Her silver-blue eyes focused on Harlowe, then roved slowly down over her form. Harlowe's cheeks got warm. She was suddenly very aware of the strip of belly her cami top revealed and how it clung to her breasts. She wasn't even wearing a bra! Tatum must think she was incredibly sloppy. Flustered, Harlowe yanked the front of her bunny robe closed. Tatum suddenly looked away. It might have been a reflection from the towel, but Tatum's cheeks looked slightly pink under her natural bronze.

Harlowe asked, "How are you feeling? A little better?"

Tatum took off the towel and ran her fingers through her damp hair, roughly combing the black lengths of it. Harlowe guessed she put her head under the faucet to cool her headache or something. Maybe she threw up. That seemed to be one of the side-effects her search on concussions revealed.

"A little."

"Good," Harlowe said, even though she was pretty sure Tatum was just putting on a brave front. "Now try and get some sleep." She cringed inwardly at the super-cliché sentence. She backed up, heading toward the door, unable to stop adding more platitudes. "Goodnight, sleep tight, don't let the bedbugs bite!" she said brightly. Harlowe backed over the threshold, nearly tripping in the process. She closed the door and stood still for a moment, unwillingly replaying the awkward moment over in her mind.

She nearly missed the whispered "goodnight" from the other side of the door. That simple acknowledgement made her ridiculously happy. Harlowe skipped back to her room and burrowed under the covers again.

****

The next morning, Harlowe stood in the little kitchen with oven mitts on, poised over the oven. Instead of yesterday's blue suit, she was in cheerfully patched jeans and her Elizabeth Coleman College sweatshirt. The timer beeped and she sprang into action, pulling out a loaf of fruit bread. It had split down the middle, revealing the moist cakey insides, richly studded with blueberries and cranberries. A light dusting of chopped pecans crowned the golden loaf.

The entire kitchen was filled with the sweet scent. Harlowe took a deep, happy breath. She carefully tipped the hot pan over the cooling rack. The loaf popped out smoothly, perfection itself.

"A masterpiece," Harlowe announced.

"I agree."

The voice was low and smooth, rich like melted dark chocolate. Harlowe squeaked and whirled. Tatum stood in the arched doorway to the kitchen. Her ominous black presence clashed terribly with the homey atmosphere of the kitchen. Still, she looked a lot better than the previous night. Harlowe's face broke into a wide grin.

"Great timing," Harlowe said. She grabbed two mugs from the cupboard and put them down on the breakfast bar. "Sit down, I've got some green tea ready."

Tatum remained standing, looming over Harlowe as she poured two mugs of tea and set out thick, warm slices of the fruit bread.

Harlowe looked up at Tatum's impassive face. She said, "Um, you know you're a little intimidating, standing there all scary like that."

Tatum flinched. She looked down at herself as if seeing the battle-suit for the first time, then she turned the full force of her laser beam eyes on Harlowe.

"Do you want me to leave?"

"No," Harlowe said. "I want you to sit down and drink your tea. I looked it up last night, and green tea is good for people with concussions. So are nuts and berries. Do you want this yummy bread to go to waste? Okay, it won't go to waste, I'll just eat it all and then it'll go to *my* waist."

The stark expression on Tatum's face softened a fraction. She folded her long body and took possession of one of the chairs at the counter. Encouraged, Harlowe grinned and slid a mug across the worn wooden surface. After a moment of hesitation, Tatum reached out and wrapped her hands around the mug. Harlowe's attention was drawn irresistibly to those delicate, but capable-looking fingers, long and strong with short, cleanly trimmed nails. The mug's logo, "Don't be shy, your mother wasn't," peeked out from between those gorgeous, tempting digits. How would they feel on her skin? What would it be like to walk beside her, would their fingers naturally twine together? How warm would Tatum's skin be next to hers? What if they ventured into a private corner? Would she reach out and gather Harlowe into her arms, holding her tenderly before stealing a kiss? Harlowe's temperature slowly began to rise. She frantically looked for something to do in an attempt to stop her brain from overloading with dangerous thoughts.

Hurriedly, Harlowe grabbed her own mug, which was decorated with daisies and quite the opposite of tantalizing. She waved it in a kind of salute before chugging the entire mugful of steaming tea in one go. Red-faced and sweating, she set down her mug with a long sigh and pulled at her sweatshirt, fanning herself. Tatum looked at her with a deeply puzzled expression on her face.

Harlowe tilted her head cheekily. "Nothing like a bit of green tea in the morning to get things off to a good start."

Tatum didn't reply, but she raised her own mug to her lips and sipped with much more restraint than Harlowe. Reassured her houseguest wasn't going to die of dehydration, Harlowe started in on her bread.

"How are you feeling today?" Harlowe asked.

"Better," came the clipped answer. "I'll leave. I won't impose on you anymore."

"What?" The morsel of bread fell from Harlowe's mouth and landed in her tea. "Shit! No, I mean, you're not imposing. One day isn't enough to recover. I think you should stay at least three more days, until the end of the week. It's either that or I follow you back to your place and sing '99 bottles of beer on the wall' until you let me in. Deal?"

Harlowe stood up and stuck out her hand. She tried to give off an authoritative vibe. Tatum put down her tea mug and raised a brow.

"You'd really sing for me?"

"Yup," Harlowe declared. "That's something you *don't* want to experience. When I was in college, I was banned from six different karaoke bars."

"In that case," Tatum said with a gleam in her eyes, "I have no choice but to accede to your wishes. It's a deal."

With a twitch of her lips, she reached out her hand and clasped Harlowe's. The sudden warmth and pressure of skin to skin sent a shock of electricity from where their hands touched straight to Harlowe's heart. She couldn't stop the gasp of surprise, but she didn't want the contact to end. The fingers gripping hers were strong yet gentle. She felt completely enveloped, protected and safe. The handshake was getting long. Harlowe steeled herself to end it when Tatum glanced down at their joined hands. She let go and backed away, Harlowe clasped her hands together, trying to forget the heady kiss of Tatum's palm to hers.

"Good," Harlowe said, trying to sound calm and in control even as her insides were quaking. She got out a spoon and attempted to fish the soggy hunk of bread out of her tea before giving up and slurping the entire thing down. She caught Tatum looking askance at her. "I told you, I don't want it to go to waste."

"Evidently." Tatum stood and started to gather up the dishes. "Thank you for a lovely breakfast."

"You're quite welcome," Harlowe said. She moved to intercept Tatum on her way to the sink. "None of that, you're still on bedrest. Actually, on living room rest. Your mission is to go out there and make sure nobody steals my sofa."

"All right," Tatum said in her gorgeously sexy voice. Harlowe felt it humming through her knees. "But only because you know my weakness."

"Weakness?" Harlowe shook her head, confused. "What's that?"

"I would hate to have my favorite song butchered by your singing it." With that, she turned and strode out of the room.

"What?" Harlowe squawked. She flapped after the tall, black-clad figure who incidentally had a really nice back-view. "'99 bottles of beer on the wall' is totally not your favorite song. It's nobody's favorite song! I bet the person who wrote it doesn't even like it! Not even his mom likes it!"

Tatum just threw a smirk over her shoulder before she draped herself regally over the sofa. Harlowe pouted with her hands on her hips for a moment, before she gave up and plopped down on the sofa, just out of reach of Tatum's outstretched arm.

"Will you be all right in here for a while?" Harlowe asked. "I want to get some work done on that overgrown jungle out back. You shouldn't read or do anything strenuous, but how about I put on some music? I promise it's not me singing '99 bottles of beer on the wall.'"

"That would be nice, thank you."

Harlowe grinned, feeling her cheeks get warm. What was it about Tatum being so damn cool and sexy and polite all at the same time that just got her going? Harlowe was going to have to put a kibosh on that sort of thing. What if Tatum found out? Harlowe would be a shish-kabob in an instant. She bowed her head to hide her blush behind her hair. Head down, Harlowe put her phone on the portable speaker and set up one of her playlists, the selection was calm instrumentals that she used to help her study.

"Okay then, I'll just be out back," Harlowe said. She got an idea and scampered off. She came back, triumphantly bearing a large handbell, which she set on the coffee table with a flourish.

Tatum's brow furrowed and she looked from the bell to Harlowe.

"Just give me a ring if you need me," Harlowe said.

That earned her the patented Tatum Edwyn sardonic

eyebrow raise.

"Just like in the song, when you ring me, I'll be there? Interesting concept."

Harlowe threw up her hands. "I thought it was a good idea. Anyway, you stay here and chill and I'll go whack some weeds."

Chapter Three

A volley of swear words came from Harlowe as the weed whacker's whirling string caught on something buried deep inside the thick brambles and the handle jerked clear out of her hands. Cursing at length, Harlowe scrambled to grab it again. She cut the engine and examined the weeds choking out the decorative hedges that ringed the large garden. The weed whacker wasn't any match for them. She needed something stronger. Harlowe grabbed the hedge trimmers and hacked away at the worst of the mess, getting leaves and bits of things in her hair and all over her clothes. Once she cut enough of the brambles, she grabbed the weed whacker and yanked at it. She got it most of the way out, and in a burst of inspiration from the less-intelligent part of her brain, she fired up the motor again. The shredded vines whipped around, nearly yanking the weed whacker out of her hands a second time. While the engine whined and vines strained, Harlowe threw herself backwards, shaking the whacker like a dog playing with a chew toy. The vines snapped. The weed whacker shot out of the bushes like a rocket. Harlowe went sprawling onto the damp ground, kicking up a storm of fallen leaves.

After a moment of lying dazed on the ground, she stood and inspected her butt, which had new and exciting mud-stains on it.

"Fucking fuckers," Harlowe spat.

"Looks like you need a hand."

Harlowe looked up and nearly landed flat on her ass again. Tatum was beside her, blades out and suit powered up. She looked lethal and stunningly gorgeous. While Harlowe tried to get her brain to function well enough to make words come out of her mouth, Tatum reached over the overgrown hedge. A subliminal hum started up from the blades, as if they were vibrating faster than the eye could see. Branches and brambles melted off the main mass, falling softly to the ground in drifts.

In only a few passes of the blades, the entire section of the hedge was free of weeds and returned to a pristine curve. Almost as an afterthought, Tatum picked up the weed whacker and leaned it against the large oak tree dominating the garden.

"Holy shit," Harlowe said. She clapped a hand over her mouth. "I mean, that's amazing. But I don't want you to overexert yourself."

"It's nothing," Tatum said. "I was going stir crazy lying on that sofa with all those toodly doodly sounds going on while you're having fun out here."

"You call battling wildly overgrown bushes fun?"

Tatum shrugged. "Bushes can be fun. Both wild and nicely trimmed." A wicked smirk crossed Tatum's face before she fired up her blades and continued working.

Harlowe froze, mouth half open in shock. Was that on purpose? Did Tatum just make an innuendo? About bushes? And that damn sexy smirk—what was that all about? Harlowe huffed a stray piece of hair out of her mouth and grabbed the weed whacker.

"Okay, since you insist on trying to kill yourself," Harlowe said to Tatum's back, "I'll trim around the trees and you do the bushes. But you have to promise to stop the second you feel dizzy or sick, capiche?"

"Aye, aye sir," Tatum called back. She paused and looked at Harlowe. "Do you have any design requests?"

"Oh, I don't know," Harlowe said. She waved a hand, encompassing the wilderness explosion that was once a well-kept English garden. "Carte blanche. Whatever you want, just don't overexert yourself. I'm counting on you to know your limits, got it?"

"Got it," she drawled with just the slightest hint of attitude.

For the remainder of the morning, Harlowe resolutely focused on her task, with only a few stolen glances at Tatum. She moved with efficient elegance, deadly and beautiful at once.

Harlowe got distracted by a pair of squirrels, who came over to investigate when she was raking up the cut grass and weeds. Harlowe stopped raking and held herself still. They came quite close, almost close enough to touch her outstretched fingers before they darted away and scampered up a tree. Harlowe followed their path with her eyes and saw a feeder in the tree's branches. She made a mental note to order some seeds for her new little friends.

By the time the watery winter sun was high overhead, Harlowe was tired and hungry, and more than a little sweaty. The wind was cool, but the sunshine was still warm. She was certain Tatum, in her best condition, could keep going full-blast for hours more, but Tatum wasn't at her best. They both were due for a break. Harlowe finished raking the last bits of cut grass and leaves into a pile and wiped her sweating face on her sleeve.

She made a move to go over to where Tatum was working and stopped. The wall of untamed hedge was gone. In its place was an entire menagerie of animals, all cut from the bushes. Harlowe turned slowly, unable to comprehend the wonder of the transformation. A pair of deer were caught in mid-leap, next to a crouching bear. Smaller bushes were cut into koalas and whimsical shapes. The pièce de résistance, though, was a huge, roaring Asian dragon that took up the entire back hedge.

"Like it?"

Harlowe stopped her slow tour and faced Tatum. She blinked and shook her head. "It's the most fucking amazing thing I've ever seen in my entire life. How did you do all that? I mean, that suit looks like it could sure blast a hole in something or take out an army, but hedge sculpting? Really?"

"I have many skills," Tatum deadpanned.

"Yeah, that's for sure," Harlowe said. "Um, look, I'm thinking we should call it a day. I'm hungry and all sweaty. You don't look it, but you must be too."

"Actually, I am," Tatum said. She held out her arm and tapped at a tiny display on the inside of her wrist. The blades folded tight against her arms and the blue light dimmed. "I think I'd like to take you up on the offer of a change of clothes, if that's all right."

"That's totally fine," Harlowe said. She grinned. "Okay, you go clean up and I'll find something for you to wear. I'm thinking something pink and cute, with pompoms."

Tatum leveled a dangerous look at her. She growled, "I don't wear pink. Or pompoms."

"Just kidding," Harlowe said. Buoyant with happiness, she threw a wink at Tatum before she skipped into the house. She went up to the second floor, a big open space under the sloping roof used mainly for storage. Rockwell confided that her great-uncle planned to make it into something but could never make up his mind what, so it became a catch-all for their extra stuff.

At that moment, all it contained was the small stack of cardboard boxes of things to be donated. Harlowe shoved aside the ones of books and household items until she found the two boxes she wanted. One was labeled "clothes (new)" and "clothes (gently used)". The new clothes box held a lot of essentials, like socks and underwear, that for whatever reason didn't make the cut to be taken with them. Harlowe wasn't sure what was in the other box, but both her great-uncle and Rockwell had always been into fashion and both were clothes-horses, so Harlowe was certain everything they left was of impeccable taste. Rockwell especially cared to present a debonaire appearance, and he was about the same height and build as Tatum so his things would probably fit her. Whether it matched Tatum's style, though, was anybody's guess. There was no way she'd even fit into anything of Harlowe's, so for the time being, it was their only choice.

Harlowe dragged the boxes down to the first floor and left them in the hallway near the bedrooms. She found Tatum in the living room, resting on the sofa. Without thinking, Harlowe plopped down beside her. She inwardly cringed when Tatum twitched back away from her.

"Sorry," Tatum said before Harlowe could. She rubbed a hand over her forehead. "I wanted to make sure I was centred before I went in the shower and I kind of zoned out."

"Oh, I'm glad it was that and not because you got a whiff of me," Harlowe said. She lifted her arm and fanned her armpit. "Kind of swampy in here today."

"You're fine," Tatum said.

"Ugh, not really, I'm heading for a shower too." Harlowe jumped up and gestured broadly. "I brought down a couple boxes of clothes for you, I hope you don't mind, it's all guys' stuff."

"Not at all," Tatum said. She stood and rotated her shoulder.

"Good," Harlowe said. She scrambled to get the boxes, but Tatum beat her there. She easily lifted the two of them, much to Harlowe's dismay at her overexerting herself, and deposited them on the floor of the walk-in closet. Without another word, Tatum turned and vanished into the bathroom.

Dismissed, Harlowe ran into the kitchen, thinking about lunch. She peeked into the fridge and found the massive container of homemade kimchee Mrs. Che gave her as a going-away present, which gave her an idea. She started the rice cooker then scampered into her room, which was conveniently located next to the main bathroom, complete with a tub and separate shower stall. Not wanting to use up all the hot water, Harlowe kept her shower short and soon was back in the kitchen nook, singing happily to herself while overseeing a couple of fried eggs.

"You actually have a very nice voice."

Startled, Harlowe flushed and turned around. For the second time that day, she was rendered speechless. Tatum stood in the doorway, leaning casually against the wall with her hands in the pockets of the charcoal grey trousers. They had a few wrinkles, but the pleats were still sharp. A crisp white shirt and suspenders gave the outfit a vintage air, while the open buttons at the collar gave it a rakish charm that suited Tatum perfectly. The rolled-up sleeves revealed an intricate tattoo of interlocking gears on Tatum's left forearm. She'd tied her hair back into a low ponytail and her long bangs swept down to trail into her face. While she was formidable in the battle-suit, Tatum was stunning in menswear. She looked born to wear it. Her long, strong body complimented the tailored lines, but her curves tempered any severity. Harlowe gulped. Pretending she wasn't soaking through her panties with lust just got much more difficult.

Under Harlowe's speechless scrutiny, Tatum shifted her weight from one foot to the other, looking enchantingly nervous. She ran a hand through her hair, self-consciously tucking it back behind her ear.

"Bad?" she asked.

"No way," Harlowe said. She shook her head to clear it. "Extremely gay, um, good! Very good! You look very, um, perfect. Glad everything fit."

"Pretty much," Tatum said. Her silver-blue eyes focused on Harlowe, who had changed into a plaid skirt with a body-hugging long-sleeved T-shirt. She felt incredibly young and girly in front of Tatum's timeless, gentlemanly presentation. Tatum tilted her head and said, "You don't look old enough to have an ex-husband, so I'm guessing these are either your older brother's or your father's?"

"Actually, they're from my great-uncle Florian and his boy, uh man friend, Rockwell."

She should have been relieved that Tatum assumed she was straight, but she only felt disappointment. It was for e silly teenager with a crush and drive Tatum away.

"Man friend?"

"We don't say 'boyfriend.'" Harlowe waved her hands around as she babbled. "Both of them are 'confirmed lifelong bachelors' from what they tell everyone. Nothing more, nothing less."

"Ah," Tatum said with a note of understanding. She tugged down her cuffs and buttoned them. "I guess that's why everything is so…dapper."

"Yeah," Harlowe said dumbly. She swallowed hard. Fuck, why did Tatum have to be so hot in suspenders? Harlowe could barely form a coherent thought. To distract herself from staring at the talented fingers that lingered over the pearl buttons, Harlowe dished up the fried eggs onto two small plates and set them on a tray along with a pitcher of cold green tea and two cups. "How about some lunch, then?"

"Sounds good. After you, my dear." Tatum bowed. With a courtly gesture, she guided Harlowe to the living room, where the rest of the lunch was waiting for them on the coffee table. Harlowe gave Tatum the sofa, while she sat across from her on the floor. Curiously, Tatum studied the array, which consisted of two bowls of steamed rice flanked by smaller dishes of various veggies Harlowe had cut into thin strips and sauteed in sesame oil, along with a cup of fiery red sauce and a large leaf of kimchee for each of them. Kitchen shears, chopsticks, and spoons completed the setting. Feeling shy, Harlowe put the fried eggs down beside their bowls of rice and poured the tea.

"Um, I thought we'd have bibimbap," she said. "When I lived in an apartment, my awesome Korean landlady was terrified my future husband would starve, so she always had me over and taught me a bunch of traditional recipes. The kimchee's from her, actually. It's pretty spicy, but really good. The sauce is too. I put it all separately so you can doctor your own, you know, depending on how hot you like it. I like things really hot." Harlowe flushed. That sounded like as innuendo. She hastily added, "I mean, hot like as in spicy hot not like sexy hot, no of course not, because it's from Korea and Koreans like things hot. Spicy. Peppers. Chili peppers. Yeah." Harlowe stopped talking abruptly and wiped her forehead with her sleeve.

Tatum raised a brow before she shot a smirk across the table. "I can take some heat," she said in that low, throaty tone that made Harlowe forget all about lunch as her mind was hijacked by the wish that Tatum would purr those words into her ear. Tatum lowered her eyes to the dishes and asked, "So how does this all work? I'm afraid my knowledge of Asian cuisine is lacking."

"It's super easy," Harlowe said. "Just add whatever you want to your bowl, mix and eat. I've got more rice if you want a refill."

Tatum picked up her kimchee leaf and effortlessly shredded it with the shears. The way her long, talented fingers worked the shears was mesmerizing. Although she wanted to watch the process for longer, Harlowe's stomach was growling, so she got busy, helping herself to the various vegetables. She picked up the kimchee leaf with her chopsticks and awkwardly snipped at it with the kitchen shears in her left hand. The kimchee got stuck between the blades. No matter how many times she snipped, she couldn't get a clean cut. Harlowe stuck her tongue between her teeth in concentration.

A low chuckle surprised Harlowe and she stopped cutting to blink across the table. Had Tatum actually laughed? Harlowe couldn't contain the smile that exploded onto her face. Tatum was also in mid-snip, but her strips were considerably neater than Harlowe's, whose bowl looked like it had been attacked by angry chihuahuas. Tatum's stunning face was relaxed, her eyes sparkled with life and mirth.

"What?" Harlowe faked annoyance. "Okay, yeah, so you're the expert at cutting things, I get it. Everything still tastes the same, no need for all that smirking over there."

Tatum put down her utensils and held her hands up. "I was just going to offer you some assistance. Or at least advice."

"Don't need it." Harlowe angrily snipped her fried egg in two. Half of it landed in her bowl and the other on the table. She scowled at it and tried not to swear. "No comments from the peanut gallery, okay?"

"Not a word," Tatum said.

Harlowe managed to complete her bowl without further incident and soon was blissfully shoveling in her bibimbap. She looked up at one point to see Tatum also chewing with the happiest expression she'd worn so far. After a while, she felt Tatum's gaze on her. Harlowe swallowed her mouthful and put her spoon down. She rested her elbows on the table and propped her chin on her clasped hands. Tatum studied her with a gentle curiosity. It was nice, if a little unnerving, having Tatum's full attention on her.

"What do you do all the way out here?" Tatum asked without preamble.

"I work for a newspaper, *The Maritime Gazette*," Harlowe said.

"Journalist?"

Harlowe's shoulders drooped. "Maybe someday, but for now I'm just a door-to-door salesperson. You know, for subscriptions. That's what I was doing at your place yesterday. I wasn't snooping, really. See, I only just started there and my boss says that if I make my goal, he'll consider letting me proofread, and maybe even write some articles. Not like that's going to happen anytime soon." Harlowe sheepishly wrinkled her nose.

Tatum leaned forward, hands loosely clasped in front of herself. "What's your goal?"

"Fifty."

"How many more do you need?"

"Fifty."

A slow smile brightened Tatum's features. Harlowe's heart nearly stopped. Tatum said, "Well, now you only need forty-nine. Consider this my promise to sign up for whatever your top-of-the-line service is, of course verifying it was you who recommended it."

"Really?" Harlowe squeaked. "That's super nice of you, but you don't have to do that. Our premium package is like twenty-five dollars a month."

Tatum just shrugged as if it was no big deal and picked up her spoon again. "How long have you worked for the *Gazette*?"

"Let's see, I've been there since, hmm." Harlowe made a show of looking at the calendar. She fixed her gaze on Tatum and intoned, "Yesterday."

That tiny, crooked grin appeared on Tatum's lips. "And here?"

"I drove down from Toronto, and I got here on Sunday."

"That's a big move. Why here? You mentioned a great-uncle."

"Yeah, this was his home and he left it to me."

Tatum's face crumpled in sympathy. "I'm sorry for your loss. Were you close?"

"Oh no! I mean, yes, but he's not dead," Harlowe said. "He and Rockwell, the man friend I told you about, are on a round-the-world-trip before they settle down in a nice retirement village. Apparently the place they picked has a movie theatre that only plays musicals, and every Thursday is Drag Night. You know, a perfect place for two heterosexual gentlemen to retire."

"It sounds nice for anyone," Tatum said. "So, you

went to Coleman?"

"How did you know that?"

"Your sweatshirt this morning."

Harlowe fought the manic grin that wanted to take over her face. Tatum noticed that! She looked at her and thought about her enough to remember her sweatshirt! Harlowe sobered. Of course, she was probably trying to figure out who this crazy person was who had practically kidnapped her.

"Oh yeah, that," Harlowe said. She forced a laugh. "I did, but it could have been my ex-husband's. Or boy-friend's."

Tatum lowered her eyes. Her beautiful lips thinned. She put down her spoon without taking a bite of her lunch. When she looked across the table again, it was with a cool, detached expression. Harlowe ached inside, wondering what caused that, if she'd inadvertently said something wrong. Was it the ex-husband joke? Oh shit, maybe Tatum had an ex-husband? Maybe he died or hurt her. Harlowe felt awful, mostly jealous as hell of the man who got to kiss those gorgeous lips, whose hands caressed the curves of her body, who knew what Tatum's ecstasy sounded like. The man who possibly hurt her enough that she hid away from the world and made death-ray sword-wielding battle-suits. Even though she'd just made him up a minute ago, Harlowe wanted to hunt down that asshole and kill him, if he was still alive. If he was already dead, she'd just have to reanimate him and kill him again.

Wordlessly, Harlowe attacked the rest of her lunch. Chewing furiously, she sloshed more tea into both of their cups before she chugged hers, washing down her huge bite of bibimbap. After the last spoonful was down, Harlowe patted herself on the chest, satisfied for the time being.

After lunch, Harlowe left Tatum resting on the sofa and puttered around in her room, unpacking the things she'd brought from her tiny apartment in Toronto and making her room homey. A shadow crossed her threshold and she looked up. Tatum stood in the doorway, calmly gazing at her.

"Did I kick you out of the master bedroom?" she asked.

"Nah," Harlowe said. She sat back on her heels and brushed back a stand of hair that fell into her face. "That room felt too big for just little me."

"Well, you *are* little," Tatum said. "But you've got a big—"

"Mouth, yeah I know," Harlowe said.

"I was going to say big presence. Your smile alone can fill the entire room with light." Her tone was warm, almost affectionate. Harlowe glowed with pleasure. Whatever went wrong at lunch was not bothering Tatum anymore, it seemed. Tatum studied her for a moment longer before she asked, "Can I give you a hand with that?"

"Absolutely not," Harlowe said, wagging a stern finger at Tatum. "I don't want you lifting anything more after all the work you did this morning. But you can come in, take a sit, and keep me company so I don't get bored and slack off."

"Sounds fair," Tatum said. She went over to the antique writing desk in the corner and spun the chair around before she dropped into it. She crossed her legs and leaned back, casually gorgeous. In order not to stare at those long legs that went on forever, or anything else that might give her away, Harlowe shook out her fuzzy blanket and draped it over the foot of her bed. She itched to ask Tatum all sorts of questions, but worried if they weren't welcome. The last thing she wanted was to undo the progress they'd made so far by pushing her. Harlowe glanced at Tatum, who was idly studying one of Harlowe's knickknacks, a wooden owl she got as a souvenir from somewhere, turning it carefully in her fingers.

Harlowe decided to take the chance. She dragged out another box and, kneeling down in front of Tatum, she ripped off the packing tape. Inside was her collection of sweaters and socks. Harlowe was glad she'd already unpacked her "unmentionables."

"How long have you lived up there?" Harlowe asked.

Tatum stared at her for a moment, then said, "About seven years."

"And you lived there all alone for all that time?" Harlowe asked. She remembered the fictional ex-husband and wanted to take the question back. Her stomach clenched. She felt like she was going to throw up.

"Yes," Tatum said softly.

"Oh wow," Harlowe said. "It must be lonely, you know, being away from other people."

Tatum stood. She went to the window and peered outside. Harlowe got the feeling she wasn't really seeing the view of the front porch and driveway with Harlowe's little bright blue hatchback in it. Harlowe was about to change the subject and blather on about something else when Tatum spoke.

"I didn't come here to get away from people," her voice was soft, heartbreakingly so. "I came here to keep myself away from others. I didn't want anyone to be hurt by me."

"But you're so nice, I can't believe you're dangerous," Harlowe blurted out. Tatum whirled and fixed her with a cold, hard glare. The new, friendly Tatum was gone in an instant. Not to be intimidated, Harlowe stood her ground and glared back.

"You don't know who I am," Tatum snapped.

"I want to know," Harlowe said. She got to her feet and took a step toward the tall woman, who looked brittle, as if a touch could shatter her. Like one wrong word would cause her to bolt, vanish into the mist. Harlowe kept her voice gentle and her posture open. "Tell me."

Tatum paused, as if hovering at the edge of a cliff. Her hands were clenched at her sides. Her breathing was labored. Harlowe kept still and waited for Tatum to speak.

Finally, she did.

"I was eighteen when I joined the military. I trained in mechanical engineering and was deployed to the middle east, working on tanks and helicopters." She stopped and looked away.

"Go on, I'm listening," Harlowe said.

Tatum paced up and down the room, her eyebrows drawn and her expression fierce. "I was never good at trusting people. I grew up having to look out for myself. Protect myself at all costs. I thought that was over when I became a soldier, but I was wrong." Tatum stopped pacing. She rubbed a hand across her forehead. "I now had to protect myself from both sides, enemies and so-called allies. Being a woman in the armed forces is no joke. Bad things happen when you let your guard down."

"I'm sorry," Harlowe breathed.

"I never felt safe, and I never let my guard down, not for a moment." Tatum's shoulders slumped. "I became good at protecting myself. Lethally good. When I got out, all I wanted was to be somewhere I was safe from attacks—and attacking."

"Were you?" Harlowe asked gently.

"Yes," Tatum answered. The word was a sigh of pain. "For a price. I made that old mill into my fortress of solitude. I hid away, losing myself in my world of robotics and theoretical science. The outside world doesn't fit me anymore." Tatum looked defeated, empty. "What I thought was my safe haven became my prison."

Harlowe looked at her, so strong but so broken. Tears welled up in Harlowe's eyes. She clasped her hands in front of herself, schooling her thoughts into words. "Tatum," she said. "Maybe you needed time alone to heal, but the world is still out there, waiting for you. It's not a war zone. Maybe it's time to let yourself live again."

Tatum fell to her knees. "I don't know if I can."

Harlowe didn't even think before she was at Tatum's side. She gently placed a hand on Tatum's shoulder. The muscle under her palm was corded and hard. Harlowe couldn't help but be impressed.

"Thank you for sharing this with me," Harlowe said.

"I shouldn't have," Tatum whispered. She balled her fists, clenching them on the material of her trousers. "This burden is too heavy for one person to carry."

"You're right," Harlowe said. "That's why you need me. I'll take half of the burden from you. Wait, do you have a person you talk to regularly? Like, someone professional?"

Tatum nodded. Some life and color came back into her expression.

"Revised," Harlowe declared. "I'll take thirty-three

percent."

The tiniest smile tugged at Tatum's lips. "You don't have to do that."

"Too late," Harlowe said. She knelt down on the carpet to be on the same level as Tatum. It was the closest they'd gotten so far. Harlowe could barely breathe with the emotions that gripped her. "You're going to be okay. And we're going to veg out on the sofa with snacks and the TV show of your choice and the first person to take a nap is the winner. Sound like a plan?"

Tatum nodded, then grimaced and pressed a hand to her forehead. "At least my lunch doesn't come back up when I do that anymore. I must be still a bit jostled though," she said. She softly prodded Harlowe's cheek with a long finger. "Because I totally agree that vegging out with you sounds like an amazing idea."

"Great." Harlowe leapt to her feet. She couldn't believe Tatum touched her! There was no way she'd ever be able to sleep now, Tatum's victory in the nap contest was assured. "I'll grab the snacks and blankets and you are needed back on the sofa. Stat!"

Tatum stood as well and bowed her head in agreement before she strode out of the room.

Chapter Four

"She should just forget about that dork, James," Harlowe declared, waving her carrot stick at the screen. "She and Kara are way better off without guys."

"You don't say," Tatum drawled from her end of the sofa. "Like, they should join Team Alex and date each other?"

Harlowe froze. Shit! She'd gotten so used to making blatant gay comments during *Supergirl* with her cheerfully rainbow-hued college friends, it just popped out. She was surprised when Tatum chose the show in the first place. Harlowe was certain she would have gone for something that wasn't packed with women in skintight leotards. Harlowe forced a laugh.

"No way, what a weird idea, they're obviously not that way. I just meant they are better off being besties, gal pals, platonic life-partners." Worriedly, she gnawed on her carrot and hoped Tatum overlooked what her big mouth blurted out.

"Maybe they are," Tatum said. She leaned forward to stab a cocktail wiener with her chopstick. "I always thought Cat and Kara were a better match. What do you think, too far apart in age?"

Was this a test? Harlowe faked another laugh. "I don't have a problem with age-gap, I actually think it's kinda hot. But Cat's the boss and she can't even remember Kara's name, for crying out loud. Nope, don't see it happening. Besides, they both are all about chasing the dong." Harlowe paused, then clarified, "Getting their fill of man-meat. Jonesing for the johnson. Receiving the schlong. Vaginally swallowing the hot scrotum soup." Harlowe finished and mentally congratulated herself for her unequivocally heterosexual-sounding answer.

"You're probably right," Tatum said. She grimaced and put down her wiener without even taking a bite. Glancing over, Harlowe wondered if there was something wrong with it. She hadn't had them long enough for them to be freezer-burned yet.

They lapsed into silence. Harlowe's eyelids grew heavy and she snuggled deeper into her blanket. The familiar voices of the *Supergirl* cast relaxed her. She was about to win the nap battle when she heard a tiny snore from the other end of the sofa. Harlowe leaned over to check on Tatum. She was fast asleep, arms crossed and chin down. Harlowe resisted the urge to stroke back the trailing bangs that hung down into her face. Her expression was peaceful and pain-free in sleep. While she was probably exhausted, Tatum falling asleep next to her filled her heart with joy. She wouldn't do that if she didn't trust her, right?

Harlowe turned the volume down and curled up in her blanket.

****

Clouds surrounded her, Harlowe gazed around in wonder. She wasn't cold, far from it, she felt toasty warm and completely safe. But she realized she wasn't alone. A figure was coming through the clouds towards her. Harlowe held her breath. The clouds parted to reveal Tatum in her white shirt and suspenders outfit, impossibly gorgeous. The look she leveled Harlowe with was far from chaste, fire shouldered in the depths of her intense gaze. It hit Harlowe right in the gut.

Harlowe gasped and rocked back. The cloud under her feet was getting thin. Already she could see the far-away ground underneath her, spread out like a map.

Fear seized her. Harlowe reached out, desperately clawing at the clouds around her, but they melted away. "Help, I'm falling," Harlowe cried out.

Tatum grabbed the front of her shirt and ripped it open to display the stylized *S* emblazoned on deep blue.

"Don't worry, I'll catch you." Harlowe felt the words vibrate through her rather than heard them.

With a sick lurch, the ground gave way.

****

Harlowe jerked awake. Stunned, she lay still for a moment, trying to process where she was. She was on her side, on a firm, warm surface. A gentle hand brushed her hair away from her face.

"Good morning, Goldilocks," a low, amused voice said.

Harlowe bolted upright. She clapped a hand over her mouth to keep the swear words in while she scrambled back to her end of the sofa. She'd not only fallen asleep, but she'd managed to get herself on Tatum's lap in the process.

"I'm so sorry," Harlowe said. "I totally didn't mean to do that. You should have just shoved me off onto the floor."

"Why would I do that?" Tatum shrugged one shoulder. "You were obviously tired, and you looked so peaceful. I didn't have the heart to move you."

"I didn't make you uncomfortable?" Harlowe scrunched up her face.

"Not at all. I'm getting used to having you around." A shadow passed over Tatum's face. "In fact, it's going to be weird not having you around when I go back to my place."

"That's why you need to invite me over for tea, right neighbor?" Harlowe scooted over to poke Tatum in the side, very gently, with her elbow. She looked up into that beautiful but pained face with the cutest, sweetest smile she had.

Tatum moved back almost imperceptibly. "That's not a good idea," she said in a whisper. Harlowe's smile faded. Their eyes locked. Tatum's were filled with anguish. She raised a hand and very carefully brushed back a strand of hair from Harlowe's face, tucking it behind her ear, echoing Tatum's own habit. She murmured, "I would die before I—"

Harlowe held her breath. She couldn't move. She felt like she was falling into a silver-blue maelstrom. The doorbell rang and Tatum recoiled. She got to her feet, tensed as if expecting an attack. The gentle, sometimes amused expression she sometimes let slip was gone. Her eyes were hard and angry, almost fearful.

"Anybody home?" a cheerful male voice called out. "Hello in there!"

Harlowe glanced toward the front door. In that instant, Tatum was gone. The ringing continued, interspersed with knocking. Harlowe raced to the door, desperate to still the noise before it upset Tatum any more.

"I'm coming, jeez, impatient much?" Harlowe muttered as she unlocked the door and opened it, but kept the screen door closed. On the other side of the screen, a smiling, bearded man with a bit of a paunch, who appeared to be about forty stood with a basket in his hands. Behind him was an older, grey-haired woman, also smiling. She was in what looked like her Sunday-best purple dress with matching hat.

"Sorry, I don't want any," Harlowe said. She started to close the door when the man spoke.

"Miss Tremaine, we're not selling anything, just wanted to bring a warm welcome to Mister Florian's great-niece."

Harlowe eased the door open once more. She channeled Tatum and crossed her arms over her chest.

"All right, state your business."

"Feisty little thing," the woman said. She slapped at the man. "Introduce yourself properly, Jim. You forget, she's from away, the big city where they's all murderers and pickpockets."

"Sorry." Jim shifted the basket to one hand and sheepishly doffed his ball cap. "Jim Peebles here, partner of the volunteer firefighter chief and head of the family auxiliary. This here's Mary McIntyre, our secretary."

"Pleased to meet you," Mary said. She looked kind, like the type of person who was the default grandma of any group. She reminded Harlowe of Mrs. Che.

Harlowe stepped out onto the porch and let the screen door swing closed behind her.

"Please accept our welcome basket," Mary said briskly. With a warm smile, Jim held it out and she continued, "We make one of these up for anyone new to Brooksville and surrounding area. It's got a bunch of goodies we hope will come in handy for you. Some local preserves and baked goods, plus a book of coupons I'm sure you'll want to use. They've even got a two-fer down at the Lo-Kost Mart."

"Wow, thanks." Harlowe took the basket. It was wrapped in clear plastic and tied with a bright pink ribbon. Shredded colored paper lined the basket like it was for Easter, cushioning the small cluster of jars and paper-wrapped package. An envelope was tucked into the side of the basket. While she was happy for the gift, she hoped they didn't want to stay for a long chat.

Jim put his cap back on over his thinning brown hair. "You're welcome to drop by the station anytime," he said. "Check out some of our events. Maybe you'll find a couple you'd like to go to."

"The biggest one is coming up just next month," Mary said with a conspiratorial wink at Harlowe that confused her. "Brooksville Days commemorates the founding of the town and there'll be events all week, ending off with a Strawberry Social for you young people to enjoy. Think you'd be interested in something like that? There are several eligible young fellows in town you might take a fancy to."

Harlowe groaned inwardly. "Actually, it's not the fellows I fancy." She pointed to herself and said, "Lesbian."

"Oh my," Mary said. Harlowe braced herself for a homophobic barrage. Instead, Mary patted Harlowe on the wrist. "I apologize for assuming. We at the Brooksville Volunteer Fire Department make every effort to be inclusive of our LGBT plus members and friends. You are still more than welcome to attend any function, either alone or with the partner of your choice."

"Yeah, uh, good to hear that," Harlowe said. She hefted the basket and said, "Thanks again for the welcome gift. I'd like to chat longer, but I'm still unpacking, and..." She shrugged and made a "what can you do?" gesture with her head.

"No problem, we won't keep you any longer," Jim said. "Nice meeting you, and hope to see you in town. I meant it about the station. I've always got a fresh pot of coffee ready for any friends who come around and you're officially one of our friends."

"Sure," Harlowe said, already on her way back inside. As she locked the door, she heard Mary saying: "What a lovely young lady. Seems the apple doesn't fall far from the tree, eh Jim?"

Harlowe let out a sigh and sagged against the door. She tiredly dropped the welcome basket on the coffee table and fell onto the sofa, only to bolt upright in panic the next second. Shit! She'd just outed herself to anyone within hearing distance! She was pretty sure Tatum was in her room, which was at the back of the house away from the front porch, but what if she'd peeked out of Harlowe's window to see who was visiting them and heard? Harlowe gnawed on her lip. That was not good. At any rate, it was too late to do anything about her slip, so Harlowe unpacked the gift basket. It really did have a lot of "goodies" as Mary put it. Her mouth watered at a pack of brownies and Nanaimo bars. Already Harlowe was picturing what tasty dishes she could whip up to try out some of those jams.

Her bangs hung into her eyes, not nearly as long as Tatum's but just at that annoying length where, if they got any longer, she'd need to get a hairband or cut them. Harlowe settled for blowing them out of her face a couple of times.

A soft footfall made Harlowe turn. Her face broke into a huge smile. Tatum was back, looking a bit skittish, but still as gorgeous as ever.

"Come and check out these treats from the volunteer firefighter's auxiliary," Harlowe gushed. She held up a jar, the contents glistened deep pink in the afternoon sunlight. "These peach preserves look awesome. I've got a waffle iron just begging for me to fire it up. What do you say? Waffles for dinner? With…bacon?" Harlowe drew the last word out nice and long, ending with a flourish.

"I'd say, that sounds wonderful," Tatum said. She settled down in what was becoming her accustomed spot next to Harlowe on the sofa. Harlowe glanced at her, trying to gauge if Tatum was acting more ill-at-ease than usual around her. Maybe she heard, maybe she didn't, either way, she seemed the same as before. Harlowe let out a sigh of relief. The tension in her shoulders eased.

"Good," Harlowe said. "Are you feeling up to continuing the *Supergirl* marathon, or do you want to lie down for a bit? I promise I won't sing or fall asleep on you."

"Pity," Tatum said. "I'm fine just sitting here. If you have other things to do, don't let me keep you from them."

"Are you trying to subtly tell me to leave you alone?"

"Not at all, I enjoy your company," Tatum said in her old-world gentlemanly way. Harlowe glowed. A shadow of sadness crossed Tatum's face. "It's going to end soon enough," she said softly.

"None of that," Harlowe said. She playfully slapped at Tatum's knee, just brushing the material of her trousers. "We're going to watch *Supergirl* and then we're going to stuff ourselves with waffles. No arguments."

"None here." Tatum held up her hands.

"Good," Harlowe said. She got them more chilled green tea and cued up the episode they were in the middle of watching. Harlowe curled up with her blanket and let herself become absorbed in the show. She thought the gay innuendos instead of saying them aloud, which was almost as satisfying. A few times her mental comments caused her to sputter in laughter and Tatum gave her the old side-eye, but didn't seem to mind otherwise.

"You're a good singer," Tatum said abruptly. "Why were you banned from all those karaoke places?"

"More for my choice of tunes than my singing," Harlowe admitted. "I don't know what people have against Ghibli songs. I mean, the movies are classics. Everybody loves them."

"Oh no, let me guess, *that* song," Tatum said. "That fish one that *never* leaves your head."

Harlowe resettled herself in her blanket with the air of affronted royalty. "So, what if it was? It's better than *'99 Bottles of Beer On the Wall.'*"

"Only marginally," Tatum said in a low growl.

"Just for that, I'm not going to sing for you."

"Thank God," Tatum muttered.

Harlowe pretended not to hear. She kept an eye on Tatum and noticed when she smiled or chuckled at something. Evening fell, bringing the promise of waffles. Harlowe was in the middle of mixing up the batter when Tatum came into the tiny kitchen.

"Is there anything I can help with?"

"Are you sure you're okay? I don't want you pushing yourself."

"I'm doing all right." Tatum rubbed a hand over her forehead. "My head's still a bit fuzzy, but I think doing something easy and repetitive might be better than nothing at all."

Harlowe crossed her arms and tapped her foot, thinking. "Okay, you're in charge of the waffle iron and I'll make the salad. Sorry I didn't ask before, but do you have any allergies or foods you don't like?"

"No allergies," Tatum said. "And I've been pretty much living on peanut butter sandwiches and boiled vegetables for the past seven years, so anything is great."

"That means you're way overdue for a trip to Chez Harlowe, then." Harlowe handed over the bowl and spoon. "It's the only five-star restaurant where you have to make your own."

"Then it's going to lose a couple of stars with me in the kitchen," Tatum said. She faced the waffle iron like she was facing down an enemy. The knuckles of the hand that gripped the handle of the spoon whitened.

"It's not going to bite you," Harlowe said. "Just lay the batter down, nice and easy, right in the middle." Encouragingly, Harlowe made scooping gestures with her hand and Tatum obligingly followed.

"Is that enough?"

"Perfect," Harlowe declared. "Now just close the lid and let the iron do its magic."

The first batch came out golden brown and smelling heavenly. Unable to resist, Harlowe tore one piping hot waffle in half.

"Test batch," Harlowe said around a mouthful of waffle. She giggled at Tatum's look of concern. "It's okay, we're not going to run out. And I need the opinion of my sous-chef." She handed over the other half of the waffle.

Tatum's face relaxed. She carefully took the treat

from Harlowe's hand.

"It's wonderful," she said softly after her taste. While the next batch was cooking, she leaned back against the counter and watched Harlowe preparing the salad. Her expression was thoughtful, with a hint of melancholy.

"Dinner is served," Harlowe said, when the last waffle joined the pile on the Willow Ware platter. She set it down on the counter beside a big bowl of salad and a mountain of bacon. She had a great time trying all the preserves and finding good combinations with the leftover berries and other random things she pulled from the fridge. Tatum alternated between watching Harlowe and doctoring her own food, which she did in increasingly creative ways. She finished with a waffle topped with peach jam, bacon, black olives, pickles, whipped cream and lemon curd with a sprinkle of paprika.

"You are not going to eat that, are you?" Harlowe asked in amazement.

"Sure," Tatum said. She took a big bite and chewed with obvious enjoyment. She mimed a chef's kiss. "Mm! That's perfect, five stars, if I do say so myself."

"No way," Harlowe said. She scooted her chair closer to Tatum. "I demand proof."

Tatum looked at her in confusion. Harlowe opened her mouth and pointed at it. Tatum shook her head and chuckled. Indulgently, she prepared a good-sized portion on her spoon and held it out for Harlowe, who swooped in and snapped up the mouthful. She chewed thoughtfully and carefully licked the cream from her lips before she crossed her arms and bowed her head.

"And?" Tatum asked with a raised brow. She smirked, brash and confident.

"That was the best waffle I've ever tasted in my entire life." Harlowe looked up, at once realizing how close they were. Her face flooded with heat. The way Tatum looked at her, at once with kindness and something more, almost affection, made Harlowe want to stay in that moment forever.

Tatum's expression grew thoughtful, that familiar melancholy settled down.

"I'd forgotten," Tatum murmured. Her shoulders fell. She turned away and stood, plate in her hand.

Harlowe felt the sting of the dismissal but didn't let it show. She got up as well.

"It's okay, I've got this."

Tatum just nodded and left the room without protest. Harlowe suspected the day was catching up with her, especially her foray into gardening. Guilt gnawed at her. She shouldn't have let Tatum exert herself like that, but honestly, she didn't think she could stop her.

Chapter Five

That night, Harlowe lay in her bed and thought about Tatum. She wanted more than anything to know what was behind those wistful glances she sometimes sent Harlowe's way, those moments of closeness that were usually followed by a withdrawal and sadness. What was Tatum thinking when she touched Harlowe? She wanted to know what Tatum forgot. Was it laughter? Fun? Just the pleasure of being close to someone? She had been alone for several years, after all. Even with a counselor, that was a long time to live with only your own thoughts to keep you company.

Harlowe couldn't let her be all alone like that, ever again. If Tatum was ready, she'd help her come out of her self-imposed prison and get to know more people. Hell, if Tatum wanted some male companionship, Harlowe could help her find that, too. The Strawberry Social flitted across Harlowe's mind. She squeezed her eyes tightly closed, trying to drive out the image of some unshaved cowhand in gross overalls hauling Tatum, her dignified, beautiful Tatum, onto the dance floor so he could rub up on her. Harlowe seethed. Okay, that was too far. If Tatum wanted to lie down with dogs, she'd have to find her own. Harlowe would die of jealousy if she had to help her do that.

Harlowe didn't think she could sleep with those nasty thoughts, but eventually she did. She dreamed of floating on a waffle raft in a lake of jam with a big spoon for an oar. She was just at the point of figuring out how to get the spoon into her mouth when she abruptly opened her eyes to darkness. Harlowe scrabbled around and picked up her phone, squinting at the screen before she fell back into the comforter. It was only a little past one am. The wind must have blown a branch or something against her window. She burrowed into her bed and tried to return to her dream-waffle, but a muffled cry made her sit up suddenly. That was not the wind or her imagination. Harlowe grabbed her bunny robe and threw it on over her camisole and sleep-shorts. It flapped around her bare legs on her way to Tatum's room.

Like before, she knocked, and like before, there was no answer. She listened for a moment longer, not wanting to barge in unless there really was something wrong. Nothing happened and she was ready to chalk it up to her imagining things when the cry came again, unmistakably Tatum. She was in distress.

Immediately, Harlowe rushed to her side. Tatum was twisted up in the covers, her eyes were closed, but she writhed as if trying to escape from the grips of something strong and terrible.

"Wake up, it's a dream," Harlowe said. She placed her hand on Tatum's shoulder and shook. She was about to continue on in the vein of "you're safe" when Tatum seized her by the wrist and yanked her face-first onto the bed. Harlowe let go with a squeak of surprise when she landed. Tatum grabbed her other wrist, flipped her over and pinned her to the mattress.

"Stop," Harlowe shouted in panic. "Tatum, it's me."

The pressure let up. Tatum blinked a few times and looked around in confusion. She rubbed a hand across her face and took a shuddering breath. She looked so lost that Harlowe forgot all about her own shock at being manhandled. Harlowe scooted over next to Tatum.

"It's okay," Harlowe said. She didn't even think before her body moved, her arms opened and she breathed, "You're safe here with me."

Harlowe squeaked again when Tatum collided with her, curling up against her and burying her face against Harlowe's shoulder. Tatum's arms wrapped around her and held her with softness and strength. Harlowe hugged her back. Their bodies pressed together, fitting like two pieces of a puzzle that were finally reunited. Harlowe's heart pounded. She smoothed the spiky bangs away from Tatum's face. Slowly, Tatum's breathing went back to normal. With a startled jerk, Tatum pulled away. She focused on Harlowe, and that seemed to calm her some-what.

"I'm so sorry, Harlowe. I didn't mean to do that—

grab you like that," Tatum said.

"I surprised you by jumping in here," Harlowe said. "You were having a really bad nightmare, I guess. Are you okay?"

"Peachy," Tatum said sourly. She turned on the bedside light, then pulled at the sweat-soaked blue and white striped nightshirt and looked down with a twist of her lips. "I sincerely apologize. Did I toss you?"

"Yeah," Harlowe said. "Maybe you were expecting someone bigger because I really flew. Good thing this bed is so big. I had a soft landing and now I know for sure how comfy it is too, so no harm done." She stretched out and put her hands behind her head.

"It's yours for now, I need to change," Tatum said. She got up and grabbed a new nightshirt and a pair of plaid boxers from the neatly folded pile on the dresser. With an apologetic look, Tatum said, "I'll replace all this stuff I used."

"Don't worry about it," Harlowe said. "I'm the one who should be paying you for whatever I broke at your place. I bet that cost a lot more than a few shirts."

"How about we call it even," Tatum said.

Harlowe raised a hand from the comfy, warm pile of covers and gave a thumbs up. While the sound of the shower filtered into the room, Harlowe luxuriated in the silken sheets. They really were super comfortable and Harlowe grimaced slightly at the thought of going back to her small bed with its foam mattress and generic bedding. She snuggled into the heavenly depths and breathed in the floral scent of the laundry detergent, plus something spicy and unique that was Tatum's own. Harlowe groaned. She did not need to know how fucking good Tatum smelled up close. She also didn't need to know how wonderful it felt to be in Tatum's arms.

It had been a while since Harlowe hugged anyone like that, not since her first and only girlfriend in high school. They'd only gotten in a couple of good full-body hugs and a few hesitant kisses before they fought over something so stupid she couldn't even remember what it was and had a dramatic breakup at their local Wendy's. It never would have lasted. Harlowe was certain of that now. Nothing could compare to how Harlowe felt in Tatum's embrace.

The shower stopped and Harlowe guiltily leapt from the depths of the crumpled bedding. She quickly remade the bed and was just smoothing down the comforter when Tatum came back into the room attired in another night-shirt. Her long hair was up in a towel, this time a lime green one. She struck a pose and twirled around. Harlowe burst out laughing.

"What do you think?" Tatum asked. "Is it me?"

"Oh yes. Very glamorous," Harlowe replied between snickers. She tilted her head and studied Tatum as she leaned over and toweled her hair dry. "Look, um, it's kind of a weird idea so feel free to say no, but do you want me to sit with you until you're asleep again? Like, I can chase away the boogeymen and be your cute night-light all at the same time."

Tatum's hands clenched around her towel. She seemed to be struggling internally with something. She resolutely dropped the towel and crossed the room in a few strides. She sat down on the side of the bed and knitted her fingers together in her lap.

"Actually, I have a weirder idea," Tatum said. She looked up at Harlowe, exhaustion showing plain on her face. "This afternoon, when you were there, sleeping in my lap, I just felt so safe. I don't know why, but some-thing about having you there felt...right. I was wondering if you could...no, forget it." She cleared her throat and looked away.

Harlowe drew in a breath of pure wonder. She hoped she hadn't misunderstood, but there was only one thing Tatum was asking her. Joyfully, Harlowe dropped her robe and leapt onto the bed.

"Of course, I'll stay here with you tonight," Harlowe said brightly. She dove under the comforter and swam around until her head poked out again. Tatum looked shocked and Harlowe froze. Oh shit.

Harlowe said, "I totally got that wrong, didn't I?"

She was about to jump out again when Tatum put a hand on her shoulder. "No, that was exactly what I was asking. I just didn't really think about it in detail.

How…intimate that would be."

Harlowe wrinkled her nose. "I should have kept to my offer to sleep in the chair. I've done it before and it's surprisingly comfy."

"No, I couldn't ask you to do that. I'll take the chair."

"And spend another sleepless night, maybe waking up with a backache?" Harlowe sat up and batted the comforter away from her body so she could put her hands on her hips in order to back up her glare. "This bed is big enough for four people, so we can share with no problem. I don't take up a lot of room and I'm pretty sure I don't snore."

Tatum's expression softened. "All right." She folded back the cover and slipped in beside Harlowe, who obligingly backed up to give her space. Tatum settled down with a sigh. She rolled over onto her side to face Harlowe, propping her head up on one hand. "Are you sure you're okay with this?"

"Sure," Harlowe said. "Are you?"

Their eyes met and locked. Harlowe bit her lip. The silver-blue depths held her captive.

"Yes," Tatum answered. The intense mood broke with a light chuckle. "After all, you're as harmless as cherry pie."

"Yup, that's me." Harlowe covered her yawn with one hand. "Hit the lights Tae."

"Tae?" The nickname was met by a brow lift.

"Oops, sorry, that just slipped out. Sorry, Tatum. The Right Honorable Edwyn." Harlowe giggled.

"I like Tae," Tatum said softly. She reached out a long arm and switched off the light.

"Really?" Harlowe wriggled happily.

"Yes and stop squirming."

"Okay, but stop hogging the covers. My ass is hanging out here."

A low laugh echoed through the darkness. "My sincere apologies. Roll over."

Confused, Harlowe did as she was told. She twitched when a strong arm came around her waist and pulled her close. Tatum's low voice murmured in her ear, "Is this okay?"

"Uh huh," Harlowe managed to squeak out. Tatum's body was warm and firm. Harlowe thought she would pass out when Tatum pressed up against her back. She held Harlowe in a gentle embrace. This was either heaven or hell. Harlowe closed her eyes and tried to slow her breathing. She had never felt anything like that, the taut heat of Tatum's arm around her.

To her alarm, a warm, hungry buzz started up between her legs. Harlowe squeezed her thighs together. Definitely hell. But a nice hell. She reached under the comforter and ran a hand over Tatum's arm, feeling the corded muscle under her palm. Harlowe took in a deep breath that penetrated through her body straight to her core and let it out. God, if this was as close as she got to Tatum, she'd be satisfied. Harlowe couldn't believe what was happening when Tatum's hand slid over the satiny front of her camisole and rested on her belly.

Nothing felt as natural as Tatum's arm around her. Her body responded as if they'd lain like that a thousand times. Harlowe held her breath, afraid to break the spell. She softly pressed her hand over Tatum's, tacitly accepting the intimate touch. Behind her, Tatum's breaths were deep and even, peaceful.

"Goodnight Harlowe." Tatum's whispered words were as intimate as a kiss.

"Night Tae."

****

The late morning sunlight streamed into the room, golden and warm. Harlowe kept her eyes closed, basking in the comfort and fuzziness of her half-awake state. Where was she? Harlowe bolted upright and looked around. She wasn't in her room. A quick inspection concluded that, for one thing, the previous night wasn't a dream and for another, she was alone. Harlowe let out a long sigh and hugged her knees to her chest. Okay, maybe that was an unspoken agreement they wouldn't talk about the incident. To go on as if it never happened.

But it did happen. Harlowe still felt the lingering

heat and softness of Tae—Tatum against her back. She remembered how safe she felt within the circle of those strong arms, like she'd finally come home.

"Fuck," Harlowe gritted. She put her head in her hands before she raked back her pillow-tousled hair. She hoped she could face Tatum that morning without blushing a hundred shades of red and blurting out the most awkward things.

As Harlowe got dressed, she thought about Tatum's health. Mentally was anybody's guess, but physically she seemed recovered enough to take care of herself. Harlowe couldn't see her wanting to stay longer. Was there any way to keep in touch? Did Tatum have a cell phone? Would Harlowe have to resort to smoke-signals or morse code via flashlight? Harlowe gathered her hair back into a ponytail and huffed her bangs out of her face. They really were getting on her nerves.

In the kitchen, she found Tatum presiding over the coffee machine with her back to Harlowe. She was in the same charcoal trousers and white shirt as the previous day, but added a fitted vest that skimmed the clean lines of her body, emphasizing her broad shoulders and trim waist. Harlowe's gaze drifted lower and...daaaaaymn, she thought to herself in a slow drawl.

Her heart jolted. Harlowe forcibly reminded herself what happened the night before was merely a friendly interaction. As far as she was concerned, until Tatum mentioned it, it never happened.

Tatum greeted her with a steaming mug of coffee. Harlowe took it and happily buried her nose in it, inhaling the rich aroma. She peered over the rim of her mug at Tatum as she sipped her own coffee. Harlowe had to admit, she looked much better, well-rested and steady on her feet. The shadows of exhaustion and pinched look of pain were completely gone from her face.

"I was getting tired of green tea," Tatum said apologetically. "I hope you don't mind I helped myself to your coffeemaker."

"Completely okay with me," Harlowe said. "I could get used to mornings like this."

As soon as she said the words, she wished she hadn't.

Tatum's face fell. That sadness that always lingered just under the surface broke through. Maybe she was thinking about the interminable future stretching out ahead of her. Tatum probably regretted getting close with some crazy rando who was prone to come knocking at the front door of her fortress of solitude at any hour of the day, possibly singing "99 bottles of beer on the wall."

To head off the mood-dive, Harlowe went over to the refrigerator and came out with the remainder of the fruit loaf from the previous day and a carton of eggs. "What are you in the mood for today? How about some scrambled eggs?"

"That would be great, thank you."

"Sit, take the load off," Harlowe said, waving Tatum over to the chairs. With both of them on the same side of the counter, the kitchen was very close quarters. They would inevitably collide if Tatum stayed while Harlowe was at the stove. She didn't want to think about what would happen then—actually, she did, but she shouldn't.

Obligingly, Tatum took a seat at the counter and sipped her coffee while Harlowe got breakfast ready.

"Did you sleep well?" Harlowe asked, as if she didn't know.

"Yes, I did, for once," Tatum said.

"Me too," Harlowe chirped. She hadn't meant to be so cheerful about it, but it had been the best night of her life so far.

Tatum didn't say anything more. She fiddled with her mug, turning it around in a circle on the countertop. She didn't look at Harlowe, and Harlowe was intrigued to see a definite flush on those sculpted cheeks.

"I just wanted to say, thank you," Tatum said. She had her eyes fixed on the countertop. She raised a hand and massaged one temple. "I really appreciate what you did for me last night. I hope I didn't...cross any boundaries. I feel free here, probably too free."

"Nah," Harlowe said. "What's a bit of snuggling between friends?"

Tatum's answer was a noncommittal grunt. At any rate, she looked relieved. Harlowe guessed she should be too, but she felt both wired and empty.

Harlowe finished her breakfast and started to collect the dishes.

"Let me," Tatum said. Her gentle tone and the tiny smile she gifted Harlowe killed any thought she had of protest. Tatum brought the dishes to the sink. Like it had always been that way, she rolled up her sleeves and began washing the plates. Harlowe dreamily leaned her cheek on one hand and contentedly lived in the moment. Something occurred to her and Harlowe sat up suddenly.

"Tae, uh, Tatum, I was wondering if you could help me out."

"Anything," Tatum said in a low, intense voice that did nothing at all for Harlowe's spiking hormones.

"I've been thinking," Harlowe said in a rush, "I really need a haircut, but it's such a pain in the butt to go into town and I haven't checked out the salons yet so it would really help me out if you could maybe um..." Harlowe ran out of breath and nerve at the same time.

"What is it?" Tatum leaned her elbow on the counter and rested her cheek on her hand. With her sleeves rolled up and the top buttons of her shirt opened, she looked casually dashing and hot as hell. "I'm glad to help out with anything. You've been such a wonderful hostess and caretaker, it's the least I can do to help you out in return."

Flustered, Harlowe flushed with happiness. She yanked out her ponytail and shook out her long hair.

"I was hoping you could cut it for me," she said in a rush. Harlowe looked up through her bangs. Her heart thudded with apprehension. Tatum wasn't angry, in fact, she looked pleased in a hesitant way.

"Really?"

"Sure," Harlowe said. She twirled a golden strand around her finger. "I trust you."

"What did you have in mind?"

"Chop it," Harlowe said with a slow smile. She felt the light of it spilling over her face and wondered if perhaps Tatum was right about her and her ability to fill a room. "I've had it like this for way too long. I don't want to look like a kid anymore."

Tatum smirked and prodded Harlowe on her shoulder. "And how old are you, anyway?"

"Twenty-one," Harlowe said, pulling herself up proudly. "But I'm almost twenty-two. It's my birthday on Valentine's Day. Aquarius and proud of it."

"Well, this Capricorn turns thirty-six on Christmas Eve, so I still think you're a kid."

"I'm not!" That stung. Harlowe pouted. "I have a house, a degree, and a job. What else do I need to be an adult?"

Tatum held her hands up in defeat. "All right, you win. So, I assume you don't want a swan?"

"Not on my head," Harlowe said primly. "My bushes are another thing entirely."

That earned her a raised brow. Inwardly, Harlowe glowed.

"All right, give me some time to get calibrated and meet me out back."

****

An hour later, Harlowe sat on a folding lawn chair in the back garden with a towel over her shoulders. Dry leaves scudded around her feet. Behind her, a low, electric hum started up. Harlowe closed her eyes.

"Ready?" Tatum's dark-chocolate voice purred in her ear.

Harlowe sucked in a breath. Fuck, was she ever. She started to nod, but felt a softly firm pressure holding her still.

"Don't nod. I need you to be very still. Use your words, Sweet pea."

The casual nickname sounded impossibly good to her ears. Harlowe swallowed and opened her eyes. She said, "I'm ready."

Tatum didn't say anything more. The hum increased in volume. It resonated through her body, setting off a chain reaction of heat that shot to her core. The arousal simmering within her grew. She fought the urge to squirm in her chair. Glowing blades lowered on either side of her. She could barely hold in the moan of pleasure as one stroked the side of her face, not cutting, but caressing her cheek as if showing her she had nothing to be scared of.

Fear was the last thing Harlowe had on her mind. A wind started up around them, whether from the effect of the blades or not, Harlowe didn't know or care. The humming vibrations rose in pitch. Long golden strands began to cascade down around her. She felt infinitely lighter, transported to another plane of reality. Her heart sang, her body reacted instinctively, inner muscles tightening. Harlowe bit her lip. She couldn't hold the burgeoning need to let go. The sweeping rush surrounding her reached a crescendo. As if a wave of boiling water crashed over her, the painfully tight tension broke in a rush of emotions that left Harlowe shaking and empty.

Harlowe came back to reality, blinking into the late autumn sunlight. Her chest heaved with deep, shivering breaths. Her hands were clenched on the arms of her chair.

"I'm finished, you can move now," Tatum murmured into her ear.

Slowly, Harlowe eased herself to her feet. Her knees were weak and she had to grab onto the chair to steady herself. She felt like she'd been burned to ashes and was now rising from them, reborn. Harlowe had never felt as alive as she did at that moment.

Tatum stood back a safe distance, her blades still glowing. Her head was down, hair over her face, but her posture was no longer defensive. She looked shyly eager, like a rescued dog waiting for its first praise.

Harlowe raised her hands to her head. The short strands were soft under her fingers. Eagerly, she grabbed up the mirror she'd brought and looked at her reflection. She let out a gasp of joy. Free from the weight of her long hair, the new short, shaggy cut framed her face and gave her a bright, sporty look that was also cutely feminine. She twirled, full of energy. Swatches of long golden hair fell from her shoulders to the ground. Tatum raised her blades. The hum changed in a very subtle way. She made a pass over Harlowe. Instead of shearing her hair, they created a tight gust of wind that blew the loose strands from her clothing.

"There, all cleaned up. I hope you don't hate it."

"Oh my god, it's incredible," Harlowe said. "You're incredible."

"I've never cut hair before," Tatum said. She ducked her head modestly, but her eyes sparkled and her luscious, kissable lips tilted up into a genuine smile. "It helps that I had a very cute volunteer. Not only cute. Sweet, funny, and beautiful. You are a treasure that deserves the best. Never forget that."

She gave Harlowe a slow once over, from her head to her feet and back again. Her gaze was piercing, as if she was trying to memorize every detail. Harlowe drew in a breath. Her body reacted to the gaze as if Tatum was touching her. Harlowe wet her lower lip. She wanted nothing more than to fall into her arms, feel that firm body pressed hard against hers, lose herself in a crushing embrace.

"We make a good team," Harlowe said in a chirpy voice.

Tatum just gave her a tiny, sad smile and powered down her suit. "I want to thank you for everything, Harlowe. I'll never forget what you did for me. You let me remember what it was like to be human, even if just for a moment."

"Wait, wait, what?" To her dismay, Harlowe's eyes filled with tears. She shook her head. Her throat closed up.

"If I stay any longer, we'll both start wanting something that shouldn't be," Tatum said. She had an air of infinite sadness, as if she was holding all the misery in the world on her shoulders.

"Is this goodbye?" Harlowe whispered. It was too soon. She wanted one more day. One more hour. Dammit, she had only the slightest taste, but she was already addicted.

"Yes. From the start, it was always going to be goodbye."

"Can I see you again?" Harlowe asked in despair. She already knew the answer.

Tatum shook her head. "It's for the best." She took a step toward Harlowe, then curled her hands into fists, as if holding back from reaching out to her. "You'll find someone perfect for you. Someone unbroken, who can make you happy the way you deserve to be. Goodbye, Harlowe."

Tatum pressed a few buttons on her wrist keypad. The lights came back on full. She sprang away and was gone in a flash.

Harlowe fell to her knees. The wind at once chilled her. The sunlight felt like glass. She stood and slowly folded the lawn chair. Automatically, Harlowe went through the motions of tidying the garden. She was shivering and her hands were numb by the time she was finished. Struck silent, she looked at the beautiful livingsculptures that ringed the garden. They were captured in mid-motion, full of life and joy. Someone terminally broken wouldn't be able to capture that emotion, would they? The scene blurred. Harlowe dragged a cuff across her face and sniffled.

"Damn it," she hissed. Angrily, she ran into the cottage and slammed the door behind her. She wouldn't break. She wouldn't let this break her. Harlowe set her jaw and purposely bypassed Tatum's—the master bedroom without even pausing on her way to the laundry room. Some mundane chores would take her mind off things.

"I'm okay, I'm going to be okay," Harlowe said. Her voice sounded loud in the cottage, which suddenly seemed very large and very empty. She pattered down the stairs to the basement, which contained the furnace room as well as the laundry room. Harlowe was mostly in control of herself until she opened the laundry room door. Piled on top of the dryer were the clothes Tatum borrowed, washed, dried and folded. A true gentleman to the very end. Harlowe crumpled to the linoleum. Tears coursed down her cheeks. The emptiness that howled through her was more painful than anything she'd ever experienced. She hugged her arms to her chest and mourned something that never had a chance to be.

Chapter Six

Ignoring the various members of the meeting on her screen, Harlowe propped her chin on her hand and stared out of the window. It had now been two and a half weeks, seventeen days to be exact, since Tatum left her. She sighed, a deep sigh dredged up from the bottom of her soul.

The days dragged on in a grey montage of events that were equally tedious and dreary. Harlowe waited for the pain to dull, but it didn't. It mutated and came at her in different ways every time. Once it jabbed her when she found the mug Tatum had used. Another time, it reared its head and bit her when a friend sent her a bunch of *Supergirl* memes with the note "LOL too gay" attached. When the news of her first subscription came through, from none other than Edwyn Robotics Ltd., Harlowe felt like she'd been stabbed in the chest. Why did Tatum have to be so damn chivalrous? And why didn't that extend into giving Harlowe a chance? Every day, Harlowe tortured herself by gazing over the increasingly brown and bare forest to the bunker. Every day it seemed farther away. She wished she had the strength to trek up the hill and bang on the gate. If she did and got shot down again (hopefully only figuratively) she didn't think her heart could take it.

So, Harlowe kept on going, she even tried to smile, but every time she tried, more tears came. Harlowe felt like her ability to be happy had been surgically removed. The bi-weekly family group call brought generous compliments about her new haircut. Harlowe's lukewarm reaction was thankfully taken for slight regret at losing the long hair she'd been growing out since junior high school.

Her assignments from the newspaper increased to proofreading and rewriting a few articles, but none of it brought her any joy or satisfaction.

The only time Harlowe felt the slightest peace was in

the garden. She ordered a bag of seeds for the feeder, which the squirrels that she named Amelia and Eleanor, enjoyed very much. Harlowe watched them scamper around, frolicking in the fallen leaves and pretended she wasn't dying with every passing moment. The sky hung heavy with the threat of snow, yet none fell.

When Harlowe wasn't listlessly raking the rapidly falling leaves, she wandered aimlessly through the garden, trailing her fingers over the sculpted bushes. There, her mind went back to the time she'd spent with Tatum. The memories were sharp and full, much more vibrant to her than her daily drudgery.

"Miss Tremaine? Sorry, you're still on mute. I'd like to hear about your progress with those proofreads."

"Shit," Harlowe spat automatically. She jolted upright and stabbed at the keyboard. She schooled her face into a happy smile before she turned on the camera and mic. On her screen, her boss Bucky, along with a number of assorted employees of the *Maritime Gazette*, stared back at her with varying degrees of interest. Harlowe adjusted her earphones to stall for time. What the fuck was that proofreading thing about again? "Sorry about that," Harlowe said with as much sincerity as she could muster. "I forgot to unmute. Anyway, about the proofreading, I'm almost done with it. I'm just fact-checking the, um, facts. Another day and I'll have it back to you."

"Well done, that's what I like to hear." Bucky rustled some papers with his thick, ruddy fingers. In the background, somebody's baby started wailing. A couple of dogs barked and one of the sportswriters shooed his cat off the keyboard. Business as usual. Bucky said, "All right folks, we've got one thing left on the agenda. I need someone who can take over for Wanda doing the horoscopes next week while she's on family leave."

"I can't," Josh Bennet, the cocky guy who acted like he was the human incarnation of the Pulitzer fucking Prize, piped up. "I've got a really important investigative piece about those bad coupons from Zoller's department store. It's gonna knock the entire province on its ass, the entire country maybe."

"Definitely keep on doing that," Bucky said. He lowered his glasses and peered at the screen. "How about you, Miss Tremaine? How in tune with the stars are you? It'll be your first byline."

Harlowe didn't give a shit about the horoscope, but she did give a shit about getting her name out there. A byline was a byline, after all.

"Sure, I'll do it," Harlowe said. Why the hell not, she wasn't getting any closer to being a reporter, that was for sure. She might as well peddle some woo-woo bullshit while she was at it. Thankfully, that was the last item on the agenda, and the meeting soon finished.

After she left the meeting, Harlowe waited for her boss to forward her the template for the horoscope, idly spinning in her chair. She had never felt as lost as she did just then. She wanted to be angry with Tatum, but she couldn't. Leaving hadn't been easy for her. There were definitely moments when she'd shown real emotion, but she did have a concussion. Maybe once she was back to her usual self, things were clearer. Harlowe felt tears prickle at her eyes and resisted the urge to swear. They had only known each other for less than 48 hours, for fuck's sake. Harlowe had to get over it.

But how could she, now that she realized she'd never find anyone who made her feel the same ever again? It was impossible. That connection wasn't something that came along every day. Her friends back home would tell her to get over it, get out and have a fling. Harlowe snorted. Even if she wasn't in the middle of a backwoods nowhere, she wouldn't do that. Maybe before, but now? Nope. She didn't want anyone else.

At the very least she wanted to see Tatum again and talk to her, really talk and see what was going on, maybe that would give her closure and Harlowe wouldn't spend half the night tossing and turning in anguish as her mind replayed every single moment they shared.

The template arrived, along with a whole lot of notes and star charts and whatever from Wanda. Harlowe pulled herself up to the desk again and promptly ignored all of Wanda's stuff. She glanced through the examples from the previous week. Just to torture herself a bit more, she looked up her own horoscope from the day Tatum left her.

Aquarius:

Do something fun and out of your comfort zone; pair that persimmon top with your teal capris, treat yourself to a solo dinner out. A project at work that could use some tweaking is going to get back on track. Your monetary situation may seem a little blue right now, but chin up! Place a yellow item in the west corner of your kitchen for max results.

Harlow snorted. What a load of bullshit. It should have read you'll get your dreams smashed and your heart stomped on. Today you'll lose something irreplaceable. She swallowed the painful tightness in her throat.

"Just get it over with," Harlowe muttered. She tapped on the template and stared at the empty page. The first sign looked back at her. Capricorn. Tatum's sign. Harlowe bit her lip. Would *nothing* ever stop reminding her of what she'd had and lost? With her luck, she'd write something stupid and Tatum would read it and... Harlowe froze. That was it. A flicker of hope woke up in her chest. She dove into the task, typing madly (and deleting just as much). Finally, Harlowe was finished and re-read the entries for what seemed like the hundredth time.

Capricorn:

Unfinished business is an albatross around not only your neck. You don't need to rent a U-Haul, but if you ask someone cute and special to tea, something going very wrong can be set right.

Aquarius:

You know that song by M.E.? The unofficial anthem of our people? The stubborn Capricorn in your life needs to hear that. It's either that or a "*'99 Bottles of Beer On the Wall*" marathon.

Harlowe nodded in grim satisfaction. She'd see if anything came of it and if nothing did, maybe she'd try a different approach. She had the Ghibli fish song in her arsenal, after all. She finished the rest of the horoscopes with anticipation in her heart. There was a chance Tatum would see what she'd written. Harlowe could only hope. When she was finished with the rest of the horoscopes, which she'd pulled completely out of her ass, she went over the article she was proofreading and changed two things that didn't really need changing, but she wanted to show she'd at least done something.

The feeling of hope followed her into the kitchen, where she reheated the chicken soup she'd listlessly abandoned at lunchtime. Her stomach growled. For the first time in two and a half weeks, Harlowe was ravenous. She mixed up a big batch of biscuits and wriggled in anticipation while they baked.

She felt better than she had in a long time, which could explain what she did that night after dinner. Harlowe was on her way back to her room when she turned left instead of right and ended up in the master bedroom. She stood in the open doorway, hand on the doorknob. She hadn't gone in there since the day Tatum left. The curtains were still open. She didn't bother to turn on the light before she stepped into the room.

In the moonlight, the bed looked just as comfy and inviting as always. Still crumpled from that morning when she woke up alone, but with the memory of Tatum's embrace in her mind. Harlowe's happy mood dissolved. She bit her lip to keep it from trembling. She took a step toward it, intending to pull the comforter straight, but she stopped just short of touching the softness of the disturbed bedding.

"Damn it," Harlowe whispered. She sank to her knees on the floor and pillowed her head in her arms. Sobs wracked her small form. With each heaving breath, the very faint scent that haunted her dreams came back to her. When she ran out of tears, Harlowe groggily rubbed her damp cheeks on her sleeve. She was finally drained of emotion. Nothing was left except emptiness.

On unsteady feet, she made her way back to her room, where she jumped into the shower and tried to scrub Tatum's scent and memory from her skin. The fragrant bubbles from her favorite lily of the valley shower gel helped a bit, but Harlowe was still sighing and melancholy when she fell into her narrow, cold bed.

****

On the day her horoscope was printed in the paper, Harlowe felt a change in the air. Maybe it was the snowstorm the weather station predicted, or maybe it was something within Harlowe herself. Something was going to change. She managed to go through the motions of a normal day, up until bedtime.

Once more, Harlowe stood in the doorway to the master bedroom. She flipped the switch to illuminate the room before she went over to the bed. She set her shoulders and lowered her head. She needed to get over it and move on with her life. She'd strip the bed and tomorrow she would scald everything clean in the hottest water her washing machine could produce. That would be the end.

Tomorrow she would forget.

Tonight was another story. The darkness of Harlowe's soul threatened to swallow her whole. She didn't have the strength to turn off the light, so she just kept it on.

Harlowe took off her bunny robe and draped it over the armchair. Clad only in her camisole and panties, she slipped under the comforter. The sheets skimmed over her skin, the soft bedding surrounded her like a caress. Harlowe closed her eyes and breathed in the scent that still clung to the fine linen that reminded her of Tatum. She remembered the feeling of completion in Tatum's arms, how carefully and tenderly she'd been held within that strong embrace. She would never have that again. Tatum was right, there was no hope for anything other than goodbye.

Tears gathered behind her closed lids. Harlowe let them fall, dampening the pillowcase.

Her dreams were chaotic and unsettling and Harlowe

woke after only a few fitful hours. She sat up, heart pounding. She had the distinct feeling she wasn't alone. She eased the comforter off and swung her legs around to sit on the side of the mattress. The garden outside was dark, the glass reflected the room back to her.

It must have been a remnant of her dream or some random neuron misfiring in her sleep-deprived brain. Harlowe reached out to turn off the light and froze, listening. Nothing more than the rustling of the branches outside came to her ears. Harlowe shook her head. She was imagining things. She needed to sleep and forget.

Harlowe pulled her feet up and flipped the light switch, throwing the room into darkness. Outside the glass, an unmistakable blue glow outlined a black form.

With a cry of joy, Harlowe switched the light on again and leapt clear across the room. Fingers scrabbled at the lock before she threw the window open. Freezing air poured into the room and grabbed her ankles, but she didn't care. Tears rained down Harlowe's cheeks, this time of joy. Outside, standing on the bare ground in full battle-gear was Tatum. The wind whipped her long hair around her body like a cape. She looked exhausted, her eyes were smudged with purple and her cheekbones were sharp against her ebony hair. A rose of pain blossomed in Harlowe's chest. Tatum raised her head and looked directly at Harlowe. Her gaze was hungry and desperate.

"I couldn't decide," Tatum said. "Which song you meant, *Come To My Window* or *Yes, I Am*. Congratulations on your first byline, by the way."

Harlowe clapped a hand to her mouth. She impatiently scrubbed at the tears on her cheeks before she leaned out and said, "It was *Yes, I am*. Yes, I am gay. Yes, I am head-over-heels for you. Yes, I want to see you again. And yes, I am sure."

Tatum bowed her head. Harlowe ached at the weariness in her movements, the sadness in her stance.

"Do you have any idea what time it is?" Harlowe sighed and rubbed her chilled arms. "The least you could do is get your butt in here before we both freeze ours off."

While Tatum clambered into the room, Harlowe

dashed to wrap herself in her bunny robe. She closed the window and shut the curtains before facing Tatum.

"Why did you leave me?" Harlowe asked in a small voice. She impatiently rubbed the cuff of her robe over her watering eyes.

"I wanted to protect you."

"So you just decided to ditch me without any warning?" Suddenly Harlowe was seized by rage, as she ran up to Tatum and raised a fist. "How dare you leave me like that," she said through choking sobs. Her voice ratcheted up as she spoke. "You didn't even ask me, you just decided. You didn't even give me a chance."

"Harlowe, *no*," Tatum cried out as Harlowe's fist connected with her shoulder. A blinding blue flash was the last thing Harlowe saw before blackness closed over her head.

****

The next thing Harlowe knew, she was lying on something so soft she was almost floating. A gentle hand was on her forehead. She blinked up at Tatum's concerned face.

"What happened?" Harlowe asked. She struggled to sit up in the bed. Tatum helped by wrapping an arm around her. Harlowe slouched back against the pillows.

"The suit," Tatum said in a sheepish voice. "Sweet pea, I should have warned you. It has several automatic defense systems. You set one of them off."

"Shit, so I stun-gunned myself," Harlowe said. "I shouldn't have punched you."

"I deserved it. I caused you pain. It was a mistake and I'm sorry."

Harlowe let her gaze rest on Tatum. She didn't have the words to describe the anguish she'd felt. Now, she could barely summon the memory. Tatum was back. She was real and right there, perched uneasily on the edge of the mattress with her hands twisted together in her lap.

"It's okay, I forgive you." Harlowe pulled her robe around her body and smiled at Tatum. She couldn't hold it back. She felt like she was champagne, full of bubbles and sparkling. She tilted her head. "So, why did you come back?"

A crooked grin pulled at Tatum's full lips. "I was just checking my horoscope and it told me I was overdue to invite a certain special someone out to tea. I saw your light and I had to go to you. Then I remembered I don't have any tea, so I'd like to ask you," Tatum paused and took a deep breath. She shook back her trailing bangs and fixed Harlowe with her intense gaze. "Ask if you'd care to accompany me into town in preparation for a tea party for two this afternoon."

"Yes," Harlowe cried out. She jumped to her knees and launched herself at Tatum. This time, she managed to do it without stunning anyone and they tumbled into the fluffy comforter. Harlowe buried her face against Tatum's shoulder. Strong arms came around her. Harlowe thought she would melt. Once more, tears welled up in her eyes.

Harlowe pulled away and sat up. She dabbed at her eyes with the fuzzy cuff of her robe.

"So, what kind of tea party are we talking about?" she asked. "Like, a friendly kind of tea party, or..." Harlowe trailed off. She lowered her head and looked up at Tatum through her lashes.

Tatum met her gaze squarely. "Whatever kind you want."

"Oh wow," Harlowe breathed. Her heart hammered against her ribs. Her entire body felt electrified. "I don't want to be just friends. I want more. A lot more. Are you okay with that?"

"I shouldn't be," Tatum said. She stood and crossed her arms, turning slightly from Harlowe. "I don't know if I'm good for you, but I couldn't...leave you like that. I couldn't work. I couldn't sleep. Nothing was the same."

"I know," Harlowe said. "It was like that for me, too."

Tatum's gorgeous mouth curled into a wry grin. "I guess you're stuck with me, then."

"Good, I want to be stuck with you," Harlowe said. "But it's not even three am." She stood and planted herself directly in front of Tatum. "We have a few hours before the stores open. How about spending them with me in a more comfortable setting?"

Deliberately, she let the robe slip down her arms and fall to the floor. Tatum's quick indrawn breath was loud in Harlowe's ears. Under Tatum's devouring gaze, she flushed and looked away. Her nipples were hard points under her camisole. Harlowe was incredibly aware her modesty was protected by only the small triangle of clinging cotton between her legs. She was not prepared for the emotions that came from simply standing there.

Tatum took a step back. She looked uncomfortable. She held out a hand, as if to block Harlowe's half-dressed form from her eyes. "Harlowe, Sweet pea, I'm extremely flattered, but it's much too soon to take that step. I can't—"

Harlowe's knees buckled and she nearly fell over in surprise. "Oh God, did you think I just asked you to, oh no, oh my God," Harlowe blathered. She grabbed her robe and held it in front of herself. "I just meant to, you know, snuggle." She huffed and blew a strand of hair out of her red and sweating face.

Tatum relaxed. "I'm sorry, I misunderstood."

"No, it's my fault. I didn't think about how it would sound, you know, to someone experienced," Harlowe said. She tried to take a step but her feet got tangled up in her robe. She tripped and pitched forward with a squeak. Tatum moved faster than thought and Harlowe landed neatly in her arms. Harlowe sagged into the strong, firm but chaste hold. She hid her blushing face against Tatum's body-armor-clad chest in embarrassment. God, Tatum must think she was such a child! She hadn't thought her words implied she wanted to do *that* with Tatum at all, but apparently that's what it looked like.

Tatum lifted Harlowe's chin with a gentle finger. "You don't have to answer if you don't want to, but you haven't been with anyone before? Intimately?"

"Um, no," Harlowe said. She nervously wet her lips and shrugged. "I have extremely high standards, like unless you can knock me out me with your clothes and trim my bushes into dragons and stuff, I won't give you the time of day," she said in a joking tone.

Tatum chuckled. The low sound rippled through Harlowe. "All right, and I will take you up on your offer of snuggles."

"Good," Harlowe said. She ditched her robe and bounded into the bed, where she busily made an inviting nest out of the fluffy comforter. "If you want to change, everything's where you left it."

Tatum stood still for a moment, and Harlowe felt her gaze rest on her. Harlowe canted one shoulder forward and pursed her lips. "No blades in the bed is one of my rules. So, either you strip by yourself or I help you. I'll probably stun myself again, but if that's the price I need to pay, then so be it."

"That won't be necessary," Tatum said. "Give me five minutes."

"Okay," Harlowe said. She burrowed into the bed and squirmed around, making sure there were no cold spots as far as her short legs could reach.

Tatum returned in the blue and white striped nightshirt and slipped into the bed beside Harlowe.

Tatum leaned over and murmured into Harlowe's ear, "Roll over." The low, husky tone caused a full-body shiver. The mattress shifted as Tatum reached out to turn off the light. She came back to Harlowe's side and pressed up against her back. Strong arms came around her and Harlowe gave an involuntary moan as their bodies settled together. She knew there wouldn't be any funny business that time, but her body hummed with arousal. Just being near Tatum was enough to turn her insides to hot jelly. Being held in her arms, feeling the incredible softness of her breasts and the hardness of her muscular belly and legs was like falling into molten gold.

"Thank you for coming back," Harlowe whispered. She slid her hand down Tatum's arm and guided her hand under the hem of her camisole, asking for a more intimate hold than the previous time. Harlowe drew in a breath as Tatum slipped under her top and allowed her palm to press against Harlowe's bare skin. The contact caused Harlowe to wriggle her backside just the slightest into the heat between Tatum's legs.

"God, Harlowe," Tatum's voice was strained. She

pulled Harlowe tight against her. A strong thigh slipped between Harlowe's from behind. Unable to help herself Harlowe let go with a tiny whimper. Tatum whispered into her hair, "Too fast?"

"I'm okay," Harlowe said. The pounding heat between her legs didn't let up. She had never been that close to anyone before. Her body screamed for more, but her mind wouldn't let her go any further. Harlowe bit her lip and willed herself to stay still. "Um, yeah, I'm extremely okay. Are you comfortable? I tried to warm up the bed for you but I may have missed a spot."

"Everything is perfect," Tatum murmured. She dropped a quick kiss behind Harlowe's ear and whispered. "Goodnight, Sweet pea."

"Goodnight Tae," Harlowe replied. She closed her eyes and relaxed into the warm darkness. For that moment, everything really was perfect.

Chapter Seven

Harlow backed the little blue car into the parking space and shut off the engine. She jumped out and inhaled the crisp morning air with gusto. She adjusted her cheerful knit cap with the rainbow-colored pompom and clapped her mittens together before she circled the car and peered worriedly into the passenger's side window. Tatum sat still as a block of ice in the trench coat Harlowe found for her after she refused to take off the battle-suit. The only sign of life was the jumping muscle in her jaw. One hand clutched onto the holy shit handle. Harlowe ached at seeing the look of stark fear on her face. She couldn't imagine how hard it would be to suddenly be thrust back into society after seven years alone. Tatum had been tense and withdrawn since that morning. Harlowe woke up alone again, and found Tatum brooding over the coffee machine. Since then, her mood hadn't improved one bit.

Harlowe knocked on the window very gently. Nevertheless, Tatum flinched violently and brought her arms up in a defensive pose. Harlowe sprang back even though they were separated by the steel-reinforced car door. Tatum sagged and buried her face in her hands.

"Tae," Harlowe said softly. She braced her hands on her knees and leaned forward. "Are you okay? We don't have to do this."

On the other side of the window, Tatum shook her head. Her shoulders rose and fell with her rapid breaths. She waved a hand and opened the door. Harlowe stepped back and waited for Tatum to unfurl her long legs, almost too long for Harlowe's little compact car. Her boots hit the asphalt, and she rose to her full height. Not exactly looking confident, but at least she was upright.

Tatum glanced around nervously. Harlowe purposely chose a parking lot in one of the less busy areas of Brooksville, behind a row of souvenir shops that were closed for the season. Their goal was the small supermarket, known as the Lo-Kost Mart, to which Harlowe had a number of coupons.

"Are you okay?" Harlowe asked.

"Fine." The taciturn, withdrawn Tatum was back.

"All right, let's go," Harlowe said. She took a few steps and when Tatum didn't follow, she turned around with her hands on her hips. "I know you might like that whole 'five steps behind' thing but we're living in the 21st century now and I insist we walk side by side. Even though I'm a pipsqueak compared to you."

That seemed to do the trick. Tatum raised her head and stepped up to Harlowe, where she offered her arm.

"My apologies," she said. "Allow me to escort you, my lady."

Harlowe giggled and threaded her arm through Tatum's. As they navigated the short walk from the parking lot, Harlowe felt Tatum flinch a couple times, but her pace didn't falter. At that hour of the morning, the supermarket was empty except for a single cashier and one worker behind the tiny deli counter. Tatum kept her head down and let Harlowe take charge of the cart. Like every single other cart Harlowe had ever pushed, one wheel would randomly mutiny and jerk them off course.

"What do we need for the party?" Harlowe asked. The cart squeaked through the produce section. The selection was limited, but what they had looked fresh and the prices weren't exorbitant.

"Tea," Tatum said. She glanced around nervously as a trio of elderly women came in. They stopped in their tracks in the entrance and bolted out again. Tatum didn't appear to notice their looks of terror, and Harlowe was glad.

"Okay, we've got tea," Harlowe said and steered the cart into the tea and coffee aisle. She held out a few for inspection and they ended up getting a box of assorted herbal teas. Harlowe kept finding items she wanted to share with Tatum, and soon the cart was full.

"Is that everything we need?" Harlowe asked.

Tatum looked up from her list and nodded.

"Great," Harlowe said. "Let's go check out."

Tatum froze. She nervously smoothed her hands down over her coat.

"What's wrong?"

"I forgot about paying," Tatum said in a defeated tone. Her lip twitched in anger.

"It's okay," Harlowe said. She placed her hand on Tatum's forearm. "I forget my wallet all the time, too. Don't worry, I'll get this one and you can get the next one. All right? Besides, I'm the one with the coupons."

Tight-lipped, Tatum nodded. They got everything paid for and bagged without incident. Tatum gallantly took both cloth bags. As they left the supermarket, a squat brick building caught Harlowe's eye.

"Ooh, hang on a sec," Harlowe said. She reached up and patted Tatum on the shoulder. "I think I see a liquor store over there. How about I get a little something to spice up our tea party?"

"I don't drink," Tatum said. "But feel free to get something for yourself."

"Okay," Harlowe said. She dug out her key fob and pressed it into Tatum's hand. "Could you take those back to the car? I'll be there in a couple of minutes."

Tatum looked torn between staying with Harlowe and escaping. The latter won out and she made a beeline for the car. Humming to herself and thinking about wine, Harlowe went into the liquor store. She stood in the entranceway and looked around, mentally calculating what would go best with the ingredients they had.

"Excuse me, girlfriend." A guy about Harlowe's age with a nametag that read "Nabeel" on his polo shirt parked himself in front of her. He extended one hand with a flourish. "Show me your deets, sweetie."

"Sorry," Harlowe said. She dug out her ID and held it out for his inspection.

Nabeel looked from the card to her face several times and let out a low whistle. "You certainly are a cute little thing. I bet you get carded everywhere you go."

"Pretty much," Harlowe said.

"You're okay to come in. Have a peek at the garden of delights we have here." Nabeel leaned one hip on the turnstile and gestured dramatically to the interior of the store.

The selection was dizzying. Harlowe pursed her lips,

deep in thought. "Can I ask for some advice?"

"Certainly honey, ask away."

Harlowe tapped her lower lip with a finger. "See, I'm looking for something non-alcoholic but festive. It's for a date. A very important first date."

"Oh?" Nabeel perked up. "Well, you can't go wrong with mango juice for that special man in your life."

"Special woman," Harlowe clarified. She flushed and smiled at the thought. "And I was thinking of something...sparkling."

"In that case, I know just the thing." Nabeel sashayed over to a display case and came back with a slim bottle in his hands. "Your lady will love this. Sparkling strawberry cordial."

"That looks super," Harlowe took the bottle and studied the label. "Thanks," she said.

"Anytime." He dismissed her with a flutter of his fingers.

Harlowe got a cart and headed over to the red wine section. As she shopped, Harlowe had a strange feeling of being watched. Besides Nabeel, who was playing on his phone, there was only one other person in the store, a husky woman in a red and black lumberjack shirt who pushed her cart around slowly. It was filled with cheap beer. Her hair was dirty blonde and cut into a shaggy mullet, and her eyes never left Harlowe for a moment. Harlowe had no idea who she was and she didn't really care to know. She looked mean and scrappy, like she'd trip you just for shits and giggles. Harlowe saw an open can of beer in the child seat of her cart. Every so often, she'd slurp at it, Classy, Harlowe thought as she looked over the selection of imported cheeses. The other customer seemed to be following her in a predatory way. Harlowe squirmed, feeling like she was a field mouse being watched by a hungry hawk.

Her suspicion was confirmed when she bent over to get a box of crackers from a low shelf. A wolf whistle cut through the piped-in pop music. Annoyed, Harlowe ignored her and hurried to the checkout. She had just finished paying when a harsh voice interrupted her pleasant thoughts.

"Hey, new girl."

Harlowe just picked up her stuff and left the store. Unfortunately, the woman ran out after her and cornered her in the parking lot.

"What do you want?" Harlowe asked. She glared at the other to get her to back off. It didn't work.

"I haven't seen you around before. You new?"

"Yes," Harlowe said slowly. "And you are?"

"Shelby Stevens." She didn't extend a hand or any other pleasantry, but her eyes roved over Harlowe's body in a way she didn't like at all.

"Not nice to meet you and goodbye," Harlowe said. She tried to dart around Shelby, but her escape route was blocked by the other woman shoving herself into Harlowe's path. Annoyed, Harlowe stopped and sighed.

"Ya wanna eat me?" Shelby asked in a mean voice.

"What?" Harlowe's face froze in an expression of complete non-comprehension.

"I heard you talking to that fruit in there. You're one of *those*, arent'cha," Shelby said loudly. "You don't do it with guys, so you must wanna do mine, right?"

"No," Harlowe replied. She shifted her load to her hip and used her free hand to stab a finger at Shelby while she spoke. "I don't know who you are, but I don't appreciate being talked to like that. Sorry, I have to go. Somewhere far away from you." Harlowe made one last attempt to get past Shelby, who bent down like a linebacker and caught Harlowe in the middle of her chest with her shoulder., Harlowe went down. She landed sprawled on the ground, winded. Her purchases burst from the bag and scattered over the packed earth.

Harlowe rubbed the aching spot on her chest and glared up at Shelby, who was gloating over her.

"Little people with big mouths are gonna get what's coming to them," Shelby said. She yanked a hand out of her pocket and suggestively rubbed her crotch. Disgusted, Harlowe looked away. Shelby squatted down next to her, close enough for Harlowe to smell the beer on her breath. She grabbed Harlowe's face with the same hand that had just been between her legs and dragged Harlowe to face her. Harlowe recoiled, but that only made Shelby grip her harder. "Look, you little bitch, I'll give you one chance. Let's go back to my place and you do your thing and maybe I'll make sure your life here isn't a living hell."

"Not a chance. I'd rather eat an actual, live beaver," Harlowe said. "Without salt."

With that, Shelby released Harlowe and shoved her away.

"Your loss. If you change your mind, I'll give you my number." Shelby pulled out her phone and waved it in front of Harlowe.

"Excuse me?" Harlowe asked. Anger overrode her fear. She slapped the phone away. Shelby cursed and dived after it. Harlowe pulled herself up and planted her hands on her hips while Shelby stuffed her phone back into her pants pocket. Harlowe said, "Let me clarify. Even if we were the last two living beings on earth, there is zero chance I would ever voluntarily even be in the same room as you. You're going to have to accept that and move on. Maybe go home and cry about it."

"Shut the fuck up," Shelby lunged and grabbed Harlowe by the front of her jacket. Harlowe struggled, trying to kick Shelby's knees, but Shelby just laughed nastily and held her at arm's length.

The air split and three glowing blades shot in front of Shelby's florid face.

"What the fuck?" Shelby hollered.

"Let her go." The words were delivered in a low growl that held a dangerous note. Tatum stood between them with the shredded remains of one sleeve fluttering in the wind. The blades glowed brilliantly blue around the edges, humming with energy. Tatum lowered her chin and fixed Shelby with the full force of her icy silver-blue glare. She bared her teeth and gritted, "Now."

"Jesus Christ, aggro much? Okay, I'm going," Shelby let go and backed up a step. "Who the fuck are you?"

"Someone you don't want to piss off," Tatum growled. She brandished her blades and advanced on Shelby, who tripped over her own feet and stumbled, then awkwardly ran off. Tatum watched her leave, then swooped down and gathered Harlowe up in a fierce, protective embrace. Tatum's shaking breaths echoed Harlowe's own. Tatum released her and looked into Harlowe's face, "Are you all right?"

"Yeah, I'm okay. Physically, anyway," Harlowe said. "Mentally, I want to punch something."

"Who was that? Do you know her?"

"I never met her before in my life," Harlowe said. She bent down and gathered up her scattered purchases with shaking hands. Tatum gently took the bag from her. Harlowe straightened up and wiped her watering eyes on her cuff. Now that the danger had passed, the shock was wearing off and her emotions were in turmoil. She sniffled. "She just came out of nowhere, saying stuff about going back to her place and doing—stuff," Harlowe said. Her voice cracked and broke.

"I apologize for not coming sooner."

"You were just in time," Harlowe said. She blinked back her tears and tried to summon a brave smile.

"Do I need to eliminate her?" Tatum asked. Harlowe stared at her. She was completely serious.

Harlowe shook her head. "No, that's not a good idea. I don't want you to get in trouble."

"I wouldn't leave any evidence."

"No, no killing, okay?" Harlowe said. She took a few deep breaths and blew her nose into a tissue from her pocket. She looked up into Tatum's face. "Let's go back home now."

The cheerful jingling of the bell preceded Nabeel pattering out to them. He had a small cannister in one hand and waved it about.

"Are you all right?" he asked. "I found my pepper spray. Where is she?"

"Gone," Tatum growled.

"Oh, well, that's probably for the best." Nabeel pocketed his cannister with a sour expression. "So, you met Miss Congeniality."

"Oh yeah," Harlowe said.

"Shelby pulls this stuff all the time," Nabeel said. "She acts like she can do anything she wants to anyone. That's what happens when your parents own the factory that employs three-quarters of the town."

"Ugh , seriously?" Harlowe asked.

Nabeel nodded. "You don't work for them, I hope. Stevens Paperworks?"

"No way."

"You should make a report, then."

"Nah, it's not worth the hassle," Harlowe said.

While Nabeel flitted around, Tatum very gently took Harlowe by the shoulders and looked into her face. "I saw her shove you and grab you. I didn't hear what she said to you, but I have an idea." Her eyes were hard. "That's assault and sexual harrassment. At the very least, you need to let someone know officially what happened. If anything else happens, we've got evidence she started it. I'll be right there beside you every step of the way."

"You're right," Harlowe said. She set her shoulders and shook out her short hair. She gave Tatum her bravest smile. "Thanks," she murmured. She gazed up into Tatum's face. Her eyes were hooded and her lips looked incredibly soft and inviting. Harlowe's breath caught in her throat. She couldn't move.

"The fire station's just over there." Nabeel's voice cut into Harlowe's happy bubble. Both Harlowe and Tatum looked at him. He pointed and twirled his finger around. "The nearest RCMP officer's an hour away and they don't really get involved in our local stuff. You're better off telling them here."

"Okay, I guess I can do that," Harlowe said.

Tatum was silent, and Harlowe could feel the tension coming off her. Even though she looked like she could bolt at the slightest provocation, Tatum stayed at Harlowe's side as promised.

"Good luck to you two," Nabeel called after them. "Come again soon!"

The fire station was only a block away. Harlowe breathed a sigh of relief when Mary appeared at the front desk. She rose and bustled out to greet them.

"Why if it isn't little Harlowe from over the creek and up the hill," Mary said. Her soft, voluminous hand enveloped Harlowe's much smaller one. She peered around Harlowe at Tatum, who hovered by the door, looking like an extremely tall and unfriendly umbrella stand. "And who is this?"

"My friend, Tatum," Harlowe said with a smile and a twinkle. She sobered. "Actually, I'm not here for a fun reason. I was, um, attacked and wanted to file a report."

"Of course, dear." Mary's face crumpled. "You poor thing, come on, into the office where it's more private." She hustled Harlowe into the small, cluttered room behind the desk and sat her down at a table with a bunch of papers to fill out. Tatum followed and hovered protectively behind Harlowe as she reluctantly wrote down the details. Halfway through, Mary came in with two cups of coffee. Harlowe gratefully sipped at hers, while Tatum ignored the cup Mary hesitantly slid toward her.

Mary glanced at the page and sighed. "Shelby is up to her old no-good tricks again, it seems."

"She's done this before?" Harlowe asked, dismayed.

"Unfortunately," Mary said. She took off her glasses and let them hang around her neck by their chain. "She was a bully all through school and never grew out of it. From the get-go we all tried to tell her parents to do something about it, but they never saw anything wrong with her behaviour. They encouraged it, even. I'm sorry she's set her sights on you. Please let us know if anything else happens."

"Okay," Harlowe said. Her belly cramped with anxiety. She glanced up at Tatum, who had her fists clenched at her sides.

Just then, Jim bustled in with the cordless phone tucked in the crook of his shoulder. He leaned over a desk Harlowe assumed was his and rummaged around in a pile of papers. His face was drawn and worried.

"That's really unfortunate. Uh huh, yeah me too. No hard feelings Earl, okay later," he said. With a muttered oath, Jim cut the line and threw the phone down on the desk. He looked up and gave a start. "I apologize. I didn't realize we had visitors. Miss Tremaine, nice to see you again." He stood and lifted his hat to Harlowe, then extended a hand to Tatum. "I don't believe we've met. Jim Peebles, head of the auxiliary. My partner Chrissy is the chief here."

Tatum looked at the outstretched hand as if he was

offering her a flaming turd on a stick.

Mary broke the awkward silence by putting down a cup of coffee on Jim's desk. "Was that call from Earl McAllister? It didn't sound like good news."

"It wasn't," Jim said. He pinched the bridge of his nose and sat down heavily in his chair. "Looks like the hall in Greenvale's not big enough for us. The kids are gonna be real disappointed if we can't find a place for Discovery Day."

"What's that?" Harlowe asked.

"Oh, it's part of Brooksville Days," Jim said. He clasped his hands over his belly and leaned back in his chair. "We always kick off with Discovery Day and it's really popular with all the kids. A bunch of people in town make booths with posters and activities to teach them about different aspects of the town's history and also to introduce some of the small businesses here. It's a pretty big event, even bigger than the Strawberry Social. We usually hold it in the church hall, but a family of porcupines moved in and we don't have the heart to move the critters when it's so cold outside. They're so cute, just take a gander." He whipped out his phone and eagerly showed Harlowe a number of pics of the little family.

"They're adorable," Harlowe said. She clasped her hands under her chin and squealed in glee at a video of three baby porcupines eating bits of sweet potato.

"What are your specs?"

Harlowe jumped, startled when Tatum suddenly spoke.

Jim and Mary looked just as surprised. They seemed to have forgotten Tatum was there. Jim straightened up so fast his ball cap fell clear off his head and into his lap. To his credit, he recovered quickly and passed over a piece of paper while settling his cap once more.

"Take a looksee," he said. "D'you know a place that could accommodate us?"

Harlowe looked at Tatum with slowly dawning understanding. Her heart filled with joy and something deeper, something that came from her very soul.

"I have a storage bay that fits these requirements.

Would you be willing to relocate to those premises?"

"Where exactly are you?" Jim asked slowly, eyeing Tatum.

"Up on the hill. Edwyn Robotics," she said.

"At last, we get to put a face to that castle up there," Mary said. She fixed Tatum with a pretend stern glare. "And was that you who sent out one of those flying things that clear blew up our welcome basket all them years ago?"

"Yes." Tatum's lips twitched almost imperceptibly. "I'll be sure to disable the security drones when invited guests are present."

"Robotics, eh?" Jim said. He snapped his fingers. "Why don't *you* make a booth? I'm sure the kids would love to see some of your robot stuff."

Tatum stepped back. She lowered her chin. "No, they wouldn't," she said with an air of finality.

Harlowe piped up, "Do you need anything else, or can we go home?" She was impatient to get back to having quality time with Tatum. Just the two of them. Her heart beat a little faster. Her palms got damp and she scrubbed them on her jeans.

"You're free to leave," Jim said. He snapped his fingers again and said, "By the bye, Miss Tremaine, I heard from Nelly at the drugstore you're with the *Maritime Gazette*?"

"Yes, I just started, though," Harlowe said. She perked up and asked, "You wouldn't be interested in getting a subscription, would you?"

"Actually, we are," Jim said. He lifted his cap and smoothed back what was left of his hair. "See, the paper we got before went to all digital and our folks here in the station prefer actual paper. They're really into the crosswords and those number puzzle things."

"*Maritime Gazette* at your service," Harlowe said. She didn't miss the affectionate gaze Tatum gave her. "We have both digital and hard copy options. If you go to the site and put my name in the 'referred by' spot, you'll get a free one-week trial plus a ten percent discount for the entire year."

"Sounds good," Jim said. "Much obliged."

"Anyway, thanks a lot, but we should be going," Harlowe said. She had to admit, she felt a whole lot better now that she'd made the report.

Mary made a move as if to either pat Harlowe on the head or give her a hug. Harlowe scooted away, not particularly wanting either.

On their way out, they met a short but powerfully-built woman who identified herself as Fire Chief Chrissie Peebles. When she extended her hand, Tatum actually briefly took it. When she let go, Chrissie winced.

"Quite a grip you got there, Edwyn," she said. "So what are you all here for? Got your Welcome Basket okay?"

After Harlowe gave a super-abridged version of that day's events, Chrissie made sympathetic noises and made Harlowe input emergency and non-emergency contact information into her phone, "Just in case". Not wanting to waste time by arguing, Harlowe did and soon they were on their way.

Back in the car, Tatum slouched in her seat and closed her eyes.

"That was exhausting," she said. She pressed a hand to her forehead. "I'm not used to…people."

Harlowe glanced at her worriedly. "Are you all right?" she swallowed and asked in a small voice, "Do you need some downtime, you know, away from everyone?"

"Including you?" Tatum surprised Harlowe by very gently placing a hand on her knee. "Absolutely not."

"Good," Harlowe said. She wriggled happily in her seat. "Because you promised me a tea party and I'm totally looking forward to it."

"So am I," Tatum said. She looked at Harlowe for a long moment. "I was okay with being alone before I met you. Now, it hurts to be alone, away from you."

Harlowe had no answer to that. Tears welled up in her eyes, and she instinctively squeezed Tatum's hand.

Tatum squeezed back. "In many ways, I feel like I'm waking up. I feel ready to be part of the world once more, in some capacity anyway."

"Like volunteer your Fortress of Solitude to be overrun with kids for Discovery Day?" Harlowe asked.

"Like that." Tatum brushed back her trailing bangs and sighed. "It's not going to be a smooth or easy transition. I've been on my own for so long, just going to the store feels like being in a foreign country where I don't speak the language. I hope you don't get frustrated with me."

"No way," Harlowe said. She started up the car. "To tell you the truth, I'm more of a homebody too, and not a big fan of crowds. I'm glad you talked to me about this. I don't know what I did, but I'm glad you're comfortable enough to want me around."

The drive back was quiet , but the tension that gripped Tatum on the way in was gone. When they arrived at the bunker, Tatum directed Harlowe to an automatic door that accessed an underground garage, built into the side of the hill. The garage was vast, but only held a pair of motorcycles, both in various states of disassembly. A little metal box skittered up to them and stopped in front of Harlowe. Curious, she bent down to inspect it.

"That's Jeeves, um, three I think," Tatum said. "He and his brothers take care of the floors. Don't worry, they've got proximity sensors so they won't trip you."

"We'll see about that," Harlowe said. "Because I'm really good at tripping over things. Wait, did you make him?"

Tatum nodded, "Yes. I've made a bunch over the years. They work here and help me to keep this place clean and running. If you're lucky, you might meet a couple more of them. They're harmless and I'm sure they'll take a liking to you."

"I hope so," Harlowe said. "It's always good to be friendly with the in-laws."

Tatum smiled faintly and directed Harlowe to the entrance hall just off the garage where Harlowe took off her jacket and hung it up next to Tatum's borrowed trench coat, which had definitely seen better days. That morning, she layered a body-hugging sheer top with a bustier made from pink eyelet lace that was cute and casual, with the slightest hint of sexy. It had a heart-shaped neckline that revealed a tiny bit of cleavage, and the form-fitting bodice showed off her curves. Her jeans and sneakers were casual, but fit her well. Harlowe caught Tatum subtly checking her out and congratulated herself on her outfit choice.

Harlowe was fiercely curious about the place where Tatum lived. She looked around eagerly as Tatum led her over to an elevator and pressed the call button. While they waited, Tatum explained the living area was located on the top floor of the building. The elevator dinged. The doors opened and another one of Tatum's robot helpers flew out. This one was a drone with a clear dome at the front. Inside, a lens swiveled and focused. It buzzed in a circle around them. With a frown, Tatum shooed it away.

"Hotaru," she said in a low growl. "You're supposed to be in the west wing today."

The drone hung in the air. Harlowe swore it looked sheepish. It let out a few beeps and soared away.

"That's Hotaru," Tatum said, ushering Harlowe into the elevator. She pressed the button for the sixth floor. "She takes care of all the lighting, checking that everything's working properly and replacing bulbs and things like that when necessary. She's very curious about everything, though. The AI I gave her is pretty advanced, and she likes getting into trouble."

"She's amazing," Harlowe said. "I can't wait to meet more of your robot family."

"I'm certain they'll like meeting you, too." The elevator reached their destination. Tatum gallantly held the doors open and ushered Harlowe into a bare hallway. "The kitchen's through that door, the bedroom and washroom are down the hall. Those doors at the end go to the sunroom. Um, I guess that's all."

"This is a wonderful place. Thank you for inviting me here," Harlowe said.

"You're very welcome. Please make yourself at home."

Eagerly, Harlowe trotted off. She parked herself in the kitchen. It was long and narrow, with a rectangular window that took up one wall and looked out over the forest. A slim concrete island occupied the middle of the room. The walls and counter were also concrete. The entire place had a monastery-like feel, thoughtful but not cold. In fact, the room was toasty warm. Tatum introduced her to Oscar, the recycler/garbage disposal unit that lurked in the corner like a bad-natured cabinet. A compact bread-maker sat on the counter, the only appliance in the room besides the four-burner stove. Tatum placed the shopping bags on the island while Harlowe mentally reviewed what she wanted to make.

"Leave the prep to me," Harlowe said. With an almost imperceptible smile, Tatum bowed her head in acquiescence.

"It's not much, but you are welcome to everything here," she said.

"What are you talking about? Not much? It's great," Harlowe said. She paused and looked at Tatum, looming like a tall, black bat in her battle suit, with her hair trailing down her back. She couldn't believe where she was—and who she was with. The mundane task of making sandwiches made the moment seem even more surreal.

Tatum hovered for a moment before she excused herself and swept from the room. Harlowe looked for a radio or something, but the walls were bare except for something that looked like an intercom. When she put away the juice and wine, Harlowe discovered the large, silver fridge was also bare except for several bottles of water.

She resisted the urge to snoop in the cupboards. Instead, she washed her hands at the sink, and helped herself to a knife from the block on the counter to start slicing the fruit they bought. The kitchen didn't look as if it had seen much use; the stove was spotless, as was everything else. Even though it was spartan, Harlowe liked being there. She felt blessed to be allowed entrance into Tatum's private space. Her sanctuary and safe place. Even more, Harlowe was eager to spend time with her, and get to know her. Hopefully, with hugs. Lots of hugs.

Harlowe fashioned the fruit tray and got started on making the sandwiches. As she worked, her mind wandered. What would it be like to make Tatum breakfast there? Which meant... Harlowe froze, clutching the pack of sliced turkey, heart pounding. What would it be like to lie down beside Tatum, pass the night in her arms as a lover? Harlowe squeaked and twirled. She felt like she was one second away from bursting into a million sparkles. What would it be like to kiss

Tatum? A real one, not just a little peck here and there. She pressed her fingers to her lips. Her entire body turned on like she had a live wire running through her. When would they take that step? Wild giggles bubbled up in her throat.

"Calm down, girl," Harlowe said aloud. She put down the deli meat and splashed icy cold water from the faucet on her face. That certainly shocked her back to normal. "Better," she declared and patted herself off with a paper towel. Able to concentrate again, Harlowe made several sandwiches and cut the brownies they'd bought into neat squares. She arranged everything nicely on a tray and had just plugged in the kettle when Tatum returned.

The box of tea in Harlowe's hands slipped and she had to lunge after it before it tumbled to the floor. She stood in mute shock, once more floored by the gorgeous vision of butchness that appeared in front of her. Tatum's long, muscular legs were in camouflage cargo pants and she had a khaki tank top over that, which showed off her finely muscled arms and clung to her firm and well-shaped breasts. Her hair was pulled back into a military-style bun, except for the long bangs which trailed down into her piercing eyes. She noticed that in addition to the gear tattoo on her forearm, Tatum also had a double-headed axe on her shoulder of the same arm. Harlowe swallowed hard and fanned herself with one hand.

"Wow," she said, not hiding her appreciation. "You make cammo look hawt. Mm! Mm!"

"Oh please," Tatum said. She blew her long bangs out of her face in a shy gesture Harlowe found adorable. "Let me know what I can do to help."

"Nothing, just be your usual handsome and gentlemanly self," Harlowe said.

Tatum looked flustered but just a little pleased by Harlowe's blatant attention. She indicated the tray. "Why don't we go out to the sunroom? It's got a better view than here, plus it's got chairs." She looked around the bare room and gestured weakly. "I usually camp out there or in my workshop. I never expected I'd have anyone I'd want to bring here."

"I'm not intruding, am I?" Harlowe asked in a small voice. She couldn't imagine how difficult it was for Tatum, who had lived a solitary existence, to suddenly be faced with a noisy, frivolous houseguest.

"Absolutely not." At once, Tatum was at Harlowe's side. She very carefully enfolded Harlowe's hand in both of hers. "I'm very happy to have you here. You're welcome to stay as long as you like, consider my door permanently open to you."

"Really?" Harlowe asked. She bit her lip and looked up into Tatum's face. "You better be serious about that, because I'm going to do my best to wear out my welcome."

"You could never do that."

Harlowe flushed under the intense gaze. Tatum could win any argument with that look.

Chapter Eight

The sunroom was homey and surprisingly cute, with a glass-topped table flanked by wicker loveseats. The chairs were piled with cushions and plants hung in the corners, soaking in the sunshine even on that grey day. True to its name, the sunroom was entirely enclosed in glass, giving a spectacular view of the forest around them. Harlowe could even see her own little cottage from there, although the opposite wasn't true because Tatum told her the sunroom's glass was one-way, coated to look like the rest of the building from the outside, the same as the larger windows. The privacy and warmth made for a pleasant atmosphere. She could see why Tatum spent a lot of time there. She sipped her tea, deep in thought until a gentle touch on her shoulder roused her.

"Why journalism?"

Harlowe swallowed her sip of tea and tilted her head. Tatum had her chin propped up in one hand, her elbow resting on the tabletop. Her eyes were trained on Harlowe, her attention unwavering.

"Journalists tell stories," Harlowe said. "Every moment we live is a story. Every day, things happen, people do brave things and stupid things, funny accidents happen and all sorts of interesting moments. I want to make sure those stories get told and remembered. I'm not interested in prying and making people uncomfortable or admit things they'd rather not. I want the stories to come to me naturally, and then I can share them with the world."

Tatum raised her eyebrows and leaned forward, closing the distance between them. "That sounds wonderful. I'm impressed."

Harlowe leaned forward as well, focusing on Tatum. Her heartbeat got faster at the intimacy of the moment.

"That's me, but what do you do here? What's Edwyn Robotics? Do you make whimsical little mechanical friends for people?"

"No, that's just a hobby," Tatum said with a tiny smile. She folded her hands and gazed out over the sprawling forest around them. "I specialize in landmine detection and disaster rescue technology. I have a number of contracts with various governments and peacekeeping groups."

"Wow," Harlowe said. She settled back in her wicker chair and pulled her feet under herself.

"Look Harlowe, snow."

Harlowe raised her head, then jumped up with a happy shout. All around her was a swirling spiral of snowflakes, whirling all around them like they were in the middle of a giant snow globe. The effect was breathtaking and magical.

"It's beautiful," Harlowe said in wonder. She threw her hands wide and spun, reveling in the joy of the first snowfall. Harlowe stopped, breathless in front of Tatum. Shyly, she held out her hands.

"Dance with me?" she asked. Her heart jumped when Tatum's fingers closed over her own in a warm grip. Tatum rose in an elegant motion and bowed with the greatest gentility. Harlowe stepped forward into Tatum's open arms. In the silence of the snowfall, Harlowe leaned into the slow spin. She couldn't hold back the wild grin. She was giddy with freedom, nearly floating with happiness.

Tatum's low chuckle filled her with pleasure. They stopped their spinning dance and stood still. The expression on Tatum's face as she looked down at Harlowe was pure, none of the pain remained. Harlowe caught her breath. Tatum's hands were on her waist. Harlowe's rested on Tatum's shoulders. They were only a breath apart. Harlowe caught her lower lip between her teeth and looked up into Tatum's eyes. The intense look she received in return weakened her knees. Harlowe lowered her attention to Tatum's mouth. She wanted those lips on hers, hungered for them like nothing she ever had before. She ached for Tatum to lean her head down and take her. Harlowe instinctively swayed forward.

Every nerve in her body tingled with anticipation. Just as she thought she'd made her wish clear, Tatum let go of her and stepped back. Harlowe swallowed the bitter groan of disappointment.

"Your tea is getting cold," Tatum said.

"How about a refill?" She topped up their cups from the Thermos. Steam rose from the cup and Harlowe wrapped her hands around it, breathing in the scent of the herbal tea.

Tatum, meanwhile, took her cup over to the window, standing with her back to Harlowe while she looked out over the forest below. Harlowe tried not to ogle too much, but the view was spectacular. Tatum suddenly glanced back over her shoulder and Harlowe knew she was busted. With a knowing smirk, Tatum returned to the table and took her place across from Harlowe once more.

"It's really coming down out there," Tatum said. Her face was drawn and sadness weighed on her shoulders. "You should get back before the road gets blocked. Who knows when the ploughs will get through? This area isn't really a priority."

Harlowe put down her tea and squeezed in next to Tatum, slipping cozily under the arm she had resting on the back of the loveseat. She let out a happy sigh when Tatum's arm came around her shoulders and pulled her close.

Harlowe put a finger on her lower lip, as if deep in thought. "You're right, it looks like there's already quite a lot of accumulation on the road already," She looked up into Tatum's face, unable to contain the mischievous grin. She said, as innocently as she could, "I wouldn't want to risk it. My car's not that powerful, it would be a shame if I got stranded halfway between here and my place."

Growing understanding dawned on Tatum's face.

"You have a point," she said slowly. "It could be slippery too. How about staying here and waiting it out?"

"I'd love to," Harlowe answered quickly. "That is, unless you have something important you need to do."

"Nothing is more important than you, Sweet pea. I would be honored to have you here. I'll make sure you get home safely tomorrow," Tatum said. She pulled Harlowe into a hug and pressed a kiss to her temple. Harlowe wriggled happily.

"I hope this won't affect your work at the *Gazette*," Tatum said. "If I can get you anything, just let me know. I'll give you the access codes for my satellite uplink, and I've got a few tablets and other devices kicking around if you need to do anything."

"I'll take you up on the offer of a tablet," Harlowe said. "All my stuff is already in the cloud. I just have to finish some things and send them in."

Tatum nodded. "How about something to wear? It'll probably be huge on you, but I can lend you some clothes to sleep in."

"Actually, I've got a change of clothes in my gym bag in my car. I'm fully prepared to make myself at home."

"Please do," Tatum said.

Harlowe snuggled closer. She never wanted to move from that spot. Under her cheek, Tatum's chest rose and fell with her breaths, her warmth stole through Harlowe and lodged in her heart. She was full. Packed to the brim with emotion. She had never been so happy to be stranded in a snowstorm before.

But one thing still pricked at her conscience.

"I'm sorry," Harlowe blurted out. "For not being honest with you from the start, for letting you think I was straight. Maybe you wouldn't have left if I had told you."

Tatum shook her head. "I left for my own reasons. My selfishness and my concern that if I stayed, I'd hurt you. Now I realize I did worse by leaving."

"It's okay, I understand why you felt that way. I just feel bad for, well, not exactly lying to you, but not telling the truth."

Tatum chuckled. "You forget my age and my background. Not telling is standard operating procedure." She drew a tender finger over Harlowe's temple, brushing back a strand of hair. "For the record, you're not very good at acting straight. It's like it never occurred to you to be in the closet."

"I guess because I never was," Harlowe said. She broke out of Tatum's loose hold just long enough to corral her tea and plate of food near to her. She nibbled on a bit of brownie before she spoke again. "When I was little and my parents read me fairytales, I would insist they change the ending to the princess ditching the prince and finding another princess to be 'best friends' with." Harlowe did the air quotes. "I guess that's why they weren't surprised when I introduced them to my girlfriend when I was sixteen. It didn't last, you know how stupid teenagers are."

"*She* was stupid," Tatum said. "For letting you go. But I'm glad she did so I could have you."

Harlowe flushed at the note of possession in the words. She fiddled with her fork. "She was my first and only girlfriend and we only kissed like, twice. I must seem so inexperienced to you."

"Actually, no. I'm the one who should be saying that." Tatum cleared her throat and seemed a bit uncomfortable. "I've never actually come out, never actually said the words *I am gay* aloud." She paused and fixed Harlowe with a crooked grin. "Not before today anyway. Anyone who needed to know figured it out. I never had a relationship, either. It was too risky and I was always on the move. I never tried to suppress it, but I never had anyone worth coming out for."

"Now you have me." Harlowe said through her brownie. "Resident weirdo and awkward person for all your comic relief needs."

"You're much more than that," Tatum said with her usual intense delivery. "I want you to promise me the next time we watch *Supergirl* you'll say out loud all the funny things you were thinking."

"Sure," Harlowe said. "Get ready for no-holds barred gay innuendos."

Tatum affectionately ruffled her hair and Harlowe glowed. She finished her snack and tidied their plates.

"How about a tour?"

"That sounds great." Harlowe jumped to her feet.

"Leave those," Tatum said, indicating the tray and stacked dishes.

Harlowe did with a tiny twinge of guilt, but that was soon forgotten as Tatum lay a gentle hand on the small of her back, guiding her to the elevator. Tatum flashed her a quick smile that turned all of Harlowe's thoughts into happy puffs of cotton candy.

Their first stop was Harlowe's car, where she retrieved her luggage. Tatum surprised her by summoning a drone, which she affectionately called Rover, and directing it to carry her stuff upstairs.

"Let's start with the heart of this place," Tatum said. "The control room."

"Okay," Harlowe agreed.

The control room was small, but packed with various monitors and displays. Harlowe looked over the complex array with interest.

"This is the solar panel input and output," Tatum said, indicating one of the displays. "These are the environmental controls. Water and heat, air conditioning and circulation is also taken care of here. This building is completely self-contained and off the grid. I've been working on it since the day I moved in."

"Very cool," Harlowe said.

They went back into the elevator. Tatum paused with her hand on the control panel.

"Where would you like to see next, the hydroponics garden or my workshop?"

"Your workshop," Harlowe said without a moment's hesitation. Tatum smirked and pressed the button for B3. As the elevator descended deep into the hillside, Harlowe bounced on the balls of her feet in anticipation. The doors opened and Tatum gestured.

"After you," she said.

Harlowe cautiously entered Tatum's workshop. Like the rest of the building, it was concrete and cavernous. Unlike the rest, it had a definite lived-in feeling, with schematics and maps posted on the walls, benches of machines and half-assembled components. It was similar to the hall Harlowe entered the first time she was there, but smaller and a lot more hospitable. One of the Jeeves brothers was busily scooting around under the table, but zoomed off when they arrived. The room was bathed in light that seemed to come from great overhead skylights, even though they were three levels underground. Harlowe eagerly took everything in. She felt like she was seeing into Tatum's mind.

"Do you do all your inventing and stuff here?" Harlowe asked.

"Yes," Tatum said. She tucked her hands under her arms and looked nervous. "It's kind of a mess, and not really interesting..."

"This is your passion," Harlowe said. She turned around, face alight. When Harlowe's attention came back to Tatum she paused. "You feel safe here."

Tatum looked surprised, but slowly her raised eyebrows came down. "You know, you're right. I have only felt safe in two places. One of them is here."

"And the other one is?" Harlowe tilted her head.

"I think you know the answer to that. Now, go have a look around if you like."

Harlowe pattered off, inspecting everything in delight until she came to a glass case that held a display of weapons, mostly blades but a few handheld pistols and a line of things that looked like futuristic grenades. Harlowe looked at them, deep in thought. She sensed Tatum's presence behind her.

Without turning, she said, "Teach me how to use these. I want to learn how to fight."

"Absolutely not," Tatum said.

Harlowe whirled. Tatum stood with her arms crossed and a hard look on her face. Harlowe held out her hands and said, "But you know how to fight. I just want to be able to defend myself from assholes like Shelby. Why won't you teach me?" Harlowe's throat tightened. She stood her ground against Tatum.

"If you pull a weapon on someone, you have to be ready to use it," Tatum said. Her eyes were like silver chips of ice. "And once you use violence against another person, you've already lost."

Harlowe hugged her arms to her chest. "But what should I do if she comes back and you're not around to protect me?"

"Run," Tatum said in a clipped tone. "Your only and ultimate goal is to get away. You are a born storyteller, Harlowe. You have the gift of words, use it. You can never get an advantage over violent people by using violence. But you can out-think and out-talk them. And out-run them."

"Okay," Harlowe said. "I guess you're right."

"You guess?" Tatum asked. Her tone was slightly warmer than before. She relaxed a fraction and regarded Harlowe with that soft, tender gaze she got sometimes. "No need for guessing. In this case, I am absolutely right. It's too late for me, but not for you."

Harlowe nodded, deep in thought. Her eyes caught a tall half-cylinder that glowed with an unmistakable blue light. She decided to investigate. Within it was the battle suit, hooked up to numerous wires and readouts. Excited, Harlowe leaned in to look more closely.

"Recharging," Tatum said when she joined Harlowe.

"Are you thinking of making these for people to use?"

"No, it's a personal project," Tatum said. She tapped at a digital relay and frowned at it. "The suit is too complex for physical controls. Most of the functions rely on a symbiotic connection between the user and the AI inside. Critical damage to the suit causes critical damage to the wearer. It's a cost I can't ask anyone else to pay."

"Why did you make it?" Harlowe asked.

Tatum crossed her arms and looked away for a moment. When she came back, her face was set. She took a deep breath and said, "The reason I joined the military was because I aged out of the foster system. I was in it from day one. Over the years, I was placed with a number of different families. I learned young I had to look out for myself. Foster kids are so vulnerable, and a lot of the time the system isn't on their side. There are a lot of good people, but also a lot of predators who know how powerless kids in the system are. I spent my entire life protecting myself, making sure nothing awful happened to me. I kept myself safe, but at a price." Tatum reached out and traced the line of the arm-bracers, with raised insets where the blades would spring out. Harlowe waited, knowing there was more. "That price was my ability to trust. It felt natural to make this. The ultimate personal protection."

"That's a really sad reason," Harlowe said. She swallowed the lump in her throat. "But this is super cool. I love the way the blades glow. Can you fly?"

"In a way. It's got a system built into the back," Tatum said, excitedly pressing a few buttons to rotate the suit. She waved to a glowing raised pack that stretched over both shoulders. "I call it WINGS, Wearable Internal Null-Gravity System. It lets me hover, move fast, and jump. Micro-thrusters built into the suit control the actual 'flying.'" Tatum grabbed a tablet and called up a floating display in front of them, where she proceeded to go into a long and detailed explanation of the system, using complicated diagrams and long equations that looked like a bunch of random numbers and letters to Harlowe.

Tatum glowed with passion as she spoke and Harlowe drank in every moment.

"I'm not boring you, am I?" Tatum asked suddenly. "This must be Greek to you."

"No way," Harlowe said. "Okay, I don't really understand it, but I do get that it's incredible and amazing and complicated as hell, just like the person who designed it."

Tatum didn't recoil from the compliment as she had before. She chuckled and playfully nudged Harlowe. "Flattery will get you nowhere," she said, although Harlowe noticed her cheeks were just the tiniest bit pink. Tatum shut down the display. "How about something more analogue? I'll show you the pool."

"You have a pool?" Harlowe asked.

"Yes, just through here," Tatum said. She led Harlowe past her work-area and through sturdy-looking steel doors. She gestured to the tunnel, which was carved into the bedrock. The walls were smooth and the floor sloped gently downward. "It's more like a hot tub, but the heaters aren't turned on at the moment, so I guess it's just a tub. I made it to test out some tunneling machines I was working on and modeled it after natural hot springs. Here it is."

"Oh my God," Harlowe said. She stopped in her tracks and stared. The view at the end of the tunnel was breathtaking. Surrounded by moss and wildflowers was a waterfall at least three meters high, carved from the surrounding rock. It cascaded into a round pool that was larger and deeper than a standard Jacuzzi. Under the water, the floor was tiled in blue and green and a ledge ringed the pool like a bench. The room was bathed in light from the same skylight-like panels. A rainbow hung in the air. The effect was magical.

Tatum knelt by the side of the pool and trailed her hand in the water with a slight wince. "I can have the heaters working by the next time you visit, if you fancy a dip, that is."

"I do," Harlowe said. She got down beside Tatum and gazed around in wonder. "This is amazing, I love it here." She flushed and cringed at the childish eagerness on her words. Tatum just smiled and playfully flicked a handful of water at Harlowe, who scooted away, brushing the drops from her sleeves.

"That's freezing," she gasped. "Ugh, the nipple-ome-ter is going off the charts."

"I'm not sorry," Tatum replied with a cocky smirk.

Harlowe pouted for a moment before she lunged and splashed Tatum back. The water soaked her tank top and she looked down, mouth hanging open. Harlowe couldn't help but notice the twin hard points that tented up Tatum's shirt front, a testament to the chill.

"Gotcha," Harlowe said. She stuck her tongue out, then dove away, shrieking in laughter as Tatum retaliated with a huge double handful that hit her back. The water drenched her top and jeans. Shivering and pretty much soaked through. Harlowe got a very evil idea. She scrambled up onto the wall of the pool, just next to the water-fall. Tatum stood with her hands on her hips, chest heaving, watching her with a look of confusion. Harlowe let out a shout and jumped into the air, cannonballing into the very middle of the pool. Her venture was rewarded by a shout and wild sputtering. When Harlowe emerged from the water, a soaked and dripping Tatum met her.

"I can't believe you did that." Tatum raked her long bangs out of her face and shook her head with a wry grin.

Harlowe's teeth chattered. She managed to say, "You admit I win?"

"Okay, you win, but you're drenched too."

"Winning is good," Harlowe said. She rubbed her

arms and clenched her jaw. "Pyrrhic victory, but still."

"Come on, you're sopping wet. I want you stripped and heated up ASAP," Tatum said, then stopped. She pressed one hand to her forehead and waved the other one as if trying to erase the words. "No, no, that came out wrong. You know what I mean."

"Uh huh," Harlowe said, too cold for any kind of banter.

"Sweet pea, you're shaking like a leaf," Tatum murmured before she hoisted Harlowe in her arms. Harlowe squeaked in surprise to be scooped up like a princess, but she didn't protest. She looped her arms around Tatum's neck and admired the corded muscles of her shoulders and biceps. Harlowe couldn't breathe. She felt like she was on top of the world.

When they were in the elevator, Tatum let Harlowe down, who landed with an audible squelch.

Harlowe clapped a hand over her mouth, but that didn't stop her from bursting into giggles. Tatum joined her, first chuckling, then letting go with a full-bodied laugh. They staggered out of the elevator. Harlowe fell down and rolled on the floor, cackling madly, while Tatum sagged back against the wall. When they both calmed down, dabbing at tear-filled eyes and trying to slow their breaths, Tatum leaned down and offered a hand to Harlowe.

"Come on, you'll feel better off the floor," she said.

"Yeah, I think I left a wet spot." Harlowe put her hand in Tatum's and allowed herself to be hauled to her feet. She didn't let go. She was incredibly aware of how close they were, each breath that brought them even closer. Harlowe's body reacted, her heart pounded, her knees got weak. She couldn't think of anything more than how much she wanted Tatum to kiss her. Harlowe pressed forward, desperate for more.

"Harlowe, beautiful, sweet girl," Tatum breathed. She reached out her free hand, as if in a trance, and gently cupped Harlowe's cheek. She brushed her thumb over Harlowe's lower lip. Her brows drew together.

"Fucking hell," she whispered under her breath.

Stunned, Harlowe blinked. She hadn't expected that.

It was also the first time she'd heard Tatum curse. She found it kind of hot, actually.

"You're turning blue, Sweet pea," Tatum said. She ran off, leaving Harlowe chilled and alone. She returned a minute later with a thick, grey blanket which she wrapped around Harlowe.

"Sorry, this is my fault," Harlowe said. The euphoria from her laughter wore off and the cold gripped her hard. She started shivering in earnest. Harlowe clenched her teeth and gritted out, "I shouldn't have been such a dumbass."

"Not at all," Tatum said. She gave Harlowe a sideways glance and a nudge. "You only finished what I started. Now you are off to a hot shower. There's a hamper in the bathroom, chuck your wet stuff in there and I'll send Rover in later on to clean and dry it."

Harlowe was too cold to protest and soon she was sighing in pleasure under the hot spray. As she was toweling herself off, a soft knock filtered into the room.

"I left your change of clothes outside," Tatum said through the door.

"Thanks," Harlowe called out. There was no response, which Harlowe assumed meant Tatum had done the gentlemanly thing and left. She eased the door open and found her gym clothes, neatly folded, with the addition of a sweatshirt that had to be Tatum's own. Harlowe wriggled into her workout clothes, yoga pants and an oversized T-shirt. She was glad to have dry socks and sneakers, along with fresh underwear too. The sweatshirt was comically big on her, and she had to roll up the cuffs several times. She paused to hug her arms to herself, as if feeling Tatum's embrace. She closed her eyes and breathed in the scent which had tormented her before, but now felt like home.

The bundle also included a new toothbrush for her. Harlowe grinned at the little show of hospitality. If there was one thing she learned about living in the middle of nowhere, it was to keep a stock of daily necessities. Apparently that held true for Tatum as well, She helped herself to toothpaste and covertly studied the bathroom. Like the kitchen, it was concrete-walled and spare. Feeling a bit guilty, but consumed with curiosity, Harlowe peeked into the medicine cabinet. She found Tatum had a stockpile of dental floss that would probably outlast the end of the world, and was on the moon cup side of the fence. Harlowe pursed her lips around her toothbrush and made a mental note to either keep some of her own products in the car or leave a stash there.

Harlowe spit, rinsed her mouth, and checked her hair in the mirror. Satisfied, she went to the kitchen and found Tatum stirring something on the stove and looking murderous.

"I'm trying to make soup, but it's not really working out," she said as soon as Harlowe entered. Tatum's expression changed instantly and she gave Harlowe a slow once-over. "You look cute as a button in my sweatshirt."

"Thanks for lending it to me," Harlowe said. She went over to the stove and looked into the pot. "Okay, I've got this, you're next for the shower."

Tatum gratefully handed over the spoon and made her escape. Harlowe inspected the soup, which didn't look bad at all, just needed some careful stirring. She added some salt and pepper and kept an eye on it while she made grilled cheese sandwiches from the groceries they bought that morning. Tatum re-entered in new cargo pants and a T-shirt that was just tight enough to grab Harlowe's attention but not enough to make her drop the bowls she was carrying.

"I feel much better," Tatum declared.

"Well, you're looking as good as ever," Harlowe said. While Tatum shook her head and smiled at the compliment, Harlowe set down a plate with their sandwiches on a tray along with bowls and cutlery.

She was debating about what to do with the pot of hot soup when Tatum went over to the intercom and said, "Cartlyn to the kitchen."

"Cartlyn?" Harlowe asked in askance as a motorized cart rolled purposefully into the kitchen.

"What? She's a cart. It fits."

"Yeah, I guess you're right." Harlowe lowered a finger at Tatum and said sternly, "But I get to name our future kids, and by kids I mean pets, got it?"

Tatum just gave her a sardonic eyebrow raise and loaded their lunch onto Cartlyn.

In the sunroom, Tatum served the soup and Harlowe dug in happily. She paused mid-chew and declared, "Tomato soup and grilled cheese is the best comfort food. My dad would always make it for me on rainy days." She stopped, horrified and said, "I mean, sorry, I didn't think."

"It's okay," Tatum said. "Just because I didn't have a regular family doesn't mean I don't enjoy hearing about yours. I'd really like to know. Tell me more about them."

"Okay," Harlowe said. She launched into a long family history, including her parents, aunts, uncles, assorted cousins, grandparents and of course her infamous great-uncle. "We've all been waiting for him and Rockwell to get married or at least come out, but they insist they're 'simply companions' and point out there's two bedrooms in their cottage." Harlowe snorted. "Yeah, okay."

"They're from a different generation," Tatum said. She clasped her hands and gazed out of the window. The air was still white with the falling snow. "Maybe they don't want to make waves with the older folks. Maybe they like having privacy, there could be any number of reasons."

"You're right," Harlowe said. "I didn't think of it that way." She chewed on her sandwich. Maybe Tatum had no plans to come out either. She said she'd never done it before. What would it be like to be in a relationship with someone in the closet? Harlowe wanted to be with Tatum, she couldn't bear the thought of living without her. If Tatum wanted them to be discreet, Harlowe guessed she could try. She really hoped it wasn't a deal-breaker because the longer they were together, the chance of Harlowe screwing up and outing them both approached 100 percent.

"What are you thinking about, Sweet pea?" Tatum's eyes were trained on Harlowe.

"I can do that whole 'just friends' thing in public if you want," Harlowe blurted out. "I'm not good at pretending, so if people get suspicious, we can say we're cousins. Very close cousins. I don't think we could pass as sisters."

A look of understanding crossed Tatum's noble features. She said, "I wasn't talking about myself. Did you forget I hugged you in front of that guy at the liquor store?"

"No, but that was a special situation," Harlowe said.

"I'm not in the military anymore, I don't have any family to offend, and I don't give a shit about what anyone in town thinks of me," Tatum said. She continued in an intense tone, "I only care about you. I would be proud to stand beside you, have everyone know I'm yours."

"Really?" Harlowe squeaked in joy. She said, "Same goes for me. So, does that mean we're officially a couple? Like, I'm your girlfriend?"

"If that's something you're comfortable with," Tatum said.

"I sure am," Harlowe replied with a big smile. She turned the information over in her mind, savoring the fact Tatum liked her They were a couple! Harlowe's pulse jumped. She finished her soup, hoping that Tatum attributed the flush on her cheeks to the hot food.

The rest of the day passed in a slow, pleasant way. Tatum retired to her workshop while Harlowe set up camp in the sunroom with a tablet Tatum lent her. It was more advanced than anything she'd ever seen before and was more like a prop from a science fiction movie than a regular computer. As promised, Tatum shared the number of the portable satellite phone she'd made and Harlowe had fun sending and receiving text messages that bordered on flirty at times.

Harlowe finished her work and curled up on the loveseat to indulge in her daydreams. She was in the middle of a very nice one about Tatum being a superhero and herself being a journalist who got into trouble a lot when her phone chirped.

Hungry?

Harlowe smirked. She could work with that.

I do have quite an appetite. It depends on what you have to satisfy me.

Food, my funny girl. Dinner is served in my work-shop. Hope you're in the mood for Greek.

Harlowe just responded with a happy stamp and scrambled to the elevator. On the way, she stopped by the kitchen and grabbed the bottles of wine and cordial. She found Tatum in her workshop, doing something intricate with what looked like a mechanical elbow joint. Her worktable was covered in gears and components. A large paper bag sat across from her. She looked relaxed and happy and completely in her element.

"How was your afternoon?" Harlowe asked. She eagerly leaned her elbows on the table. "Did you get a lot of work done?"

"Yes, I did," Tatum said. "I finished a bunch of orders I was stalled on and had a breakthrough for my upgraded version of WINGS. There's this subroutine that's been giving me problems, and I think I've figured out a workaround for it."

"That's great." Guiltily, Harlowe looked at the phone on the table with their messages on the display. "I probably shouldn't have texted you so much."

Tatum paused in her work and gazed at Harlowe. "Your texts were the highlight of my day." She reached out to Harlowe, then stopped and looked apologetically at her hands. "How about I leave the prep to you? I need to wash up."

"Okay, I got this," Harlowe said. She rolled up her sleeves and unpacked the feast Tatum ordered. She was happy to see the restaurant included paper bowls and cups. She picked up the bottle of wine and looked around in dismay. "Crapola," she muttered.

"What's wrong?" Tatum was back, grease-free and faintly scented with citrus hand soap.

"I forgot the corkscrew upstairs."

"Not a problem." Tatum got that cocky grin that made Harlowe's tummy clench. She picked up the bottle in one hand and a blade in the other. With a flick of her thumb, the blade hummed to life, glowing red. She swished it through the air. With a clunk, the top of the wine bottle fell to the table. The glass was perfectly cut, on an angle. A single drop of wine tracked down the side. Tatum placed the opened bottle in front of Harlowe with a courtly bow. "Your wine, my lady."

"Showoff," Harlowe said.

Tatum gave her another smirk, this time with an arch of her brow before she brought her hand to her lips and slowly licked the burgundy droplet that had spilled from the bottle to her fingers. The movement was sensual, inviting and tantalizing all at once.

"Woah nelly," Harlowe whispered in awe. A warm tension awoke between her thighs, causing her to squirm in her seat. She froze and looked at Tatum in alarm. "Are you sure you should be tasting alcohol? I mean, even a little..."

"It's all right," Tatum said. "I can drink, I just don't. I got out of the habit years ago when I was on medication. I'm not on it anymore, but there didn't seem to be any point in drinking alone. Now, however..."

"In that case," Harlowe held up the bottle. "Can I interest you in sharing a sip with me?"

"That would be lovely," Tatum said. She held out her cup and accepted a small measure of wine. They touched their cups together before they drank.

"Mmm, good," Harlowe said. She swirled her wine in her cup like she was a professional sommelier enjoying a premium vintage. "I detect hickory smoke with a hint of blueberries and bacon."

Tatum snorted into her wine and patted herself on the chest. "I'll take your word for it. I was always a whiskey drinker. Whiskey or tequila, whatever was the strongest thing they had." She dropped her gaze to the table and grimaced, as if some unpleasant thought surfaced. She recovered so fast that Harlowe wasn't sure if she'd imagined the look. Tatum dished up the food and they dug in.

"This is amazing," Harlowe declared through her mouthful of flaky spinach pie. "I'm definitely going to be a repeat customer."

"I'm glad you like it," Tatum said. "Made in Amphipolis is the only place that will deliver out here. And nothing stops them. Aris came over on his snowmobile. Okay, there is one other place, Larry's Fish Shack, but I'm not a fan of botulism so it doesn't count."

"Ugh, me neither. No thanks, Larry," Harlowe said. She took a big mouthful of salad and hummed in pleasure. The wine went exceedingly well with the black olives and feta. Tatum chose the perfect dinner. Curious, Harlowe peeked at the receipt stapled to the bag. She blinked and fixed Tatum with an incredulous look. "You tipped him a hundred and fifty dollars?"

Tatum shrugged. "I don't usually tip that much, but tonight he went above and beyond the call of duty."

"Yeah, but…really?"

"Really." Tatum put down her cup and gestured around. "Besides spare parts, what am I going to spend my money on? I appreciate their attention to quality and the caliber of service and respond accordingly. I get good service and Aris gets to put more away in his new car fund. It's a win-win situation."

"True," Harlowe said.

"And it was either the Greek dinner special or…" Tatum aimed a thumb over her shoulder to a shelf where a half-empty jar of peanut butter sat next to a bag of home-made bread. "You deserve the best I can offer."

"I would have been just as happy with peanut butter sandwiches," Harlowe said. "As long as I'm with you."

Tatum looked adorably pleased. She lowered her head and concentrated on her dinner. Harlowe finished her cup of wine. She poured herself some more and offered Tatum a refill, but she declined and opened the strawberry cordial instead, which she declared outstanding.

After dinner, they played cards and talked about everything and nothing. Harlowe felt like a wall between them had fallen. Tatum was still withdrawn at times, but the winces of pain, the raw anguish she displayed before vanished. She was courteous and respectful, indulgent of Harlowe's jokes, and at times even seemed amused. Harlowe was grateful to see this side of her, a side that was buried for a long time, it seemed. As bedtime approached, Harlowe tried not to get too bouncy and excited. She wondered if Tatum would continue her decorous manner and provide a separate room for Harlowe, or would she invite Harlowe to lay down beside her and spend the night in her arms? Harlowe couldn't help but get a happy buzz from that image. Ever since the first time she felt Tatum's arms around her, Harlowe couldn't get enough.

"It's getting late," Tatum said. She put her cards down and stretched both arms over her head. She lowered them with a grunt and pulled one foot up to rest on her knee. She looked across the table at Harlowe, who was blinking and stunned at the lithe beauty she'd just seen. Tatum's silver-blue eyes were hooded and warm, with a spark of humor as if she knew exactly what she'd just done.

"Shall we call it a day?"

"Sure," Harlowe said. She gathered the cards and tapped the deck on the table. They stubbornly resisted going back into a neat rectangular shape, even with her best effort. Harlowe bit back the swear words that wanted to pop out. Long-fingered hands closed over her own. Harlowe looked up into Tatum's face. She swallowed hard and moved back.

"I've got this," Tatum said. As if her fingers were magic, the cards returned to their neatly organized state in an instant.

"You sure do," Harlowe said. "So, off to bed?"

Mischievously, she got up and stretched, just like Tatum did a moment before. Tatum stared at her for a moment before she hurriedly looked away.

"Sorry," she said, one hand over her face.

"Why?" Harlowe asked. "You can look at me all you like. I want you to do more than just look. I mean, if that's what you want too."

"Sweet pea," Tatum breathed. She knit her fingers together. "You don't know how much I want that. But I'm not used to, well, I don't want to rush things."

"Don't worry, if I want you to stop I have no problem letting you know," Harlowe said. "I want you to be comfortable with the pace too. Tae, I like being with you, and being close to you. I'm going to be here for a while, so don't stress about that. This isn't just some fling, I know it. I feel like there's some kind of connection between us, like a force pulling us together." Harlowe paused and scrunched up her mouth. "Ugh, that sounds dumb. It's not a line, I promise."

Tatum relaxed. She said, "I know. I...feel it too."

The words struck something deep inside Harlowe. It wasn't just her imagination.

"I hope you're not going to be virtuous and put me in the guest room," Harlowe said. She tilted her head and innocently fluttered her lashes. "Because it's my first night in a strange place. I might get scared or lost."

"Don't worry," Tatum said softly. "I don't even have a guest room."

"Good," Harlowe said. "I want you to promise me one thing."

"Anything," Tatum said with her usual panty-destroying voice.

Harlowe put on a fake pout. "Don't run off and leave me all alone in the morning. You always get up first and I appreciate the coffee, but you know, I'd like to see what waking up next to you is like."

Tatum grimaced. "Sorry, I've never been one to sleep in. How about this, I'll get up and do whatever I have to do, and then I'll go back to you. Sounds good?"

"That sounds great," Harlowe said. "I don't want to wreck your morning routine, though."

"I could do with a new routine," Tatum said. She stood and offered her arm in the courtliest of gestures. "Shall I show you to the bedroom?"

Unable to reign in her enthusiasm, Harlowe crowed out, "Hell yeah!"

That night, in the warm circle of Tatum's arms, Harlowe closed her eyes and tried to calm her thoughts. She couldn't help but tease herself with the fantasy of what would happen if she turned around, parted Tatum's thighs and pressed her body between them. Claimed Tatum's mouth with hers and guided Tatum's gently seeking hands to cup her breasts. Her heart pounded, her sex throbbed. Harlowe squeezed her eyes shut. All in good time.

Lulled by the regular breaths behind her, Harlowe eventually managed to fall asleep.

****

Tatum was true to her word and Harlowe was treated to the nicest wake-up of her entire life so far. She stirred and opened her eyes. The spare lines of the bare concrete walls were illuminated very slightly by the morning sunlight filtering through the blinds. She snuggled back into the heavenly nest of warm blankets and even warmer embrace of the woman who dozed beside her. A soft kiss on her temple woke Harlowe up the rest of the way. She felt incredible, buoyant and safe, and most of all, she felt loved. Wait, was that right? Tatum's low voice interrupted Harlowe's whirling thoughts.

"Good morning, sweet pea," she purred in Harlowe's ear.

"Ooh, my." Harlowe moaned softly. She ran her hands over the forearm across her belly and arched into the softness behind her. Tatum's long legs brushed up against hers, bare skin to skin. Harlowe drew in a breath at the sensation. "I'll say it's a good morning," she said.

"How about a cup of coffee?" Tatum asked. She nuzzled into Harlowe's hair and murmured against her skin. "I turned the machine on when I got up the first time. After I did my morning workout, started the bread, checked the perimeter, and recalibrated the environmental systems. I also read the newspaper, looked up the weather in the Farmer's Almanac, gave Hotaru a tune-up, plus did three Sudokus and today's word puzzle."

"Okay, yeah I know I'm lazy," Harlowe said, playfully slapping at Tatum's arm. "But it's so warm and comfy in here. Especially with you."

"I agree, it is very nice, but we have to get up," Tatum said. "Come on, let's get moving. There you go." She lifted off the comforter and, grumbling, Harlowe rolled out. She found a small pile of the clothes she wore the day before on a chair beside the bed, cleaned and dried. She only got a fleeting flash of Tatum's muscular behind in boxer briefs before Tatum pulled on her cargo pants. With her head down, tacitly giving Harlowe privacy, Tatum laced up her boots before she took her leave, loping out of the room and leaving Harlowe to get changed.

A few minutes later, Harlowe rejoined Tatum in the kitchen, who poured her a large mug of coffee and placed a couple slices of fresh bread on a plate next to her. Harlowe stood at the island with her mug and felt completely rested and happy.

Harlowe sipped and let out a deep sigh of contentment. "Now, *this* is a good morning," She eyed Tatum. "Did you sleep all right? No nightmares?"

"Not a single one. I don't get them every night, but I've never had one with you. You have something I don't that keeps the bad thoughts away."

"Well, you know what they say," Harlowe said, waving her mug around, "Cuteness triumphs over brawn any day."

"Are you saying I'm not cute?" Tatum said, pressing a hand to her chest as if terribly offended.

"Hey, if the shoe fits," Harlowe retorted. She had to put down her coffee and flee, shrieking with laughter as Tatum charged her. She made a wrong turn and ended up in a dead end. Harlowe had only one second to let out a squeak of surprise as Tatum caught up to her. Strong arms came around her and Harlowe found herself pressed up to Tatum's full length. Her vision went fuzzy with the feeling of Tatum against her. Snuggling was not like that. This was hot and hungry. Tatum held her with possessiveness and desire. Harlowe caught her breath at the look in Tatum's eyes, as if she was barely holding herself in check. The feeling rippled through Harlowe, sent on a tight beam straight to the centre of her being. Harlowe wanted her too. She ached for Tatum to grab her and kiss her, rip her shirt off, suck her nipples hard, touch her everywhere and take possession of her entire self. Harlowe was desperate for more. Instead, Tatum let go and stepped back with both hands held up.

"I'm sorry if I scared you," she said. "I didn't mean for that to happen."

"I'm perfectly fine," Harlowe said, even though her lower belly was heavy and tense. She smiled up at Tatum to prove it.

"Good," Tatum said. She glanced over her shoulder and gestured vaguely to the window. "I checked the road conditions and nothing's getting through until at least tomorrow. How about I drop you home? I'll come get you again when the roads are clear and you can pick up your car."

"That's fine," Harlowe said. Disappointment warred with curiosity. "But how are you getting me home if the roads are impassable?"

Tatum just let a slow, mysterious smile play over her features.

****

"Are you ready?" Tatum asked.

"Nooo," Harlowe replied. She pressed her back against the cold concrete wall and tried not to think about the six-story drop in front of her. Tatum had opened one side of the sunroom to reveal a flat, open balcony she called the launching pad. Reluctantly, Harlowe followed her out onto it and was regretting every step just then. Tatum hovered in front of her, suspended in the air and standing on nothing at all. The wind whipped around them, sending glittering sprinkles of snow through the air. The powdery snowflakes caught the light of the battle-suit and glowed blue for the briefest of moments before they spiraled away.

"It's perfectly safe," Tatum said. She held out her arms. "I've carried payloads twice your weight, if that's what you're worried about."

"Uh, yeah about that," Harlowe said. "You know what, I changed my mind. Call me a helicopter or get me some snowshoes, okay?" She shuffled her feet, trying to return to the window she came out of without having to turn around. The new snow slid under her foot. She lost her balance and pitched sideways into the white abyss. Her panicked scream only got halfway out of her throat before she landed in a giving hold.

"I've got you," Tatum said. "Are you all right?

"Now? I'm perfect," Harlowe said. She wrapped her arms around Tatum's neck and nestled her face into the crook of her neck. "Wonderful. Lovely. I always wanted to know what it was like to have my life flash in front of my eyes."

"I scared you," Tatum's voice carried a note of deep sadness Harlowe hadn't heard in a while.

"No, I'm fine now. Ha ha, see?" Harlowe made herself relax. She raised her head and looked around. They hovered above the treetops. Tatum's arms were strong and secure around her. The material of the suit was softer than she thought, flexible and warm either from Tatum's body heat or generated by the suit itself. "This is actually pretty cool. I feel safe in your arms."

"I'm glad to hear that. Ready to go?"

"Blast off," Harlowe crowed. Tatum gave her a crooked grin and they shot through the air. Harlowe only squeaked a few times, and she managed the entire trip without falling, panicking, or peeing herself.

Her little cottage appeared below them and Tatum lowered them to a perfect landing on the front porch. She let Harlowe down, but didn't move back as she always did before. Harlowe looked into Tatum's face. Her expression was filled with longing, Harlowe ached for something too. And she was going to get it. It was more than time. She kept her eyes trained on Tatum's as she reached up and placed her hands ever so lightly on Tatum's broad shoulders. She moved forward so their bodies were flush against each other, She knew the instant Tatum's breathing hitched and deepened. Tatum's hands rested on her waist.

"You'd better go inside," Tatum said. Her voice was husky and tight. "It's freezing out here."

"I will," Harlowe whispered. "After this." She rose to her tiptoes and closed the distance between them. Her mouth met Tatum's, sealed seamlessly together. The kiss was gentle and chaste for approximately one second before the rushing desire filled Harlowe and her willpower crumbled. She dragged her lips over Tatum's, wanting to possess her. The hands on her waist tightened and melded Harlowe to Tatum's long body. Their mouths crashed together and parted, only to join once more. Harlowe grabbed air when she could, submitting and plundering in turn. Tatum's harsh breathing kicked Harlowe in the gut, her thighs turned to electricity-filled water. She felt like a hot wave broke over her, pulling her into Tatum's embrace. Harlowe had never been kissed like that, like Tatum would die if they stopped.

The dance of passion slowed and Harlowe fell back. She felt drained of energy, but filled with the most wondrous feeling of completion. She pressed her fingers to her lips, they were wet and full. She looked up into Tatum's eyes, fearful she might see regret. Harlowe didn't regret anything. Tatum looked rather stunned. Her face was flushed and she was breathing hard.

"When can I see you again?" Harlowe asked in a small voice.

"Soon," Tatum replied. She lifted Harlowe's chin with a finger and very softly pressed a second kiss to her lips. It was over too quickly and Harlowe whimpered when Tatum pulled away. "You have my info, call or text me anytime."

"I will," Harlowe said. She stepped back and pressed a hand to her chest. The burgeoning feeling was too much. She felt like she was one heartbeat away from exploding into a thousand happy bits. With one last crooked grin, Tatum leapt into the air and was gone.

Harlowe let herself into her cottage and stood still for a moment before she clasped her hands together and twirled joyously. The memory of Tatum's lips on hers, the feeling of power in her arms as she held Harlowe inflamed her. Harlowe shed her coat and hat. Her body burned, her thighs trembled and a fist of tension deep within her begged for release. Harlowe thought about the toy in her bedside table and for a moment was incredibly tempted to get it out. She decided against that. The next time she got off, she knew exactly who she wanted to get her there.

Chapter Nine

Flashing orange lights reflected on the ceiling. Harlowe quickly sat up in the narrow spare room bed and grabbed her phone. It was a little past eleven. Harlowe wondered if Tatum was still up.

"Nothing to it but to do it," Harlowe said out loud. She snuggled back under the comforter and regarded the screen of her phone. The kiss that changed her entire world had only taken place that morning, but Tatum did say Harlowe could call or text anytime. She chewed on her lip in thought. She wanted to hear Tatum's voice, she ached to see her. Before Harlowe could change her mind, she pressed the "call" icon and waited, barely breathing.

Tatum answered right away. The screen of Harlowe's phone showed Tatum was in her workshop. She had a soldering iron in one hand and what looked like a circuit board in the other. She wore an unbuttoned, cotton work shirt over her tank top, with the sleeves rolled up to her elbows. She was a bit scruffy and looked damn good. Harlowe had to refrain from licking her lips. Under the covers, she squeezed her thighs together.

"Hey there, stranger," Tatum said with a warm, affectionate glow. "Are you all right? Can't sleep?"

"Nope, I'm good," Harlowe said. She rolled over and pillowed her head on the arm that wasn't involved in holding out her phone. "I saw the plough come through just now, so if the roads are still clear in the morning, could I bother you for a lift back to your place so I can get my car?"

"Of course. It's no bother at all," Tatum said. She put down what she was working on and rested her chin on her clasped hands. "What time were you thinking?"

"I have a meeting in the morning with my boss," Harlowe said. "But anytime in the afternoon works for me." Her arm was getting tired, so she made a pile of her comforter and rested her hand with the phone on it.

"I'll be there," Tatum said. She tilted her head and

fixed Harlowe with a smirk. "Door or window, your call."

"Either works for me," Harlowe said. "I won't bother you for too long. Just zip in and out."

"You're not a bother at all. Why don't you stay and hang out for a while? I'd be glad for the company."

"Okay, yeah, I'd like that too." Harlowe's cheeks got warm. "So what do you want to do when I'm there?"

"Anything you desire," Tatum replied in her too-sexy-for-her-own-good throaty purr. Scruffy appearance notwithstanding, she oozed sensuality. Harlowe swallowed hard and squirmed. Damn, that voice hit her right on the clit. Harlowe got a wicked idea. Two could play at that game.

Leaning close to the screen, she murmured, "And what do *you* desire?"

With her phone held over her, Harlowe rolled over onto her back and let the comforter fall away from her body. Her camisole had ridden up during her squirming fest and she was bare all the way to her sternum. Tatum flushed and drew in a quick breath. Triumphant, Harlowe trailed one hand over her breast, taking her time over the hard nub under the thin material of her camisole. Her heart pounded. Harlowe had never done anything like that before, but it felt natural to do it now. The look of desire on Tatum's face encouraged her to continue. Harlowe licked her lips and slipped her hand underneath her camisole. "Do you want to kiss me again?" Harlowe asked. Her voice came out breathy. "Do you want to touch me?"

"Jesus, yes," Tatum breathed. Abruptly, she shook her head and put a hand over her face. "Harlowe, Sweet pea, you're making it very hard—uh, difficult for me to think about my work right now."

"It's late," Harlowe said with a little pout. "Work tomorrow."

Tatum leaned her cheek on one hand. Her posture softened from the ramrod-straight one she favored. Her eyes bore into Harlowe's. The very air heated, as if they were in the same room, not separated by a screen.

"And what should I do instead of work?"

"Play. With me," Harlowe said. She trailed her hand suggestively over her breast again, then drew her fingers up over her throat to her lips. "I wish you were here in this bed, pressed up next to me. I'd take your hand and put it...here." Harlowe aimed a sultry glance at Tatum before she slipped her hand under her camisole. This time, she didn't stop, and brought her hand up to cup her fullness. With a breathy moan, Harlowe rubbed her nipple into hardness. "Tae," Harlowe whispered. "Look at me. I want you to touch me like this." A glance at the screen showed Tatum was leaning forward with a look of intense concentration on her face. Her hands were clenched into fists.

"Fuck," Tatum gritted. Her breath was loud in Harlowe's ears.

"Do you want me to stop?" Harlowe asked. She bit her lip and threw her head back. "Or do you want me to go lower?"

"My God," Tatum breathed. Her voice was raw and cracking. "Harlowe, you're killing me. But...would you really? For me?"

Harlowe just answered with a little giggle that turned into a gasp as she stroked her hand down her belly, heading for the waistband of her panties, which were already soaking wet at the crotch. She was just about to delve underneath when her phone slipped from her grasp and landed on her face.

"Ow!" Harlowe sat up quickly, holding her nose. "Dammit."

A low chuckle filtered through the haze of pain.

"Your poor nose. Are you okay?" Tatum asked.

"Yeah," Harlowe replied. She huffed and picked up her phone. "Sorry for wrecking the mood."

"Sweet pea, I can't wait to see you tomorrow, in person." Tatum shifted in her seat and Harlowe swore she adjusted something under the table. "We can continue this conversation where we left off, if you're okay with that."

"Oh yes, very okay," Harlowe said. "Super okay."

They said goodnight and goodbye and ended the call. Harlowe plugged her phone into the charger and plopped it down on the mattress next to her. She rolled over and hugged her pillow, unable to find a comfortable position. Her nose smarted and her belly burned with hunger. She was a little surprised at herself, but she loved teasing Tatum. Talking like that and touching herself in front of Tatum turned her on more than anything else ever had. She rolled over again and folded her pillow in half, grumbling with frustration. The next day couldn't come fast enough. Just like Harlowe.

****

The morning meeting with Bucky nearly made Harlowe fall asleep, and by the end of it, she was ready to chuck the entire computer out of the window just so she wouldn't have to listen to him blather on about whatever stupid issue he had at the moment. At least Harlowe got to run the idea of the Gazette setting up a booth for Discovery Day by him. Bucky told her it was a great idea and promised to ship some stuff from the office for her to use.

She was so jumpy in anticipation of seeing Tatum again, Harlowe barely touched her lunch. Impatiently, she shoved the salad and meatloaf into a Tupperware container and raced into her room to finish getting ready. She didn't have a lot of clothes, so she just went with the cute plaid outfit she wore the day Tatum left her. Harlowe studied herself in the mirror. The last time she'd worn that was the worst day of her life. She had never felt an emptiness like that. Now she was overflowing with happiness. And as a bonus, her cropped hair looked super cute that day. A knock at the door brought Harlowe flying out of her room. She was halfway into her coat with her bag hanging off her arm when she wrenched the front door open. Tatum stood on the other side, dark and looming as ever, but the most welcome sight Harlowe had ever seen. Harlowe chirped with happiness and threw herself into Tatum's arms. She dropped happy little kisses on Tatum's cheek, although a few missed and got her ear.

"Woah, I guess you're happy to see me," Tatum said when the welcome-barrage was over. She set Harlowe down and pretended to wipe off her cheek. "You sure marked your territory. Nobody's going to come near me now."

"Funny," Harlowe said dryly. She quickly recovered and said, "Well? Are we going or not?"

"Sorry to keep you waiting," Tatum said. She scooped up Harlowe and cradled her tenderly in her arms. Harlowe draped her arms around Tatum's neck and pulled her close.

"Kiss me now," Harlowe ordered.

Tatum's response was definitely affirmative. She swooped down and claimed Harlow's lips with hers in a sweet kiss that left Harlowe hungry for more.

"Is your nose all right?" Tatum asked. "It took a direct hit last night."

"Totally fine, never better," Harlowe said in a dreamy voice. She came back to the present and gave Tatum a little squeeze. "Why don't we get moving? I heard a rumor you have unfinished business with me."

"I will never be finished with you," Tatum said. She pressed a quick kiss to Harlowe's temple. "Hang on, here we go."

Tatum jumped off the porch and into the air. This time, Harlowe was prepared for the experience and enjoyed the scenery. The white sunlight cast their shadow onto the glittering, sugary surface below them. They arrived at the bunker and Harlowe cheerfully greeted several of Tatum's helpers before she was invited up to the sunroom for a cup of tea.

"Is that like, 'come up for a nightcap'?" Harlowe asked innocently.

"It can be," Tatum said. She waggled her eyebrows. "But I do actually want to share a cup of tea and chat."

"I can chat," Harlowe said agreeably. She had to admit that while she was completely okay with being saucy the previous night, now facing Tatum in person, in the middle of the day, it was difficult to summon up the same feeling. Harlowe decided not to worry about it too much. Things would progress at whatever speed was best for them both. At any rate, she felt comfortable and safe. She felt like she was home.

Harlowe went up first and relaxed in the warm, sun-filled room. She wondered what it was like to live there, able to enjoy the spectacular view every day, then again, how lonely it must have been. Lonely enough for Tatum to make her team of helpers. Harlowe sobered and curled up on the love seat. The solemn mood didn't last long, though. She got a happy thrill, thinking of Tatum settling down next to her, maybe draping an arm around her shoulders, or giving her a long hug. Harlowe wriggled with anticipation.

Tatum soon entered, in her usual cargo pants and tank top combination that Harlowe found ridiculously sexy, with a tray in her hands. She set the tray down on the table.

"Leftovers," she said with an apologetic shrug.

"Hm?" Harlowe looked up from the plate, her mouth full of brownie. She swallowed mightily and accepted the cup of tea a concerned Tatum handed her. "Totally okay. I love these brownies."

"Glad to hear it."

Tatum poured herself a cup of tea and made a move as if to sit down on the chair across from Harlowe, who decided that just would not do.

"Ahem," Harlowe said. She arched a brow and pointed to the empty space next to her. "I believe there is a reservation here for a T. Edwyn."

Tatum shook her head and laughed softly before she rounded the table and sat down next to Harlowe.

"Did you sleep last night?" she asked with a teasing poke to Harlowe's shoulder.

"Oh yes, like a log," Harlowe replied archly. "Did you?"

"After that sexy show you put on?" Tatum groaned. "Every time I closed my eyes, I'd see you, lying there right in front of me, touching yourself like that and making me so fucking hot I thought I would explode."

"Not sorry," Harlowe quipped. She took a moment to savor the effect she had on Tatum. It was a powerful feeling, one she wanted to have again. A lot of times. "So?" she asked innocently.

"So, what?"

"So, are you going to continue your business with me?"

Tatum slipped from the loveseat to press her body between Harlowe's legs. Her hands rested on Harlowe's hips and she pulled them together. Tatum's mouth brushed Harlowe's ear. She whispered, "Until you beg me to stop."

Giddy with desire, Harlowe hitched herself forward until their bodies met in a breathless crush. She lowered her head and claimed Tatum's lips with a greed and passion she hadn't thought lived in her. Tatum's breath picked up, her harsh breaths when they parted drove Harlowe's arousal up in spikes. Tatum moaned against her lips, then pulled away, leaving Harlowe to gasp into the air as Tatum found the sensitive skin of her neck. Talented lips teased her. Harlowe threw her head back and closed her eyes. She couldn't help the wanton thrust of her hips, driving herself against Tatum's firm belly. The hands on her hips snaked around to cup her buttocks. From there, hot palms stroked up and down her back. Harlowe couldn't get enough.

"Yes, oh my God, Tatum," she moaned. She pressed her breasts to Tatum's. She wanted Tatum's hands not on her back, but her front. Her nipples tingled from the pressure. Her inner muscles clenched. "Touch me," Harlowe said between heaving breaths.

Tatum didn't speak, but drew Harlowe into a deep, devouring kiss. Taken by surprise, Harlowe nevertheless welcomed the intimate intrusion. She couldn't believe how deeply she felt the connection, breaths heating the air, her body responding automatically as if she already knew the rhythm of Tatum's lovemaking. A gentle hand brushed over her side and cupped her breast. Harlowe moaned with the sudden contact. She bucked her hips, desperate for Tatum, she wanted nothing separating them, she wanted Tatum on her, thrusting into her. The image shocked Harlowe enough she froze.

Immediately, Tatum drew back. Her face was unsure.

"Did I push you?" she asked. Her voice was low and husky. The hooded look of raw desire in her eyes flooded Harlowe with heat. She shook her head.

"No, you didn't. This is good." Harlowe clasped her hands and looked into Tatum's face. "Like, really good. I can't believe how much I lo—um, like being with you. It's a bit overwhelming, I guess. I hope you're good with the pace, too."

"Absolutely," Tatum said. She eased back, still on her knees. She tucked her long bangs behind one ear. "I don't want to go into the details, but while I haven't had relationships exactly, I have had, well, experience with women."

"Like what?" Harlowe blurted out. "Oh! Okay. Um, yeah I know what you're talking about."

"I'm not ashamed or regretful." Tatum looked uncomfortable. She didn't meet Harlowe's eyes. "While I did engage in risky behavior, I made sure to do it the safest way possible. Protecting myself is the one thing I excel at. You are safe with me, Harlowe. Just so you know, I've been tested multiple times since my last…night out."

"Thank you," Harlowe said. "I appreciate you telling me. I have all my shots, so I guess I'm protecting you, too."

"You don't think less of me, now you know?" Tatum asked.

"No, why should I?" Harlowe replied. "You had a life before me, and I'm glad to be here with you now."

"I am too." Tatum fixed Harlowe with an intense look. "What we have, this is different from anything I've had before. I don't want to ruin this by going too fast."

"Me neither, but I don't want to go too slow either," Harlowe said. She was very aware of Tatum's body between her spread thighs. Her skirt had ridden up, exposing her stocking-clad legs. Harlowe's chest still heaved with deep breaths. She hesitantly reached out and drew a finger down the side of Tatum's face. Tatum closed her eyes and lowered her head, giving into the caress with a look of peace. "Tae, can I ask you something?"

"Anything," Tatum said. She blinked up at Harlowe as if waking up.

Harlowe giggled and wriggled her hips a bit. Tatum

caught her lower lip between her teeth and flushed. "Are you doing anything a week from Saturday? In the evening, specifically."

Thoughtfully, Tatum sucked her lower lip into her mouth. Harlowe gulped. Fuck, did she have any clue how smoking hot she was?

"No plans. Yet," Tatum said. She lifted an eyebrow and fixed Harlowe with a piercing gaze.

"That's good because I was wondering if you'd like to go to the Strawberry Social," Harlowe said in a rush. "With me."

Tatum paused and Harlowe was just about to start babbling and take the invitation back when she spoke. "It would be my honor to accompany you."

"Really?" Harlowe squealed. She threw her arms around Tatum and dragged her into a hug. Tatum's arms snaked around her and held her tightly. Tatum lowered her head and buried her face against Harlowe's chest with a happy hum. Harlowe stroked her hands over the tightly tied back hair and rested her cheek on the silken ebony strands. "It's being held at the community center, so how about you meet me there at seven?"

"Sounds good," Tatum said. "What's the dress code?"

"It seems pretty casual, unfortunately."

"Unfortunately?"

"Yeah," Harlowe said. She wrinkled her nose. "I was kind of hoping I could wear this dress I bought for my college's graduation formal, which I ended up not going to. It's kind of fancy, so I'll just go with jeans, I guess."

"I have no problem with formal," Tatum said. She moved back to look into Harlowe's face. Her expression was serious, but her eyes danced. "Let me know the color so we can match."

"You'd wear a dress?" Harlowe asked in amazement.

"Not exactly," Tatum said. "Let's just say I wouldn't be averse to repeating the venture I had into tailored wear. Especially the way you looked at me in it."

"Oh God, was I obvious?" Harlowe asked. Her ears got hot. She remembered the dashing figure standing in her kitchen and somewhere significantly lower heated up as well.

Tatum's deep chuckle spoke volumes. She said, "Let's just say I thought you were going to grab me by the suspenders and have your way with me on the kitchen counter."

"What can I say?" Harlowe said with a shrug. "I have a weakness for a sharp-dressed woman."

This time, Tatum's chuckle bloomed into a full laugh. In that moment, Harlowe believed deep in her heart nothing could ever destroy that happiness.

Chapter Ten

One week later, on the morning of Discovery Day, Harlowe woke up much earlier than usual with a feeling of excitement in her chest. Aside from that idyllic afternoon when Harlowe went to pick up her car, she hadn't been with Tatum in person. They'd texted a lot and called every night, which was nice, but Harlowe wanted more than what they could exchange through a screen. Even there, Harlowe behaved herself admirably. For the past few days, Tatum had been out-of-sorts and rather taciturn. While Harlowe ached to go over and be with her, she understood Tatum was busy preparing physically and mentally for Discovery Day and needed space. Harlowe satisfied herself by keeping busy with her own work and playing with Amelia and Eleanor, who were now comfortable enough to take nuts from her hands. Eleanor, who was the bolder of the two, even scrambled up to sit on Harlowe's shoulder for a moment a couple times before scampering back to her treehouse.

Harlowe finished her breakfast and cleaned up without really paying attention to what she was doing. Impatiently, she wandered through the cottage, looking for something to occupy herself. She'd just finished dusting the entire living room when her phone chirped. Harlowe instantly had the phone in her hand and a big smile on her face. The message from Tatum was short.

My place?

Harlowe quickly replied.

I'll be there in five.

She put her coat on over her powder blue work suit before she picked up her overnight bag. Instead of using a convenient snowstorm as an excuse, Tatum straightforwardly invited her to stay overnight, which Harlowe didn't even consider refusing. Her body hummed in anticipation of being with Tatum. She thought of their kisses and snuggles. What would that day bring? Harlowe wondered. What would that night? To head off the giddy burst of anticipation-tinted nerves, she thought of the news she had to share with Tatum.

Practically vibrating with energy, Harlowe tossed her bag onto the passenger seat and started her car. Soon she pulled into the now-familiar bunker. The parking garage hosted several SUVs and pickups bearing the fire department's logo. Tatum greeted her in the entranceway, in her battle-suit and looking ill-at-ease.

"Are you okay?" Harlowe asked. She hung up her coat and studied Tatum.

"Yes. No. Maybe," Tatum said. She wrung her hands. "Why did I agree to this again?"

"Because you are a generous and caring person who was in the position to help out a lot of people and you did."

Tatum pursed her lips in thought. She got that crooked grin Harlowe loved before she leaned down and whispered into her ear, "Or maybe I was trying to impress a pretty girl."

"If that's your goal, it's working," Harlowe said. She draped her arms over Tatum's shoulders. "Come down here and say hello properly."

"Yes ma'am," Tatum said. She took Harlowe by the waist and drew her close. Harlowe eagerly lifted her chin and was rewarded with a soft, warm kiss that turned into several. Harlowe moaned softly against Tatum's lips. She dragged her fingers through Tatum's long hair and down the back of her neck. The hands on her waist slipped lower as well, as if in response. Harlowe's breath kicked up when Tatum's strong fingers cupped her backside, pressing their bodies together in a heated embrace. Har-lowe wanted more. She opened her mouth in appeal and was rewarded with a quick swipe of searching tongue against hers.

It lasted only the briefest of moments, but the con-nection set Harlowe's libido on fire. When Tatum let her go, Harlowe sagged against the wall and fanned herself.

"You're really good at that," she said.

"What, kissing?" Tatum said with a wicked spark in her eye. "Remember, I have many skills. You haven't seen anything yet."

"Oh wow," Harlowe breathed.

"This is for you," Tatum said. From a hidden pocket in her suit, she pulled out a plastic card and passed it over. "I've activated the security locks to keep the guests contained to the storage bay. This will get you anywhere in the building. Just swipe it in the reader."

"Thanks," Harlowe said. She slipped the card into a pocket of her suit jacket.

She followed Tatum to the storage bay. It was filled with cheerful talking and banging as the volunteers set up their booths. Harlowe glanced at Tatum. The situation had to be hard for her. She squeezed her hand, the fingers that clutched at hers were cold.

"You got this," Harlowe whispered. "Remember, you can always take a step back if it gets too much. The auxiliary is officially in charge of the event. You can vanish at any time and they'll take care of everything."

"You're right," Tatum said. She let go of Harlowe's hand and sank back. "I have some things to get ready. Do you need anything?"

"I'm fine," Harlowe said. "Hang on, does that mean you're going to present something too?"

Tatum shrugged. "I'm just setting up a few things to show the kids, nothing really special."

"I can't wait," Harlowe said. Tatum gave her a weak smile before she activated her suit and slipped away. Alone, Harlowe trotted into the vast storage bay. Someone in an orange safety vest directed her over to the cargo area where her own stuff was, delivered the previous night directly from the *Maritime Gazette's* main office. She quickly set up the backdrop of a city at night, with the words "*Maritime Gazette* Live" printed on it, and placed the two folding chairs on either side of a small table that held two microphones in their charging stand. She secured the video camera on a tripod in front of the interview space, and had to go on a rummage to find the cords she needed to hook it up to the monitor. A larger table held a few samples of the newspaper, permission forms for the parents to fill out, plus a stack of Harlowe's business cards.

When she was finished, Harlowe stood back and regarded her booth with satisfaction.

"Looking good, eh." A jolly male vice caused Harlowe to whirl.

"Oh, hi Jim," Harlowe said.

He bobbed his head and grinned. "That sure is a nice operation you got there. Real professional."

"Just our standard setup." She aimed a thumb over her shoulder. "My boss lent me a bunch of stuff they use for trade fairs. Thanks for letting me join at the last minute."

"No problem," he said with one hand stroking his beard. "You're part of the community, too. And there wouldn't be any Discovery Day at all this year if it weren't for your Miz Edwyn. She's something else, isn't she?"

"Yeah, you got that right," Harlowe said. Inwardly, she glowed with happiness at how far Tatum had come in the short time they'd known each other. Obviously, her issues wouldn't disappear overnight, and Harlowe didn't expect them to. Tatum really was a unique individual. Harlowe's chest got tight. She never wanted to be away from Tatum. Sure, they could be separated physically and she wouldn't implode, but she never wanted Tatum to leave her heart. She wondered how Tatum felt about her. It was more than just the chance at having a warm body in her bed, that much Harlowe was certain.

While Harlowe busily checked everything in her booth, Jim wandered off. Harlowe finished her preparation with lots of time to spare, just like she'd planned. Lightheaded with anticipation, she made her escape and used her card to get into the elevator. On the way, she pulled out her phone.

Meet me in the kitchen. I have something to show you.

Harlowe sent the message and smirked to herself.

She was only in the kitchen for a moment when Tatum came barreling in.

"What did you want to show me?" she asked.

"*Maritime Gazette's* newest reporter," Harlowe said proudly. She pointed to herself. "Guess who got approved to do a feature for our online digest? I'm interviewing kids about their Discovery Day experience. It's not glamorous, but it's what I always wanted to—"

Harlowe squeaked as Tatum grabbed her in a crushing embrace, then twirled her around. Harlowe's legs flew out and she held on as tight as she could, giggling into Tatum's shoulder.

"Congratulations," Tatum said into her hair. She let Harlowe down and very gently cupped her hands around Harlowe's cheeks. Tatum's face was alive with excitement, and something else, deeper and more intimate. She radiated a fierce pride that Harlowe found both flattering and incredibly sexy. Tatum leaned forward and touched her forehead to Harlowe's. Her voice was soft and husky. "This is a huge step for you. I know you'll be the best reporter they ever had."

"Not sure about that," Harlowe replied. "But I hope somebody finds my article interesting."

"I certainly will," Tatum said.

"You're totally not biased or anything," Harlowe said. Tatum just shrugged and smirked. "Still, kids say the funniest things. It's gonna be a hoot to hang out with them."

Tatum got a thoughtful, soft expression as she studied Harlowe. "You really like children, don't you?"

"They're okay in small doses," Harlowe said. "I'm an only child, but I have older cousins that spawned. I like playing with kids, but I also like giving them back to their parents. The main thing I like about them is it's fun being taller than somebody for once."

Tatum reached out and tucked a wayward strand of hair behind Harlowe's ear. "I'm sure the children of Brooksville will love you just as—uh." Tatum abruptly stopped and looked away. She seemed ill-at-ease and Harlowe wasn't quite sure why. "Never mind."

"I better get back," Harlowe said. She raised her

face, hoping for a kiss and received a quick one that didn't do much to quell her hunger for more. She practically floated back down to the storage bay, which rang with talking and laughter, filled with people bustling around doing last-minute preparations. The orange-vested firefighter was now armed with glow sticks, and he directed a steadily increasing group of people into two orderly lines at the entrance. Harlowe felt their excitement, especially from the younger members, who peered eagerly into the main event space.

Harlowe went over to her booth and settled down on one of the chairs. The folding chair wasn't the most comfortable or professional, but she didn't mind. This was her first real assignment! Her first chance to prove herself to Bucky and the rest of the *Gazette* staff. Harlowe was determined to make sure her first assignment wasn't her last. She straightened up when Fire Chief Chrissy Peebles rang her bell. The talking immediately ceased. After a short, pompous, and insincere address by a balding, paunchy man who was introduced as Sylvester Stevens, Chrissy rang her bell again. The firefighter with the glow sticks gave the all clear sign. With shouts and laughter, the children burst into the vast storage bay. Harlowe had to smile at their enthusiasm, which even outshone the calls of the people manning the various booths.

Harlowe watched several groups pass her by before she got her first visitor of the day, a sister and brother who shyly answered Harlowe's questions while the proud father took a video with his phone.

"When are you going to publish the interviews?" he asked after the two siblings returned to his side.

"It'll be available in the January edition of our online digest," Harlowe said. She suddenly realized why Bucky had been so supportive of her venture to take part in the event. Harlowe put on her best smile and said, "If you sign up for our online subscription service, you can have it delivered automatically to your inbox a week before the public can access it."

"Really? How do I do that?"

Harlowe whipped out her business card and passed it

over, while giving a brief overview of the subscription process and benefits. The next three interviews resulted in similar interest for a subscription. For the first time, Harlowe felt like she might actually be able to meet her goal in her lifetime. Gloating, she casually placed some of the few rather dog-eared free samples on the table. She felt a tug on her skirt. Behind her was a very small girl with her straw-yellow hair in two pigtails. She was hugging a teddy bear.

Harlowe crouched down to be on the same level. "Hello there. Are you lost?"

"No," she said. She darted around Harlowe and pulled herself up into one of the chairs. She placed her bear beside herself and looked expectantly at Harlowe.

"Okay then," Harlowe said. She settled down in her own chair and held out a hand. "I'm Harlowe Tremaine, reporter with the *Maritime Gazette*. May I have your name?"

The little girl squirmed and giggled. "I'm Ellie."

"Nice to meet you," Harlowe said. She used her ignored hand to pick up the microphone. With a serious expression, she pointed it at Ellie. "So, how are you enjoying Discovery Day?"

Ellie nodded enthusiastically, which set her pigtails bobbing. "I'm four," she said and held up four chubby fingers.

"Wow, really? I'm twenty-one," Harlowe said. She put down the mic in order to hold up two fingers on one hand and one on the other. The older kids usually called her out and said that was only three, but Ellie didn't take the bait. Harlowe picked up the mic again. "I see you've brought a guest to the event today. Who is your friend?"

"Bear," Ellie said. She hugged her bear and buried her face in its fur.

"I hope you both are enjoying the various booths." Harlowe mentally went down her list of questions, trying to find one suitable for Ellie. Before she came to a decision, two women came running up. One was blonde like Ellie and the other had long dark hair that fell around her shoulders in sleek curls.

"Ellie, there you are, we were worried." The blonde

knelt down and addressed the little girl. She looked over at Harlowe and said, "I'm sorry, did she bother you?"

"Not at all," Harlowe said. She indicated the TV screen. "I was just interviewing Ellie for the *Maritime Gazette*."

"Oh my God, that's so cute," the brunette said as she took out her phone. She waved her hands, indicating they should move closer. "How about a quick pic?"

Harlowe obediently posed with the small family. When the photo-op was over, she gushed, "It's so nice to meet you two. It's great to see a two-mom family even all the way out here. I never thought there would be so many other lesbians around here. Must be something in the water, eh?"

"Uh no," the blonde said while the brunette started laughing. "We're sisters-in-law."

"Oops," Harlowe said. She grimaced. "Sorry, sometimes I forget straight is the default setting. I didn't mean to assume."

"No problem, it's actually not the first time that's happened," the blonde said. She introduced herself as Andrea Marshall and her sister-in-law as Jamie.

"You never know, Andrea," Jamie said between chortles. "If things don't work out with Cody, at least you know there are options."

Andrea rolled her eyes. "Sorry hun, but don't get your hopes up."

Jamie burst out laughing again and Andrea patted her on the shoulder.

"I really hope you haven't met Shelby Stevens yet," Jamie said once she finished snickering.

"Unfortunately I have," Harlowe said with a grimace. "It was less than pleasant."

"Ugh, my condolences," Jamie said. "Don't think all of us are like that. Shelby was in my older brother's class all through school and bullied him so bad he had to go to therapy. She's always been just awful to everyone. Everyone in her entire family is like that. All of us here are just waiting for one of them to cross the line. Anyway, here's hoping she'll leave you alone."

"Too late," Harlowe muttered.

Andrea came over with Ellie in her arms and they shared a round of goodbyes before they trotted off in the direction of the sandbox the river cleanup committee was overseeing.

When Harlowe was finished cringing at herself, she turned around the poster to show the "back in ten minutes" message. She grabbed her bag and her phone and went off to look at the rest of the booths. Most of them were geared towards children, with hands-on activities and games with trinkets as prizes. Harlowe picked up a few pamphlets about hiking trails in the area and was listening to a lecture by the Clean River Society when she heard a sudden chorus of shrieks. Convinced that Tatum had something to do with it, Harlowe ran over to investigate. She stopped in her tracks to see Tatum, in full battle-mode surrounded by a crowd of children sitting in a semicircle around her. Tatum brandished her blades and they scooted back away from her. Some of the younger ones looked scared, but most of the kids had expressions of awe on their faces.

"They're not actually sharp," Tatum said to the crowd. She knelt down and showed them by touching a blade with her bare finger. "They can be calibrated to vibrate at different frequencies in order to cut different materials. This is done by utilizing a system of sonic—"

"Can you, like, slice people in two?" one of the boys near the back of the crowd shouted.

"Yes," Tatum answered matter-of-factly. "But I wouldn't unless under very extreme circumstances. Now, about the internal generator—"

"How do you go to the bathroom?" another child called out.

Tatum closed her eyes for a moment and Harlowe fought back a giggle at the look of obvious annoyance.

"I don't," she said in a clipped tone.

All at once, the kids started shouting out their questions. Harlowe clapped her hand over her mouth to keep the laughter in check as Tatum got more irritated with each one.

"Where do you keep your car keys?"

"Where do you think?" Tatum snapped.

"Does it got a zipper in the back?"

"What?" Tatum stared at the child who asked the question.

"Why is it black?"

Tatum threw her hands into the air.

"Does it come in kid sizes?"

"What's all those buckles for?"

"Can you come to my school for show and tell?"

"Are you a superhero?"

"Do you have a boyfriend?"

At that question, Tatum looked over the crowd and locked eyes with Harlowe. Her lips quirked up for an instant.

"No, I don't," she said. "I have a girlfriend."

Harlowe couldn't help the giddy rush of happiness. She glanced around to see if anyone had noticed her soul had just lit up like the sky on Canada Day. Of course, nobody did, but Harlowe felt radiant.

As one, the children said, "Ooooooh!"

"Do you kiss?"

"What's she like?"

"Are you gonna get married?"

As more questions bubbled up from the group, Tatum's cool façade broke. Her cheeks got pink and she shuffled her feet like she wanted to be anywhere but there. She turned away from her audience and grabbed a large folded square of paper. Her blades hummed and swished through the air before she whirled back and unfurled a garland of perfectly cut snowflakes. As one, the kids took in a collective breath. The air filled with clapping.

Harlowe leaned back and watched the show progress. Once she got over her initial annoyance, Tatum was actually really good with children and it was adorable to see her interact with them. One of the boys seemed particularly taken with her. He was small and scrawny, with ginger hair that stuck out in all directions and thick glasses. His questions were respectful and Tatum took extra care to answer them.

Harlowe's gaze grew soft and her chest warm. After a short demonstration of the hover potential of the suit, two drones appeared with a huge block of ice between them. Harlowe held her breath in awe as Tatum went to work, carving it with her blades. Fluffy shavings streamed into the air like the lightest snow. The crowd of children went wild, dancing in the shower and jumping on the fallen mounds, which melted instantly. The parents on the sidelines even paused in filming the scene on their phones with similar looks of wonder.

"Get away from them!" A shout cut through the fairytale-like scene. Harlowe froze, along with everyone else. The only one moving was Shelby, stomping toward Tatum with an angry scowl on her mottled-red face. She ran up to Tatum, who moved away from the ice sculpture, hands in the air.

"Step back," Tatum said. She lowered her chin and fixed Shelby with a steely glare.

"No, I gotta protect these kids," Shelby hollered. "A crazy dangerous freak like you shouldn't be anywhere near kids. You're gonna take someone's head off."

The bespectacled redheaded boy ran up to them. Harlowe twitched and wondered if she should go after him. He stood with his back to Tatum and his arms outstretched. Someone in the audience called out, "Davey!"

"She's not dangerous," he said. "She's my friend. She's all of our friends."

"Watch out, kid," Shelby said. She shoved Davey out of the way and charged Tatum, just like she had Harlowe. This time, her shoulder hit Tatum in the belly and sent her flailing backwards. A set of blades sheared through the block of ice, jaggedly decapitating the half-carved dragon. The two of them went down in a pile. The severed head hit the floor and burst into thousands of pieces with a sound like a shotgun going off.

Chaos broke out, with children running and screaming and their parents frantically trying to round them up. The floor was slippery from the melted ice. Everywhere people were tripping and falling down. A stampede for the exit trampled several booths. The firefighters leapt into action, calling for people to slow down. But not even Chrissy's determined bell-ringing and the guy with the glow sticks could stop the crowd. Someone pushed Harlowe roughly aside. She crashed into a table and went sprawling to the floor. Harlowe was rubbing her smarting leg when Jim barreled over to her.

"Are you okay?" he asked, holding out a hand to her. His ball cap was nowhere to be seen, and he was sweaty and disheveled.

"Never better," Harlowe said. She waved off his help and stood up. In the few minutes she'd been down, the chaos ended. The storage bay was silent once more. The panicked crowd had left and the remaining volunteer fire-fighters milled around, collecting broken chairs and scattered brochures. Harlowe was filled with rage. Shelby ruined everything. Harlowe said, "This isn't Tatum's fault. You saw what Shelby did."

"Yup," Jim said. He made a move as if to grab his hat, but when his hand closed on nothing, he chuckled in a sheepish way. Sobering, Jim said. "Look, I'll have a talk with folks in town and try to smooth things over for Miz Edwyn. Don't worry. More'n a few of them have had run-ins with the Stevens family one way or another. They may not be able to say anything outright, but they'll understand."

"I appreciate that," Harlowe said. She couldn't stand still anymore and pelted off to find Shelby and officially uninvite her. Angrily, Harlowe scanned the room. She saw her worst fear, Shelby and Tatum in a standoff. Tatum had her blades out and her arms crossed in front of herself in defense. "No, no, no," Harlowe said under her breath as she dashed across the room. She skidded to a halt between them and shoved herself into Shelby's space.

"Oh hey it's the little heroine," Shelby said. "Come to save me from the big bad whack-o, huh?"

"What the fuck is wrong with you?" Harlowe shouted. "This is not your home and you had no business coming in here, messing things up. Tatum is *not danger-ous.*"

"Way I see it," Shelby drawled, "is a bloodthirsty fucked-in-the-head hermit like that shouldn't be near kids. You saw what she did to that ice thing. That could'a been a kid's head."

"What are you talking about?" Harlowe planted her hands on her hips. "You obviously have no idea what actually went on and you just came here to ruin the day. Congratulations, you did. Now get out of here."

All the while, Tatum stood so still, she could have been a block of ice. Her head was down and her long bangs covered her face.

"You know you're not as cute as you think you are," Shelby said. She gave Harlowe a slow, lascivious once over that made Harlowe's skin crawl. She smacked her lips. "Even though you're a mouthy little bitch, I'll still take ya."

"What?" Harlowe shook her head. Bile rose in her throat.

"Come to the Strawberry Social with me," Shelby said. She made no effort to hide how she was leering at Harlowe's chest. Annoyed, Harlowe pulled her suit jacket tight to her body.

"No," Harlowe said. She lifted her chin and said with pride, "I'm already going with someone a million times better than you could ever hope to be."

Shelby spat on the floor. "Don't tell me you're going with *that*?" She craned her neck in an exaggerated way to look past Harlowe to Tatum.

"Yes I am," Harlowe said.

Shelby let out a dirty, rough laugh. "You really need to raise your standards. Have fun with your shut-in dyke friend."

"I don't appreciate you using that word," Harlowe said. She crossed her arms and tapped one foot. "Besides, you're one too."

"Shut your trap!" Shelby suddenly shouted. Her face got blotchy and red. Spittle flew from her lips.

"Then why don't you just get a boyfriend and leave me alone?" Harlowe asked.

"I can get any guy I want," Shelby spat. "I'm not gay, *you* are!"

"That's not an insult," Harlowe said. "I'm proud of being a lesbian."

"You sure flaunt all out for everyone to see," Shelby hollered. Veins stood out on the side of her neck. "If you're gonna act like the town bicycle, don't be surprised when people start lining up for a ride you little sl—"

Her words choked off as Tatum reached out and grabbed her by the collar of her disreputable hoodie.

"Don't finish that sentence," Tatum growled. She dragged Shelby close to her. Harlowe took an involuntary step back herself at the steely tone and primal rage in Tatum's eyes. "Apologize to Harlowe."

"No," Shelby said. She swatted at the fist that gripped her hoodie.

"I won't ask you again," Tatum said. She raised her free hand, blades gleaming. Harlowe watched in horror as the glow deepened and a dangerous hum came from them.

"Hey Harlowe," Shelby called out with a nasty smirk Harlowe didn't like one bit. "I'm sorry your girlfriend's a freak and you're a cheap ho—woooah shit!"

Tatum's blades swung through the air. Shelby flinched violently. Harlowe clapped both hands to her mouth. Tears sprang to her eyes. The blades stopped a millimeter from Shelby's exposed neck. A heavy silence fell, punctuated only by Shelby's frantic wheezing. Harlowe froze, not knowing what to do. A sick sense of foreboding lodged itself in her gut. The blades wavered, then fell away as Tatum lowered her arm.

"Get out," Tatum said in a low, threatening tone. She gave Shelby a hard shove that sent her sprawling.

"I have half a mind to burn that stupid social to the ground." Shelby made a show of hocking a fat loogie onto the floor before she shambled off. On her way to the exit, one of the Jeeves brothers zoomed over and clipped her on the shin. Cursing, Shelby kicked at the little robot, but missed.

The firefighters who had been following the exchange suddenly found other things to do and innocently looked away. Harlowe took a step toward Tatum. She was trembling.

"Come on, look at me," Harlowe said. She reached out a hand and Tatum recoiled. Harlowe's heart felt like it would tear in two. She tried to smile. "It's okay. You didn't do anything wrong. You were defending me."

Harlowe itched to draw Tatum close to her, reassure

her everything was all right, but the icy, closed look on her face kept Harlowe still. Harlowe wished she knew what Tatum was thinking.

Jim jogged over to them. He stopped a safe distance away and doffed his newly recovered cap. He held it in both hands, nervously wringing it.

"We all didn't see anything," he said. He glanced over at Tatum, instead of the fear Harlowe expected, his expression was sympathetic. "Unless Miz Stevens presses charges, none of us is gonna say a thing. I would advise you to stay clear of her from now on, though. We don't want any trouble here, and feuds like this never end well."

Tatum moved a fraction, inclining her head. Jim looked mollified. He gave Harlowe a nod.

"Off the record, but Lord knows I'd'a done the exact same thing," he said. "If it were my Chrissy bein' disrespected in my own house. Just wanted to leave that with you. Take care now."

Harlowe blinked in surprise as Jim sped off. Did that mean he accepted them as a couple? A flush of pure pleasure filled Harlowe. She sobered. Now wasn't the time for that.

"Tae," Harlowe said softly. That broke Tatum's thrall. For the first time since the incident, her silver-blue eyes lifted from the floor. Harlowe drew in a breath at the sadness in their depths, Tatum's utter hopelessness radiated like a beacon. Not caring about the firefighters who were ferrying stuff across the floor, Harlowe slipped beside Tatum and gently squeezed her hand. The tiny squeeze she got in return felt like winning the lottery. Harlowe said lightly, "Let's leave them to clean up here and go somewhere quiet. I've had enough excitement for today."

Tatum nodded ever so slightly and allowed Harlowe to gently prod her over to the elevator. Harlowe had to let go of Tatum's hand while she swiped her card, but once they were in the elevator, she found her hand grasped once more.

Chapter Eleven

They didn't speak until they got to the sunroom. Tatum sat down heavily on the loveseat. Her head bowed and her shoulders slumped.

"Talk to me," Harlowe said. She hated the air of defeat that weighed down Tatum's proud head.

"This was a mistake," Tatum whispered. Abruptly, she got to her feet. With a hum, the suit flared into life. She clenched her fists and the blades deployed with a sharp thunk. Face unreadable, Tatum strode over to the window and peered outside with her back to Harlowe. She muttered something under her breath and pounded one fist sharply against the glass. The sudden violence caused Harlowe to flinch, but she didn't even think of leaving Tatum's side. She had to be there.

"What was a mistake?" Harlowe asked. She held her breath and waited.

Without turning, Tatum said, "I traumatized those kids. They'll always remember the monster who ruined the day."

"No, that's not true," Harlowe said. She couldn't stay still anymore. She leapt up and ran over to Tatum. Without thinking, she threw her arms around Tatum's waist and hugged her from behind. At the first contact, Tatum's body twitched, but she didn't otherwise try to break the hold. Harlowe rested her cheek on Tatum's broad back, aware of the warmth and subliminal hum of the battle suit. Harlowe said, "Kids are resilient, they'll be okay. Shelby's the one who wrecked everything."

Tatum flinched. "I shouldn't have used violence. It was only words. Words should never be answered by force."

"You did the right thing," Harlowe said. "You didn't actually hurt her, and I don't think you ever intended to. She needed something big to get through her thick skull. You showed that she's wrong. You have humanity and decency that she doesn't. And you risked everything to prove it. That was the most heroic thing anybody's ever done for me. Thank you."

Tatum twisted in Harlowe's arms and broke free from her. Harlowe peeped in surprise as Tatum grabbed her in a crushing embrace. Tatum buried her face into the crook of Harlowe's neck, as if trying to block out the world. Her breaths were deep and strained. Harlowe's heart pounded. She was more grateful than she'd ever been before at the way Tatum hadn't pushed her away. She didn't think she could take another goodbye like that last one. Harlowe wrapped her arms around Tatum's shivering form and held her. She stroked one hand through Tatum's hair.

"The firefighters are good people," Harlowe said. "They wouldn't be on our side if they didn't believe in you. I'm on your side too. I always will be."

After a long moment, Tatum let go and stepped back. Her expression was more alive and peaceful than before, and Harlowe finally breathed easily again. She studied Tatum for a moment before she asked, "Are you feeling better now?"

Tatum nodded. She stowed her blades with a sheep-ish look at Harlowe, then raked back her long, trailing hair with both hands.

"Thanks," she said.

"You're very welcome." Harlowe playfully sketched a curtsey.

Tatum's expression softened. "I hope you at least got some good material for your article before it all went to hell," she said.

"Yup," Harlowe replied. "My boss had the right idea to let me interview kids. I got a bunch of subscriptions from the parents. In a way, it's a good thing I didn't do too many interviews. If I had to leave anyone out, I bet they'd complain."

"That's good." Tatum paused before she said, "Har-lowe, I want to show you something."

"What?" Harlowe was intrigued.

Tatum looked down at herself, her body trussed up and encased in the battle-suit. When she came back to Harlowe, her face was set. She held out both arms, wrists turned up to show the tiny control panels that were normally hidden by her stance. Harlowe knit her brows in confusion. She had the feeling this was a huge step for Tatum, but she wasn't exactly sure what she was supposed to do.

"Grab both my wrists," Tatum said without preamble. "Thumbs down on both sides. You see those ridged yellow patches there?"

Confused, Harlowe lowered her head to look. After a moment, she found what Tatum directed her to. "What are those?" she asked. "Hopefully not the self-destruct buttons."

"No," Tatum said. She didn't laugh at the joke, not even a tiny smile. She looked nervous. "They control the system shut down and release sequence."

"Okay," Harlowe said. She suddenly understood as Tatum took her hands and gently guided her into position. They were very close. The moment was incredibly intimate. Tatum was giving Harlowe power over her, the power to disable her.

"Give it a moment to input your fingerprint. Okay. Push down simultaneously here and here." Tatum closed her eyes and leaned back a little. She let out a breath. "Now, Harlowe."

Harlowe bit her lip and squeezed her fingers tight in order to get the necessary leverage. She felt something shift under her thumbs. A second passed and nothing happened. Then a series of clicks followed by a long hiss filled her ears. Tatum rolled her shoulders and threw her head back. The suit parted along curved seam lines that Harlowe previously thought were just part of the design. Between the opened edges, an expanse of skin grew. Whirrs and more clicks narrated the suit falling open enough for Tatum to step out of it. She was barefoot, clad only in black athletic shorts and a matching sports bra. For a moment, Harlowe couldn't breathe at the magnificence of the woman standing in front of her. She was built like a goddess of war, elegantly muscular, radiating confidence and sensuality. Harlowe swallowed hard.

Tatum raised her eyes and met Harlowe's gaze with a sheepish little shrug.

"No zipper in the back," Tatum said. "But now you know how I take it off."

"It's amazing," Harlowe said. She took a step closer to Tatum, drawn irresistibly to her. Her entire body twitched with the urge to close the distance between them. She wanted nothing keeping her from Tatum. Her heart pounded, echoing the throbbing tightness deep between her legs. "You're amazing," Harlowe whispered. The amount of emotion coursing through her choked her voice.

Perhaps in response to Harlowe's state, Tatum's expression grew sultry. Her eyes were dark and her gaze heavy. The warmth radiating from her bare skin made Harlowe shiver with desire.

"Are you cold, Sweet pea?"

"Nope," Harlowe said. She let her attention fall from Tatum's face, drinking in the sensuous line of her throat, the tempting swells of her breasts that rose and fell with her breaths, noting the hard nipples that strained the binding fabric. Tatum's long midriff was rippled with muscle, the band of her shorts emphasized the firm waist and swell of her hips. God, she was so long and gorgeous. Harlowe licked her lips when she thought about what waited for her under that body-hugging spandex. She dragged her gaze back up to meet Tatum's. The knowing smirk on Tatum's face told Harlowe she knew exactly what was going through her head. Harlowe said, "I think I'm overdressed."

"You are?" Tatum studied Harlowe intently for a moment. "In what way?"

"In the way, this isn't a bikini," Harlowe said. She wriggled her hips, wishing Tatum's hands were on them. "How is the water in your hot tub right now? I could go for a nice, relaxing soak."

Tatum ran a hand through her bangs. Her smirk turned into a genuine smile, one that stole Harlowe's breath in its brilliance.

"Towels and robes are in the bathroom. I'll go down first, meet me there in five," Tatum said. Harlowe's chirp of agreement died in her throat as Tatum spun and padded away on bare feet.

"Fuck me she's gorgeous," Harlowe whispered. She allowed herself a moment to savor the memory of the sculpted lines of Tatum's back and gloriously firm ass before she hurried to get changed.

****

The air that greeted Harlowe as she entered the tunnel to the hot tub was heavy and warm. The walls glowed with condensation as if they were alive. The smooth rock under her bare feet was silken, a change from the concrete of the rest of the bunker. Harlowe heard splashing sounds from the main grotto and picked up the pace. She trotted through the archway and stood, transfixed by the idyllic view.

Surrounded by mist and rainbows from the cascading waterfall, Tatum had her arms outstretched on the ledge of the hot tub. She'd pulled her hair back into a knot, but long strands had come loose and trailed down over the inviting lines of her neck and shoulders. She was on the carved bench that ringed the pool, and the hot water came up to just under her breasts. It appeared she was in a two-piece swimsuit, with the top being a sporty tank in a light grey. Harlowe swallowed hard at the sight of the taut buds poking up through the clinging fabric.

At Harlowe's entrance, Tatum pushed herself off from the bench and came gliding through the water toward Harlowe, with a pure, welcoming smile on her face.

"Well, hello there," Tatum said. She crossed her arms over the edge of the pool and perched her chin on them. "I don't use chlorine, so why don't you wash off over there and join me?" With that, Tatum turned her back on Harlowe and parked herself in the far end of the tub, effectively dismissing her.

Pouting at the abrupt dismissal that didn't include even one kiss, Harlowe found a cubby that had a shower stall and some shelves. Like the rest of the grotto, it was carved into the surrounding rock and looked more like a natural formation than something built by machines. She stashed her towel and hung her robe next to Tatum's before she stepped under the spray. In addition to the sandalwood body wash, Harlow found a small bottle of lily of the valley-scented body gel. It was new, just like the robe. The fact it was Harlowe's signature scent meant its appearance was no accident. Just one more facet of Tatum's gentle thoughtfulness. It was a lovely gesture, but Harlowe didn't want to waste any more time. She lathered up a puff and scrubbed herself down.

After she was free of suds, Harlowe turned off the water, patted her face dry, and rubbed her damp hair with her towel. She didn't bother with drying off the rest of her body before she skipped out to the main grotto.

Tatum sat up when Harlowe paused to stand in front of the pool. She gave Harlowe a leisurely once-over that left her skin tingling and a naughty buzz between her thighs. Enjoying the attention, Harlowe twirled, showing off her apple-green bikini, her favorite bathing suit so far. She glowed with the knowledge that Tatum was the first to see her in it. There was a reason Harlowe hadn't ever worn it in public. It was cute but also quite revealing. The bottoms hugged her butt nicely, with golden rings at each hip, holding the sides together while leaving a tantalizing peek of skin. The halter top had a ring between her breasts with a delicate sparkling charm hanging from it. Completing her turn, Harlowe tilted her head and fixed Tatum with a knowing look of her own.

"Like what you see?" she asked.

"Yes, you're so beautiful," Tatum breathed. She drew a hand over her face. "Come on in, Sweet pea. I've been waiting for you."

Harlowe obligingly sat down on the side of the pool and lowered herself into the heated water.

"Oh," Harlowe couldn't stop the exclamation. "This feels so nice."

Tatum drifted over to her and took a seat on the bench a chaste distance from Harlowe. Her face was flushed, probably from the hot water, Harlowe assumed, but she wanted to believe she was responsible for upping Tatum's temperature by at least a few degrees.

"This is one of my favorite places here," Tatum said. She trailed her hands back and forth under the water.

    Angel of Blades

Ripples of light danced over her skin. "The water comes from a mineral-rich spring under here. It's slightly acidic, you can feel how clean it is. Relaxing as well as refreshing, don't you think?"

"Yes, very," Harlowe said. She watched, enthralled as Tatum lifted her cupped hands and water cascade from them. With a happy sigh, Tatum draped both arms over the edge of the pool. Harlowe sprawled out as well, stretching out her legs and enjoying the hot water that cradled her body. The sound of the waterfall filled the air like music. She glanced over at Tatum, who had her head back and eyes closed, looking completely at ease. Harlowe got an evil idea. She smirked to herself and eased off the bench. She crouched so she was submerged up to her chin. Like a stealthy predator, Harlowe slowly circled the pool to come up to Tatum's side. Confident that the splashing from the waterfall covered the small sound of her actions, she brought her hands together, just under the sparkling surface. She cupped her hands and prepared to shoot a waterspout. Giggles threatened to spill from her mouth as she took aim and—

A split second before she squeezed her hands, Tatum leapt up, fully alert and unleased a double-handed tidal wave that crashed down over Harlowe's head. Her ease had been a ruse, and Harlowe paid the price for her attempted ambush.

"Oh you!" Harlowe sputtered. She shook herself off and looked around for Tatum, who had pushed off from the bench and swam in powerful strokes around her. "I'm gonna get you for that."

"I'd like to see you try," Tatum answered with a raise of one brow. She gave Harlowe a lightning-fast smirk before she vanished below the surface.

"Where did you go?" Harlowe spun around, trying to spot Tatum. She crossed her arms and pouted. "You know you're not funn—ee!" Something grabbed her ankle and tugged, yanking her underwater. Harlowe's squeak ended in a burble. Under the surface, she came face-to-face with Tatum, who thumbed her nose at Harlowe. She retaliated by crossing her eyes and making a funny face of her own. Harlowe couldn't hold her giggles in anymore and she surfaced, laughing. A small distance away, Tatum's black head popped up. Reacting quickly, Harlowe flipped over and kicked mightily. She was rewarded by spluttering on the other side of the white wall of water.

"Oh no," Tatum said, raking her long hair back out of her face. When she stood, the water came up to just below her waist, showing the band of her sporty swim-shorts. "I'm not going to let you get away with that."

"Let's see what you've got then," Harlowe replied. "Nyaaaa!" She stuck her thumbs in her ears and flopped her fingers up and down, which turned into a frantic front-crawl as Tatum came after her, cutting through the water like a cruiser. Giggling wildly, Harlowe changed tactics and dove toward the waterfall. Tatum was faster. She leapt out of the pool and launched herself into the air, heading Harlowe off. She dove low and caught Harlowe around the waist. Harlowe once more found herself underwater. Tatum let her go and she surfaced in a shower of droplets that sparkled in the golden light from above.

"Dammit, you cheated," Harlowe said. Her breath came hard from her burst of laughter. Tatum was chuckling as well. The mood was buoyant and Harlowe reflected how good it was to hear Tatum laugh. Their laughter slowly faded, leaving a charged silence. Tatum stood in front of her, separated only by a breath. They weren't touching each other, but Harlowe felt the weight of Tatum's gaze on her bare skin, which she was showing quite a lot of. Being that close to Tatum was electric. Harlowe shivered.

Their eyes locked. All the feelings of arousal rushed back with the heated look in Tatum's eyes. Harlowe unconsciously bit her lower lip. Her body thrummed with the need to be touched. The cheerful mood vanished, swallowed by something more urgent and raw.

Without speaking, Tatum closed the distance between them. She cupped Harlowe's jaw, tenderly moving her hand to hold the back of her head. Her eyes darkened, her breaths got deep and rough. Harlowe's heart jumped. Her body ached for Tatum. Her inner muscles trembled. She let her eyes drift into slits as she gave into the very gentle pressure of Tatum's hands and stepped forward. Harlowe let her lips ghost over Tatum's, feeling the heat of her breath, savoring the sweet tension of that moment. She hungered for Tatum's kiss, but lingering on the edge was addicting. Harlowe kept her lips just barely on Tatum's as she closed the distance between them, allowing her body to press against Tatum's long, hard length. The water cradled Harlowe's back, while her front was sealed to Tatum's bare skin.

A tiny groan escaped Tatum's throat.

"Dammit, Harlowe," she whispered in a heated voice. "I want you so fucking much."

The longing in Tatum's voice pushed Harlowe over the edge. She tilted her head and caught Tatum's mouth with hers. The kiss stole her breath and reason. Harlowe didn't need to be teased before she opened her mouth to Tatum. They were both wet as the kiss got messy, deep, and frantic. Harlowe loved the way Tatum's lips worked on hers, sucking gently, then claiming her with a deep thrust. Harlowe moaned. Tatum had to know how much she was turned on. Her nipples were tight, harder than they'd ever been. She ran her hands up and down Tatum's broad, bare back, from the waistband of her shorts over the rippling fabric of the swim top, to hold onto her muscular shoulders.

Harlowe's breathing came faster. Her body thrummed with pleasure and tension. She didn't want to stop. She wanted to give all of herself to Tatum.

Tatum pulled away. For a moment, their labored breathing filled the air. Tatum's hands rested on Harlowe's hips. Her eyes bored into Harlowe's as if trying to read her mind.

"Sweet Harlowe, my precious girl," Tatum breathed. "Stay with me tonight."

That had been the plan from the start, but the way she said it made the meaning clear. This wasn't going to be like the other times. Harlowe swallowed hard. She felt like her entire soul was sparkling with energy.

"Yes," Harlowe answered.

Tatum's lips quirked up into a grin. She said, "Come upstairs with me."

Harlowe nodded.

****

In the elevator, Harlowe leaned back against the wall and threw her head back, welcoming Tatum's hungry kisses on her neck. Every point where her lips touched ignited a thrill of electric pleasure. Harlowe never knew how sensitive she was there. She wanted more, much more. Taking Tatum's hand from where it rested on the waist of her hastily thrown-on robe, Harlowe drew it to rest on her belly. Where Tatum's hand lay, her skin burned. Harlowe couldn't stop the moan of anticipation.

Against her neck, Tatum's lips curved into a smile. She very carefully nipped Harlowe's earlobe and murmured, "Is this okay?"

"Uh huh," Harlowe replied.

The doors opened and Tatum backed out, taking Harlowe gently by the hands. Harlowe's entire world was in Tatum's eyes. She didn't look anywhere else until they were in the bedroom. Then, she glanced down at the big, inviting bed. Her heart pounded. Tatum took her by the chin and very gently drew Harlowe up to look at her.

"Stop me anytime," Tatum said seriously. "I mean it. If you feel pressured, or just need a break, I need to know. I want tonight to be a wonderful experience for you."

"Okay, so I say something like 'pineapple' to let you know?"

"If that's what works for you."

"Pineapple it is then," Harlowe said. She playfully bit her lip and glanced up at Tatum. "But tonight's not only about me, I hope you get a little something out of it too."

"Absolutely," Tatum said with a quirk to her lips. She dropped her robe and started to pull off her swim top. "How about I go first?"

"Oh wow," Harlowe said. She licked her suddenly dry lips. "Please," she said.

In one smooth motion, Tatum pulled off her top and kicked off her shorts. She stood still before Harlowe, not bothering to hide anything, and tacitly allowing Harlowe to take her time drinking in the view. Harlowe swallowed hard. Tatum was more beautiful than anyone Harlowe had ever seen. She already knew the beauty of her muscled arms and taut belly, from the first time she knew Tatum's softness. Her breasts were full and firm, her nipples were thicker and darker than Harlowe's, the areolas pebbled. Her lean body blossomed to graceful hips. A line of dark hair led from Tatum's navel to the bushy patch between her legs that didn't quite hide the full, pouty outer lips, with just the hint of slick inner petals nestled within. Harlowe found that incredibly sexy, how unashamed Tatum was of her body, just as it was. Harlowe hadn't expected to be as turned on only by looking, but she was on fire. Her thighs clenched as a wave of heat rolled through her.

Harlowe trembled with the sudden rush of arousal, coupled with the incredible feeling of how much trust Tatum put in her. Tatum raised a knowing brow and slowly sat down on the bed. She spread her legs and gently drew Harlowe to stand between them.

"Like what you see?" she asked in a husky drawl.

"God, yes," Harlowe said. She shrugged her robe down, wanting nothing between herself and Tatum. It pooled on the floor at her feet. Harlowe reached behind herself, searching for the clasp of her bikini top. Tatum's hand on her elbow stopped her.

"May I?" she asked.

Harlowe nodded eagerly. She loved the thought of Tatum undressing her. In order to reach the clasp, Tatum leaned forward slightly. Her breath was hot on Harlowe's skin.

"Beautiful," Tatum breathed. The halter top fell from her fingers to join the robe on the floor.

Harlowe's squeak of surprise turned into a moan as Tatum's hands found her breasts and cupped them. They fit perfectly into each palm, as if Harlowe was born to be Tatum's.

"Is this all right?" Tatum asked.

"Yes, but just, do something," Harlowe pressed herself against the fingers that were being too soft for her liking. "Touch me, please Tae."

Tatum did more than just touch her. She bent her head and kissed the edge of one puckered aureole before she greedily drew Harlowe's nipple into her mouth.

"Yes, oh God," Harlowe cried out. The feeling was at once so new, but at the same time, so right. She felt safe in Tatum's embrace. Harlowe wrapped her arms around Tatum's shoulders, wanting more, wishing to be devoured entirely by that talented mouth. Her hips moved instinctively, driven by the primal rhythm of Tatum's tongue on her. Tatum's hands dropped to her waist and drew Harlowe to her.

When Tatum pulled back, Harlowe gave an impatient huff, but Tatum's mouth crashing into hers took that away in an instant. Harlowe welcomed Tatum's tongue, chasing it with her own. Soft breasts and hard nipples met. Harlowe arched her back, letting her sensitive buds play over Tatum's. The feeling was beyond anything she ever knew. When Tatum's panting breath topped off with a moan, Harlowe glowed. She wanted to make Tatum feel as good as she did.

Tatum's hands drifted from her waist to her hips, slowly roving over her backside, following the line of her bikini bottoms, teasing her with the light touches. It wasn't enough. Harlowe canted her hips in a blatant invitation. Tatum's low chuckle told Harlowe she knew exactly what she was doing. Tatum leaned back. Her fingers hooked onto the rings at Harlowe's hips.

"Now or later or no?" Tatum asked. Her voice was low and husky.

"Now," Harlowe practically sang. Her entire body hungered for Tatum. Any shyness she might have had burned away by the flame of desire. Harlowe's only thought was how much she wanted Tatum. Once she was free of the garment, Harlowe's knees went weak with the look that crossed Tatum's noble features. Of course there was naked desire, but also something so intimate and affectionate Harlowe's chest got tight with emotion.

"Come here," Tatum said.

Harlowe bent her knees and straddled Tatum's lap. The move opened her. Harlowe was incredibly aware of how exposed she was, her slick sex pressed so close to Tatum's. Her own thatch was slightly deeper gold than her hair, the curls were already soaked from her juices. Her pulse thundered in her ears and resonated to her core. She was perilously close to losing control. The deep shiver of pre-orgasm flickered into life, her clit begged for attention. Harlowe couldn't wait any longer.

"Tae," she said in a whimper. "I'm really close. I need more, I need you so bad."

Tatum took Harlowe in a strong, tender embrace before, in a move quick as lightning, rolled them over so she was on top of Harlowe. "Are you okay with this?" she asked.

The move left Harlowe right where she wanted to be, spread wide under Tatum. For the first time, she felt Tatum directly against her. She fit perfectly. Harlowe felt every inch of her, soft and hot and hard with desire. Harlowe bit her lip to hold in the moan and nodded.

Tatum ran a hand down Harlowe's body, down over her hip to gently press Harlowe's knee higher, spreading her more. Tatum's voice was like heated caramel in Harlowe's ears. "How do you want me to make you come?" Tatum lowered her head and dropped a line of kisses over Harlowe's collarbone, hovering over the fullness of her breasts. Her voice thrummed through Harlowe's body as she said, "Tell me what you want."

Harlowe swallowed her gasp of raw need that Tatum's words set off. She said, "Stay on me like this, just like this." Harlowe didn't want to admit how many times she'd played the scenario over in her mind. While she entertained thoughts of a variety of acts, one always pushed its way back into her dreams. She knew exactly what she wanted Tatum to do. Reality was even better than fantasy, Harlowe soon found out. Tatum dropped one last tender kiss to her breast and raised her head.

"Your wish is my command," Tatum purred.

Her expression was intense. Harlowe felt the tension in her long body, saw the corded muscles of her shoulders ripple as Tatum levered herself up on her elbows. She bore down on Harlowe with a pump of her hips. Their connection was instant. The insistent kiss of slick lips to hers was the most intimate thing she'd ever felt. Harlowe's head went back into the pillow and she couldn't help the moans that came with every deft thrust. Tatum's hard clit raced over her in a steady pulse, sliding up and down her spread length, hitting the very spot that needed it the most at the apex.

Harlowe clutched at Tatum's shoulders, her own rhythmic cries in counterpoint to Tatum's heavy breathing, Tatum's grunt as she picked up the pace. Harlowe felt her climax coming, sparking through her, bringing her higher and higher before the inevitable plunge. Her chest heaved, her thighs clamped down around Tatum's body, begging for harder, faster.

"Let me hear you," Tatum growled in her ear. "Are you ready to come for me?"

"Fuck, yes," Harlowe gasped out. "Oh, God, *yes!*"

Her hips shuddered as the orgasm hit. Harlowe hung onto Tatum as wave after wave ripped through her from her spread-open sex, through her belly and finally sizzling like living embers through her limbs. Harlowe cried out, wantonly releasing her pleasure. Above her, Tatum thrust hard, her breaths were ragged and rough. Harlowe pulled Tatum to her, pressing their bodies firmly together. Tatum's hips started to jerk. She was close. Harlowe couldn't help the renewed burst of arousal. She was desperate for another orgasm, one shared with Tatum.

"Yes, Tae, yes," Harlowe gasped out. "Gonna come, oh fuck, Tae I'm coming—"

Once more, Harlowe lost herself. She felt the deep tremor of Tatum's own release on her and was fiercely, proudly glad. Slower, like ocean waves, Tatum rocked against her, chasing Harlowe's pleasure, wringing every last drop out. Finally, Harlowe collapsed in a sweaty, satisfied sprawl. Tatum immediately gathered her up and held her. She scattered kisses into her hair. Slowly, Harlowe's breathing got back to normal. She snuggled into the embrace, loving the feeling of Tatum's strength around her. Harlowe had never been that content. She now knew why it was called afterglow. She felt incandescent.

"Was that okay?" Tatum asked. Now, out of the throes of passion, the powerful dominance was gone. She looked softer and introspective. Harlowe marveled at the complex, intriguing person Tatum was. The very same person who gave her the most mind-blowing orgasm of her life, hopefully the first of many.

"Very veeeeery okay," Harlowe said. She trailed a finger down over Tatum's arm, idly tracing the gear tattoo. "I thought you could tell."

A low chuckle rumbled through Harlowe from Tatum's chest to hers. "I had an inkling," she said.

Harlowe basked in the intimate embrace for a moment longer. She closed her eyes and wished she could always be like that, held safe and tight in Tatum's strong arms. She wished the road ahead of them would be a simple and long one, but it felt like they were edging around a cliff where one misstep would send them tumbling to the depths.

A soft kiss to her temple brought Harlowe back to the present. She looked up into Tatum's face and stretched with a long, luxurious movement. She loved being naked with Tatum. Hopefully, they would have many more opportunities in the future.

"Hungry, Sweet pea?"

"Starving," Harlowe said, suddenly ravenous. She giggled and poked Tatum on the shoulder. "Maybe I used up a few calories."

"I did too." Tatum sat up. Looking back over her shoulder, she said, "I'll lend you something to wear. You can save the stuff you've brought for tonight."

"You mean you're not going to keep me bare?" Harlowe idly trailed one hand over her breast, teasing her nipple hard again, remembering the feeling of Tatum's lips on her. She shimmied her hips, a thick heat gathered between her thighs.

"Tempting," Tatum said. Her eyes darkened and her breath hitched. With a shake of her head, Tatum abruptly stood and grabbed a handful of clothing from her dresser. "But I wouldn't want you to get cold. What do you say, peanut butter sandwiches sound good?"

"My favorite," Harlowe said. She gave up on being a

naked pleasure slave for the time being and got into the cotton drawstring pants and sweatshirt.

Chapter Twelve

Humming to herself, Harlowe finished preening in the mirror and picked up her cashmere stole. She could barely contain her excitement about the Strawberry Social that night. The tunes she put on to psyche herself up filled the room. Harlowe took one last look in the mirror. She had to admit, she cleaned up well. Her short hair was sleek and elegant, held back from her face with a delicate wire band studded with crystals. Instead of being clear, the crystals were a light gold, to complement the topaz of her dress. They sparkled in the lamplight. Harlowe's dress was gleaming satin, cut in a retro style reminiscent of the golden age of cinema. The top was sculpted and clung to her curves, and the full skirt came to just below her knees.

When she bought it two years previously, she couldn't bring herself to wear it. Not because it wasn't flattering or didn't fit, but because she'd looked like a kid playing dress-up. Now, though, Harlowe looked at herself in awe. She carried the weight of experience on her shoulders like a mantle. She knew pain, heartbreak, and pride. Most of all, she knew love. Not even a week had passed, but Harlow felt the person she'd been before that night was a million years away. Harlowe sighed in happiness as she remembered that night. After the dinner of peanut butter sandwiches, they'd stayed up late with snacks, snuggling and talking about silly things. Tatum even finagled a floating screen in the bedroom so they could watch *Supergirl* in bed. Harlowe had never felt so comfortable, or so cherished. She'd finally gone back to her cottage the next afternoon, leaving Tatum checking the entrance every five minutes for a mysterious delivery she wouldn't explain.

Wrapped in her stole, with her beaded cocktail purse slung over one shoulder, Harlowe was ready to go. She originally wanted to wear strappy heels, but the several centimetres of snow on the ground outside told her that boots were a better choice. She zipped herself into the new calf-length fawn boots, that by the grace of the online shopping gods, arrived just in time for the dance, and ventured out into the chill evening. On the way to her car, she texted Tatum to let her know she was on her way. Harlowe filled the screen with hearts and kissy stamps, giggling to herself.

The drive was short enough that the air puffing from the vents still hadn't warmed up by the time she arrived. The community centre was located across the street from the church, both were flanked by thickets of pine trees. Their boughs were heavy with snow.

Already the parking lot behind the community centre was teeming with pickups and SUVs. Harlowe parked and got out of the car. Her breath steamed into the air and the packed snow squeaked under her feet. The community center blazed with light over the silent lot and the surrounding forest. Streamers and banners hung over the windows, and the raucous twang of a local country band filtered into the cold, still evening.

Harlowe turned from the brightly lit building and peered into the darkness, searching for a human figure. Her heart thumped in anticipation. Even after her eyes adjusted, she still didn't see any signs of life. She wondered if Tatum had decided not to show up. Her heart ached with disappointment, but Harlowe wouldn't blame her for that. Going to the supermarket had been a trial for her, suddenly being thrust into a noisy, crowded social event would be much worse. Harlowe wondered uneasily if suggesting they go to the social was a mistake.

In fact, if Tatum did decide to stay home, there was only one thing for Harlowe to do and that was go back up the hill and stay home with her. Maybe she could get Tatum to take another dip in the hot tub with her, this time with no bathing suits. The thought warmed Harlowe's cheeks and sparked happy giggles in her throat. She checked her phone for messages and found none. Sighing, she tucked her phone back into her purse and slipped it under her stole.

"Turn around, beautiful."

The soft, low voice caused Harlowe to whirl. She

froze, mouth open at the vision of class that stood before her. Tatum was in a tailored suit that fit her perfectly. It was a timeless three-piece, grey trousers and vest paired with a charcoal jacket. An amber silk necktie that exactly matched Harlowe's dress nestled into the starched collar of the white shirt. She had her hands in her pockets and looked unbelievably handsome. Her hair was pulled back into a sleek ponytail, but a swoop of bangs fell across one eye, giving her a rakish, dashing air.

Speechless, Harlowe clapped a hand to her mouth. She pressed the other to her chest, to try and still her racing heart. Tatum crossed the small distance that separated them and held out a hand.

"I apologize for keeping my lady waiting," she said with a gentlemanly bow.

"No way," Harlowe said. Her mind was blank. She blinked and said, "I just got here."

Tatum held out a hand and Harlowe placed hers in it. Those fingers she knew so well and hoped to know even better, enfolded hers in a gentle grip. Tatum lowered her head and raised Harlowe's hand to her lips, pressing a kiss to her knuckles. Harlowe's face flooded with heat. God, Tatum made that whole charming routine absolutely fucking hot. Making no effort to hide the admiration in her eyes, Tatum looked her up and down.

"Harlowe, you're stunning," she said. "That dress was made for you."

"This old thing? I just had it lying around," Harlowe said and pulled a "Who, *moi*?" pose. She tilted her head and fixed Tatum with an appreciative look of her own. "And I could say the same for you. How on earth did you get something so *damn* perfect so fast?"

Tatum shrugged. A grin tugged at one side of her mouth. "I just happened to find a tailor who takes orders online and has a lot in stock. I guess it meets with your approval then?"

"Oh, yes," Harlowe said.

Even though they were surrounded by snowdrifts and the wind whirled her skirt around her legs, Harlowe didn't feel the cold one bit. She was flushed and warm, her heart beat fast in her chest. A sudden, loud cheer from the hall rolled over the moonlit parking lot. Tatum flinched and drew back into the shadows. As if drawn by an invisible thread, Harlowe took a step after her.

"Could we just..." Tatum stopped speaking and looked around. She lowered her head, a change came over her. The suave air was gone. Now, she was a predator, sensing her prey nearby.

"Are you okay?" Harlowe asked. A cold chill crawled down her arms.

"Did you hear...never mind," Tatum said. She shook her head and fixed Harlowe with a soft expression. The warm, loved feeling flooded back. Harlowe couldn't help but return the smile. The tinny announcement from the dance faded as a slow, romantic ballad filtered out to them. Harlowe held out a hand.

"Dance with me?" she asked.

Tatum swept into a courtly bow and gently took Harlowe's hand. Their bodies came together softly and tenderly. Harlowe bit her lip and looked up into Tatum's face. She wished she had the courage to say the words, to tell Tatum exactly how she felt and how deeply she'd come to care for the reclusive genius who held her like a precious jewel.

In time to the music, surrounded by snow-laden trees, they twirled. It was as if they were the only people in the world. Nothing existed outside of themselves. Harlowe never felt so safe. She slipped her hand from Tatum's and stole up her body, to lightly join her fingers behind Tatum's neck. The move was met by Tatum gently encircling her waist with her arms and pulling them together. Harlowe rested her head on Tatum's shoulder and closed her eyes. She couldn't stop the words. They had to come out.

Harlowe took a deep breath. "Tatum, I—"

Three sharp bangs ripped through the air. Harlowe gasped and whirled in Tatum's arms just in time to see a blinding spray of sparks erupt from the community centre.

"What the—" Harlowe breathed.

"Get behind me," Tatum barked in a voice that commanded instant compliance. Harlowe peered over

Tatum's shoulder and stifled a scream. The second floor of the center was ablaze, with flames licking up to the roof. An alarm wailed. People streamed from the community centre. They gathered in clumps, black drifts outlined in red from the blaze. Shouts and screams echoed over the snowy landscape. Harlowe's gut clenched. Shadows appeared at the windows. People were still trapped inside.

"Stay here," Tatum said. Harlowe didn't get a chance to say anything more before Tatum was sprinting across the packed snow of the parking lot. She was halfway to the centre when another blast rang out. That time it came from behind Harlowe. It was so loud she bent double with her hands clapped to her ringing ears.

In front of her, Tatum fell limply to the ground and didn't move.

"No, Tatum!" Harlowe cried out. She jumped up to run over to Tatum but a thick arm wrapping around her throat from behind stopped her. Harlowe let out a fierce snarl and struggled, kicking out blindly at her attacker. A burnt, chemical stench filled her nose and made her cough.

"Simmer down before I shoot you, too."

Harlowe was released with a hard shove that sent her sprawling on her hands and knees. She looked up in horror. Shelby stood over her with a double-barreled shotgun in her hand. Smoke steamed from the muzzle.

Anguish wailed through her.

"You shot her," Harlowe choked out. "You shot her from behind like a coward." Tears dripped down her cheeks. Harlowe clenched her hands into fists. Her vision filled with red as the urge to kill rose within her. She didn't care if it wrecked her, her soul was already gone. Tatum was injured, unconscious or worse.

Shelby shrugged. "Around these parts we call that takin' care of vermin."

"Tatum Edwyn is not vermin," Harlowe said. Her voice dropped into a low, savage timbre she'd never heard before. "You are."

"You sure are pretty enough until you open your mouth," Shelby said. She casually held the gun in one hand, the muzzle pointed at the ground. Harlowe's eyes tracked the barrel of the gun as it swung lazily back and forth in front of herself. "I got a couple ways to keep it shut. Come home with me tonight and I won't finish that freak over there."

Harlowe twisted to look over to where Tatum lay. Elation filled her heart like an explosion of rainbows when she saw Tatum slowly rise from the ground. She was alive! Tatum struggled to her feet. Two steps and she fell to her knees once more. The sight hurt Harlowe more than any physical blow. A hot, wide hand came down on her shoulder.

"You got one minute to decide, startin' now." Shelby's mouth was uncomfortably close to her ear. Harlowe's entire body itched from the closeness. She felt helpless and terrified.

Tatum staggered upright once more. Her head came up. Even separated by several meters, the rage in her eyes was impossible to miss. She clenched both hands and two sets of glowing blades split the sleeves of the dapper jacket. Never breaking her stare, she started walking across the snowy lot. With each step, she sheared off more of her clothing, slashing at the white shirt and tailored trousers until they hung in ribbons over her black battle-suit. At last, they fell away from her powerful body, leaving a trail of shredded garments in her wake. Her hair came loose, falling over her shoulders and down her back. All at once the Tatum Harlowe loved was gone. Instead, was the machine of destruction from the first instant they'd met.

Harlowe swallowed the gasp of dismay. Tatum may have been up and moving, but something was very wrong. Each step was slow and dragged as if she was fighting against an incredible force. Tatum's face was frozen into a rictus of pain and anger. Her chest heaved with labored breaths. The blue glow of her suit flickered and guttered.

"Got a feisty one," Shelby said. She let loose with a guffaw. The hand that had been resting on Harlowe's shoulder rubbed clumsily over her cheek. Harlowe shook her off and wiped at her face with the hem of her stole.

Without another glance at Harlowe, Shelby shouted across the snowy parking lot, "Stop right there, freak-o. I'm not afraid to give you another helpin' of buckshot before I help myself to this bit of cheesecake here." Shelby laughed. Her meaty hand grabbed Harlowe's arm and squeezed.

"Do what you want to me, but leave Harlowe out of this," Tatum said. She stopped in her tracks, close enough for Harlowe to see the sweat tracking down her face. She reached out one hand in appeal as she went down heavily on one knee. "Your business is with me. Not her."

"Oh I got business with her all right. After all, it's gonna be me and not you who takes this little fuck toy home tonight." The hand vanished from Harlowe's arm. Shelby raised the shotgun to her shoulder once more. She closed one eye and aimed with the ease of a seasoned hunter. Her finger twitched on the trigger.

Harlowe couldn't stay still any more. She glared up at Shelby.

"God, what a pathetic chicken-shit," Harlowe scoffed. She fluffed out her skirt with a preoccupied air she didn't feel in the least.

"What did you say?" Shelby took her attention from the prey in her sights to Harlowe.

"I said you're chicken. Chi-ken," she drew the word out slowly. "Hiding behind your gun, attacking an unarmed person from behind? Oh yeah, that's really attractive. Tatum is prepared to fight for me, and all you do is wave that thing around. Where *I'm* from, we call that being a chicken." Harlowe sarcastically made air quotes with her fingers.

"Don't call me chicken," Shelby yelled.

"I call it like I see it." Harlowe inspected her nails as she spoke. "Figures a chicken like you can't even fight."

"Look, I can fight," Shelby snapped. Her nostrils billowed.

"Prove it," Harlowe crossed her arms over her chest. A siren split the air. Flashing lights played off the snowy landscape as two fire trucks stopped in front of the burning centre. Yellow-suited firefighters streamed from the trucks. Harlowe shouted to be heard over the wail, "Put the gun down and take responsibility for what you did."

"Nope, 'cause I didn't do nothing wrong," Shelby said. Her cheeks squeezed up with an ugly grin. "This is my town and I get to say who stays and who goes. They'll thank me for taking that freak out. And that eyesore community centre over there too."

"You didn't," Harlowe breathed. Her heart felt like it plummeted down to her feet. "You started that fire?"

"Sure did," Shelby said. "I couldn't'a picked a better night to do it too with all those losers and their stupid social. Now move or you're gonna be sorry. I got some ass-kicking to do. As a special favor to you, I'll do it without my gun."

Shelby spun and the butt of the gun whacked into Harlowe's shoulder and sent her sprawling into the snow. Harlowe clutched at her shoulder in helpless fury and panic as Shelby threw down her weapon and beckoned Tatum. Shelby's crude insults whipped by on the wind, overlayed by the shouted orders from the firefighters. Tatum didn't respond. Shelby went up to where Tatum stood and spread her arms wide.

"Come on, I'll give you one shot," she taunted. "We'll see who's chicken."

Tatum didn't move. Her eyes glowed with burning rage, but her arms remained at her sides. Shelby got in her face, shouting and taunting louder. Tatum still didn't move. Shelby's face suffused with anger and she raised her fists.

"No, Shelby don't," Harlowe screamed as Shelby released a punch to Tatum's gut. Her voice was drowned under another incoming siren. A red Land Rover with the fire department logo on the door pulled into the lot. It bypassed the crowd and zeroed in on the three of them, throwing the scene into harsh brightness with its headlights. Fear kicked her hard. The scene did not look good with Shelby down, knocked out cold at Tatum's feet. Tatum was doubled over and looked absolutely murderous. In the distance, the fire was still blazing. Torrents of water flowed from the building over the grounds.

Right behind the Land Rover came several black and

white cars. They pulled into the parking lot and formed an arc. Harlowe raised a hand to block the blinding light. Her thoughts spun.

"Drop your weapons and put your hands up," a tinny, amplified male voice boomed out at them. Tatum straightened up and stood with her arms limp at her sides. The clear blades picked up the flashing lights and sparkled with unearthly beauty. "I repeat, drop your weapons or we shoot."

Harlowe scrambled to her feet and threw herself in front of Tatum.

"No! You don't understand."

"Step away from the suspect," came the voice.

Harlowe shook her head. "This isn't her fault." She looked desperately to Tatum. There was no response. Tatum's head was down. Her shoulders drooped.

"Tatum, look at me," she begged. Tatum didn't move. Harlowe tried again. "Don't give up. Stand with me. Fight with me."

At last, Tatum raised her head. Through trailing bangs, her gaze met Harlowe's. Once filled with love, now, Tatum's eyes held darkness. No anger. No recognition. Only endless, hopeless sorrow.

"I can't."

The words vanished into the night.

The Land Rover chirped its siren and eased forward. Harlowe looked frantically from the car to Tatum. The flashing lights illuminated Chrissy, the fire chief, at the wheel. Her face looked carved in granite as she slowly inched the car forward.

The siren chirped again, and Tatum took a step. Away from Harlowe. Towards the road. The instant Tatum took that step, a uniformed officer grabbed Harlowe and pulled her away.

"Let go of me," Harlowe cried out. "I have to go to her. I won't leave her."

"Please calm down, miss," the officer said.

"No," Harlowe whispered. She couldn't take her eyes from the scene unfolding in front of her like a nightmare.

The Land Rover edged forward as Tatum started walking. The car followed her, lights flashing but silent.

Harlowe collapsed, unable to hold herself up. She couldn't speak. Tears ran down her cheeks and fell unheeded. The only thing she could see was the black figure being herded up the hill, back to the bunker. Despair crashed down over her. She had lost Tatum. In the background, she was vaguely aware of one of the fire trucks pulling away. A sooty smell choked the air. The charred remains of the community centre reminded Harlowe of her own heart, gutted and destroyed. If the fire was still blazing, she would throw herself into it. The pain was more than she could bear. Every moment was pure agony. Tatum left her. Again.

"Do you require medical assistance?" the officer asked.

Harlowe couldn't speak. She shook her head.

Jim came rushing over, face red and puffing. "It's okay," he said. He put both hands on his knees and leaned over, catching his breath. He took off his ball cap and wiped a hand across his forehead. "Whew, sorry, a bit busy tonight." Jim looked at the officer. "Could you give me a minute with Miss Tremaine, please?"

The officer didn't look pleased, but he moved back.

"Your friend is going to be okay," Jim said. "Chrissy's not gonna hurt her or anything. We just need folks to cool off and stay put while we work out what went down here."

"She's hurt," Harlowe said. "Shelby shot her in the back. I know she won't go to a hospital."

"Shelby did what?" Jim's eyes bulged. He dropped his face into his hands. "Okay, I'm gonna ask you to talk with one of the officers if that's all right. Just give a statement and you're free to go. Deal?"

"Do I need a lawyer?"

"That's up to you," Jim said. "'Pends on how long you want to spend here."

"I just want this over with," Harlowe said. Tears blurred her vision. "Tell me who I should talk to."

"Got it." Jim waved his arm and a female RCMP officer jogged over.

"What can I do ya for?" she asked in a broad upper-Canadian accent.

"This young lady would like to give her side of the story," Jim said. He addressed Harlowe. "This here's Officer Rhonda Wheat. She'll take care of you."

Silently, Harlowe nodded. The smoke and flashing lights were overwhelming. Almost as much as the aching blackness of her empty soul. Harlowe sniffled. She hated how weak she felt. She was trapped in the moment when Tatum turned her back and walked away from her. What did that mean? Was that the final goodbye?

Harlowe allowed herself to be led over to sit on the open tailgate of a rescue truck. A blanket was draped over her shoulders and a bottle of water pressed into her hands. While Harlowe wanted to run away as fast as she could, she made herself sit. She took a deep breath and she talked. Officer Wheat listened and took copious notes. Harlowe forced herself to remain calm, to speak with as little emotion as possible. If she let the dam holding her feelings in check crack even the slightest, she'd explode.

Just as she finished, a kerfuffle broke out across the crowded parking lot. Harlowe saw Shelby being escorted into one of the RCMP cruisers.

"You should be thanking me!" she shouted in a spittle-flecked haze. "I'm the one who got rid of that dangerous freak! You should name a holiday after me!"

Harlowe flinched.

Officer Wheat moved, neatly blocking Shelby from view. She stowed her notebook. "I appreciate your bravery and honesty. Don't worry about your friend, okay? Ms. Stevens made a full confession to all of it. Arson, assault, lying in wait. Hate speech too." She grimaced. "Piece of work, that one."

"Do you need a statement from Tatum as well?"

"It would help," Wheat said. "But I know shi-uh, stuff works differently out here. We've got the confession, plus your story. A bunch of people who were in the community centre and Jeb Gallant in the parking lot also saw what went down and we've got some security footage that looks promising. We can make do with what we got if necessary." She shrugged.

"So, can I go now?"

"Yeah," Wheat said. "Just don't leave town, okay?"

The officer turned and loped off. Harlowe didn't even wait to see where she'd gone. She leapt up and raced over to where her stole lay half-buried in a snowbank. She shook the snow off and whirled it around herself like a shield. Harlowe gritted her teeth. She wasn't going to give up.

"It's not fucking over yet," Harlowe announced to the world.

She used her small stature to her advantage as she ducked and threaded through the crowd to her car. Harlowe's destination, the bunker on top of the hill.

****

The road to the bunker had a line of vehicles parked with their lights flashing. One of the fire trucks had joined the fire chief's Land Rover, plus a black-and-white police cruiser that blocked the road to the underground entrance. Harlowe ditched her car and jumped out, ready to make a dash for the bunker.

"Hey, stop right there," Chrissy's voice cut into Harlowe's fugue.

She whirled. "What? I have to go in there. Tatum needs me."

"I know she does," Chrissy said. "Look, we aren't leaving here until we know you both are okay. If your friend is hurt, we need to get emergency services involved."

"Let me through," Harlowe said. Her vision blurred with tears. "Please."

Chrissy stepped back. "We're here to help you, okay?"

"I know," Harlowe said. She looked desperately at the ring of law enforcement vehicles. The jarring flashing lights pulsed in her brain. "Tatum's not like other people. You know that."

"Yeah," Chrissie said. She waved her arm. "Just let us know, okay?"

Harlowe barely got out a croaked affirmative before she shoved her way through the gate and into the unlocked front door, just as she had done that first day what seemed like years ago.

Where would she be? Harlowe pounded through the now-familiar space and jumped in the elevator. There was only one place Tatum would go in that state. The only place she felt safe. Harlowe jammed her thumb onto the B3 button and the doors glided closed behind her. She didn't know what she would find, or what state Tatum would be in. Harlowe only knew she was incomplete without Tatum.

When the doors slid open, Harlowe stepped into the silent and dimly-lit workshop. Her heart plummeted. Had she misjudged? Or worse, was she too late? With her fists clenched at her side, she moved past shelves and covered masses.

Then she heard it. A mechanical clicking, slow and unsteady. Harlowe hastened her steps. Tatum was huddled in a corner, much the way she'd been that first night. This time, the blades glow faded and guttered. Tatum's face was a sickly pallor, her eyes unfocused. Her breathing was uneven, shallow with too much pause.

"I'm here," Harlowe said.

At first, Tatum didn't appear to hear, then she looked up with a sharp, almost fearful expression.

"Get out." The words were faint.

"I can't do that. You need my help." Harlowe swallowed the tears. "And I need you. Please, Tae."

Tatum lurched to her feet, staggering forward a step. Her blades clacked. She lowered her chin and looked up through her bangs.

"I don't want to hurt you," Tatum said.

"You won't."

"I don't have a choice." Tatum went down on one knee, blades clumsily flailing through the air. She jerked back, one cheek sported a thin crimson line that spilled over her skin. She drew in a labored breath and growled, "The AI is taking over. I can't fight it anymore. Leave here and never look back."

"I can't do that." Harlowe didn't stop the tears that filled her eyes. "You are my heart. The other half of my soul. I love you."

"You do?" Tears streaked her face now.

"Yes," Harlowe answered. She reached out and smoothed away a newly-shed tear. "I love you more than I can say. I want to be with you. I can't lose you. I want to make a future with you. That is, if you want a future with me."

"Nobody has ever said that to me." The desolate look on Tatum's face broke Harlowe's heart. "Nobody has ever loved me."

"I do. I'll tell you every day if you let me." Harlowe threw herself down, as close to Tatum as she dared. "Will you let me?"

A long pause. Tatum's head drooped. She fell back in a clatter. Harlowe cried out and lunged. She didn't care about the blades anymore. She had to get that suit off before it deactivated and took Tatum with it. She reached out to grab the hidden yellow buttons. Harlowe jerked back as a blade swiped dangerously close to her face. A severed lock of blonde hair fell to the floor.

"Focus, girl." Harlowe coached herself. To Tatum she snapped, "Show me your wrists, dammit."

The tone worked and Tatum shifted, now fully on her back, arms spread. The movement exposed the control panel Harlowe wanted. In a flash, she grabbed and pressed. And waited. Nothing. Hissing a curse through her teeth, Harlowe tried again. And again.

"No fucking way I'm letting this pile of circuits win, come *on*."

Was it her imagination? Something gave. A hissing sound brought a triumphant shout to Harlowe's throat. The invisible seams parted and spread, showing pale, mottled flash underneath. Tatum stirred weakly, and the suit parted more. Strong hands took over from Harlowe and Tatum ripped the malfunctioning suit from her body and rolled free. The blue light flickered once, then went dark.

"Tae?" Harlowe asked, half in disbelief.

One silver-blue eye opened. Tatum reached out a hand. With tears rolling down her face, Harlowe twined her fingers with Tatum's.

"Thank you," Tatum breathed. "And yes."

"Yes what?" Harlowe hiccupped.

"Yes I will let you."

Harlowe collapsed into Tatum's embrace. Strong arms curled around her.

Nobody was going to die that day. Now all they had to do was figure out how to live.

Harlowe didn't care about the tears that ran down her face as she grabbed her phone and texted Chrissy.

It's over. Everything is going to be okay. You can go now. She'll come to the station tomorrow to give her statement

Chapter Thirteen

"It's over," Harlowe said. She smoothed shower-damp hair out of Tatum's face. They lay slightly apart on the bed. Tatum's unearthly pallor was slowly blossoming into a healthy flush. The cut on her cheek was barely visible. "Shelby confessed. I saw them taking her away. We won."

"Sweet pea," Tatum whispered. "Even without her, it's not going to be easy from here on in."

"I know," Harlowe said. She shifted closer. "That's what you do when you love each other. You stand by each other no matter what. Oh crap!" Harlowe realized what she'd implied and attempted to make sweeping gestures but ended up getting all tangled in the bedding. "Um, you know, or just feel pretty good hanging out like good buddies or something. I didn't mean to assume anything or put words in your mouth." She pressed her lips together and glanced at Tatum, who had risen up on one elbow.

"You didn't. I never thought I would feel love for anyone, but I do," Tatum said. The words broke over Harlowe like a wave. She gasped with joy. Tatum continued, "Something changed inside of me when I fell in love with you. You changed me. My precious Harlowe, please don't cry."

"Okay," Harlowe said, sheepishly wiping at her eyes. "I can't believe you said it back. Wow."

That sly grin Harlowe loved so much pulled at Tatum's lips. "I'm not good at saying stuff like that, but for you, I'll try."

"You could have fooled me." Stifling a yawn that came from the bottom of her soul, Harlowe managed to get free of the quilt and lifted a corner. "I don't know about you, but I'm beat. How about calling it a night?"

"After you," Tatum said.

When she was firmly and tenderly held in Tatum's arms, Harlowe allowed herself to relax and believe that

things were going to be all right. The soft breaths of
Tatum in near-slumber reassured her. Only then did Harlowe close her eyes and let sleep take her.

****

The sunlight poured into the bedroom in shafts, illuminating Tatum's sleeping face. Harlowe had to draw in
a breath at the scene. Tatum trusted her, loved her enough
to let down all her guards. Harlowe wasn't going to take
that gift lightly. She snuggled deeper into the light
embrace, fully intending to wait for as long as it took for
Tatum to wake naturally but her full bladder and rum-
bling tummy had other ideas. Harlowe grimaced.

"The one day she actually sleeps in and I gotta get
up," Harlowe muttered.

As gently as she could, she wriggled backwards out
of the bed. A quick trip to the bathroom later, Harlowe
padded into the kitchen. Her bunny robe hung open over
her sleepwear. She stifled a yawn with the back of her
hand, and focused on the dazzling white forest spread out
beyond the window. She wasn't going to dwell in the
past. The future was all that mattered; and it was one she
would share with Tatum.

Wanting coffee, Harlowe started the machine. Soon
she had a warm mug in her hands and a plate of fruit and
yesterday's bread in front of her. She was on the verge of
ditching her robe and jumping back into bed when Tatum
strolled into the room in an immaculately tailored white
shirt and grey trousers—with matching suspenders. Harlowe's knees nearly gave out. She was thankful she
wasn't holding anything, because it would be on the floor
right now.

"Oh my," Harlowe said. She stepped back, allowing
herself to give Tatum a thorough once-over. "That looks
good on you. Super good."

Tatum shrugged one shoulder and aimed a grin at
Harlowe. She stuck her hands in her pockets and glanced
down. "You like it?" she asked in that cocky twang that
never failed to soak Harlowe's panties.

She gulped and nodded. While the outfit bore a

resemblance to the one Tatum had worn the first time at Harlowe's cottage, the cut was more modern, with an effortless androgynous elegance that left Harlowe gasping.

"It fits you perfectly," Harlowe said. "Like it was made for you."

"It was," Tatum answered. "At least, altered for me. I figured if I'm getting one suit tailored, I might as well go all-in for a new wardrobe."

"I like it," Harlowe said. "Very, very much."

Tatum smirked, then sobered. "And I think it's time for a change."

"Change is good." Harlowe held out a hand to Tatum and asked, "Did you sleep okay?"

"Very well," Tatum replied. She crossed the room and took Harlowe's hand in hers. Her thumb brushed over the back of Harlowe's hand in a way that sent a shock of electricity straight to her heart. "Come here, Sweet pea."

Harlowe couldn't help herself. With her robe billowing like a cape, she jumped up and landed in Tatum's arms.

"Oof," Tatum said. She held Harlowe close and pressed a kiss into her hair. Harlowe basked in the closeness, breathing in Tatum's intoxicatingly inviting scent, reveling in the feeling of the crisp shirt under her cheek. After more kisses, Tatum let her go and Harlowe skipped back to her mug, with more than a few covert glances across the table.

Tatum helped herself to a cup of coffee with a knowing smirk. She looked completely different from the sorrowful person on the edge of complete despair Harlowe saw the previous night. Her posture was relaxed and she rested her elbows on the countertop, propping her chin in her hands.

The idyllic moment was ended by a compact drone flying in with an ungainly mass, which it deposited on the floor before zooming away.

Tatum straightened up, her face still. At her feet was the discarded battle-suit, looking like the gutted carcass of some dark animal. Harlowe's heart lurched at the concrete reminder of what happened just the previous night.

How close had she been to losing Tatum forever? Harlowe took a deep breath.

Tatum slowly crouched down and lifted what appeared to be part of the arm covering. She studied it for a moment before she let it fall to the floor once more.

"Can you fix it?" Harlowe asked in a small voice.

She dropped to her knees in front of Tatum, whose head was down. For a moment she was silent. Tatum raised her face and shook back her trailing bangs. "Some components may be salvageable, but I'm not sure I should."

"How about just do the fun bits?" Harlowe suggested. "Like the flying stuff and the back view." At the last, Tatum shot her a look, complete with an eyebrow raise.

"The back view?" Tatum drawled.

"It's um, very flattering to the…physique and obviously fits perfectly and seems to be quite supportive, not that I was being a perv and checking out your…um, assets," Harlowe's mouth said in a nonstop gush. She felt her face getting warm and pressed her hands to her cheeks.

"Good to know," Tatum said with a quirk of her lips that seemed like she was trying to stifle a laugh

"Of course it's up to you. I'll be with you no matter what," Harlowe said. "If at any point you decide to rebuild, or make it into something else, I'll support you. Not that you need it, but I just wanted to say that."

"Thank you," Tatum said. "That means a lot to me. I'll deal with this all later on. Now I have a very special someone to take care of." She slapped her hands to her knees and stood, resolution written on her face.

Tatum strode over to the island and snagged a grape from Harlowe's plate, holding it out in an invitational way. Harlowe jumped up and joined Tatum. Instead of eating the fruit herself, Tatum extended a long arm and playfully offered it. Giggling, Harlowe lunged and sucked the grape, as well as Tatum's fingertips, into her mouth.

"Ouch," Tatum said. Theatrically, she shook her hand. "Nearly took my arm off. Remind me never to get between you and food."

"Ha, ha," Harlowe replied. She helped herself to another grape and licked her fingers. She noticed Tatum's attention drifting to her lips. Breakfast suddenly became the last thing on Harlowe's mind. She pushed herself away from the island and slowly came over to stand beside Tatum, who was leaning back against the kitchen counter.

All the time, Tatum never took her attention off Harlowe. Her silver-blue eyes darkened with the look Harlowe was beginning to become very familiar with. Her body responded to the intense gaze. An electric flutter awoke in her belly. Harlowe's thighs grew very slightly damp where they brushed. She tilted her head and playfully bit her lower lip, then slowly and deliberately let her robe slide from her shoulders and drop to the floor, leaving her in only her camisole and panties. Unlike the first time she'd done that, Harlowe meant the invitation with her entire heart. Never taking her attention from Harlowe, Tatum extended an arm and swept the countertop bare, sending a couple of tangerines rolling into the sink. She seized Harlowe around the waist and lifted her to sit on the newly cleared surface. Her hands were gentle, but Harlowe felt the tremor of desire in them.

Slowly, lazily, she draped her hands over Tatum's shoulders and drew her lover to stand between Harlowe's spread thighs.

"God, Harlowe," Tatum said. She leaned forward until their noses were almost touching. Her fingers drifted over the satiny fabric of Harlowe's camisole until they reached the hem. Tatum lingered there, teasing Harlowe's hungry skin with her closeness. Tatum licked her lips. She said, "I have half a mind to take you back to bed right this minute."

"Only half? Let's see if I can help you make that a whole," Harlowe purred. She raised one knee and stroked her leg up Tatum's body.

Tatum replied with a raised brow. She pressed forward and slowly took Harlowe's mouth in a soft, tender kiss. Harlowe hummed in pleasure and cupped Tatum's head, demanding a harder, deeper kiss. As Tatum filled her mouth, Harlowe felt like she was floating, held to earth only by the insistent pressure of Tatum's hands on her waist. Not breaking the kiss, Harlowe reached down and lifted her camisole top, pulling it over her breasts. Her chest heaved with deep breaths and she welcomed Tatum's hands on her with a whimper. Tatum pulled away for a moment, her eyes wide and filled with passion.

"Harlowe," she rasped. Tatum gathered Harlowe against her. She lowered her head to kiss and tongue at Harlowe's neck, then even lower to suck one achingly hard nipple into her mouth.

"Yes, I like that," Harlowe said. "Oh, yes, I love your mouth on me." She closed her eyes and threw her head back, on the heels of every breath came a moan. She didn't care about being loud. Who was going to hear her anyway? Oscar the recycling can? The only one Harlowe cared about at that moment was Tatum, letting her know how much Harlowe enjoyed the affection being lavished on her.

The counter fell away from Harlowe's backside. She came back to reality, lifted in Tatum's arms. Harlowe hung onto Tatum's strong shoulders as she was carried the short distance into the bedroom. Tatum lowered her to the softness of the bed and drew back. Harlowe leaned back on her hands, extremely aware of her bare breasts peeking out from her rucked-up camisole, hard nipples swollen and deep pink, wet from Tatum's mouth. She watched as Tatum impatiently stripped off her suspenders and started to unbutton her shirt. She got it half way undone before she pulled it over her head. Underneath, she was in a simple white undershirt with nothing on underneath it. The shadows of her erect nipples inflamed Harlowe. She couldn't stay still.

"Let me help you with that," she said. She rose to her knees and eagerly scooted forward to pull open Tatum's trousers. They fell to the floor, and Tatum kicked them away.

"Help me up here," Tatum rasped in her ear. Harlowe swallowed hard as Tatum pulled off her undershirt. Her lips quirked up in a cocky grin, which set off another set of waterworks, this time a burst of wetness between Harlowe's legs. Her nipples stood, hard and ready. Harlowe ached to taste them.

Harlowe didn't hesitate. She grabbed Tatum by the waistband of her boxer briefs and surged against her. The rush of breath with the hint of a moan from Tatum told Harlowe she was doing something right. She took Tatum's proud nipple into her mouth. Her tongue stoked over the responsive flesh. Tatum's breathing quickened. Harlowe's fingers found her other breast, she circled the hardness with her thumb. Harlowe's body reacted, her own nipples tingled, and she was soaking wet inside her panties.

"Okay, enough, Harlowe," Tatum's hoarse words stopped her. Harlowe looked up, Tatum's pupils were blown wide, her face flushed. For a moment, Harlowe thought she'd done something wrong, but the hunger in Tatum's gaze assured her otherwise. Tatum licked her lips. "Fuck, I want you."

"How do you want me?" Harlowe asked. She looked up through her lashes as innocently as she could. She spread her knees and let her fingers drift between her thighs. Tatum bit her lip and groaned. Harlowe was in control and safe. The heat of Tatum's desire for her was addictive. Slowly, deliberately, Harlowe pressed her fingertips against herself, then rubbed up and down over the sodden cotton. She felt like she was riding on a cloud of pure light. Harlowe purred, "Look at me, how wet I am for you. Do you want this?"

"Yes, yes," Tatum gritted. She looked like she was on the verge of losing control. Her long fingers clenched into fists. "But only if you do, too."

In response, Harlowe lay back onto the pillows and spread her legs wider, fingers still resting on her heated mound. Her breathing picked up. Arousal burned through her. The brazen pose was one she would never do for anyone else, but she was very willing to do it for Tatum. She wriggled her hips against the comforter, silently asking Tatum to come to her. Tatum didn't move, but her throat rippled as she swallowed hard. Then Harlowe understood why Tatum was waiting.

Her cheeks grew warm, but Harlowe had to speak, to say the words that would bring Tatum to her. She said, "Tatum, I want you here. You have my permission."

Harlowe spread her fingers, framing the soft flesh that throbbed for Tatum's touch. That time, Tatum moved. Harlowe gave a low hum of approval when Tatum's long, muscular body unfurled and lay down next to her. Their eyes met, their breaths mingled. Harlowe wanted nothing between them. She wanted Tatum with all of her being. Tatum very gently placed her hand over Harlowe's, cupping her.

Tatum drew in a reverent breath. "Are you ready?"

"Yes," Harlowe breathed, afraid to break the spell. She retrieved her hand and arched her back, pleading with Tatum to take the next step.

Strong fingers slowly moved, tracing circles over her, teasing her indirectly through the wet cotton. Harlowe bit back a moan. She was already a pile of shivering jelly inside. She needed more. Tatum slipped up to the waistband of Harlowe's panties, then paused.

"May I?" she asked in a husky voice.

"Please," Harlowe answered. She bit her lip as Tatum's fingers disappeared under the soft cotton. Harlowe was aware of every millimetre as Tatum stroked through her curls, then delved deeper, meeting her super-sensitive skin for the first time. "Oh yes, that's good," Harlowe said. She couldn't believe how much Tatum's touch aroused her. At the same time, Tatum's breath got harder, her eyes brilliant.

"You feel so good," Tatum whispered. "Fuck, so good."

The fingers on her got more urgent, sliding up and down her length, circling her opening, before briefly skimming over her clit, then again, down and up. Harlowe couldn't help but rock her hips, riding the rhythm of Tatum's fingers on her, growing more urgent with every pass.

"Tae," Harlowe said between gasping breaths. "I want to see."

She whimpered with need as Tatum withdrew to tug Harlowe's panties down and off. Tatum's own boxer briefs joined them on the floor before she sprawled down once more. Harlowe welcomed her back with a happy purr. This time, she felt the purpose in the strokes that dipped into where she was wet, stroking closer every time. Harlowe looked down. The motion of Tatum's hand between her legs was urgent, incredibly hot. Harlowe spread her legs wider, hungry for more. The movement pressed her thigh between Tatum's.

"You're so wet," Tatum said.

"I'm not the only one," Harlowe said. With the next thrust of her hips, she let her thigh grind against the incredible heat between Tatum's legs. Free from her boxer briefs, Tatum's flesh pressed against her, hard and dewy with arousal. Arousal that Harlowe caused. Harlowe's bare breasts rose with her triumphant mood.

"All for you," Tatum said. The lightning-fast grin disappeared into a moan as Harlowe once more pushed against her. Harlowe's clit throbbed, begging for release. Tension clamped down deep in her belly. Harlowe was ready, she couldn't wait any longer. She wanted Tatum inside her when she came.

"Do it," Harlowe said in desperation. She held herself still, surrendering to Tatum.

Tatum kissed her once, then pulled back, allowing Harlowe to see Tatum's slick digit sinking deep within her spread wide inner lips.

"Is this okay?" Tatum asked softly. "Enough?"

"More," Harlowe gasped. Tatum slowly withdrew, and the sound was gloriously erotic, then pushed back into her with two.

"Good?" Tatum asked.

"Yes," Harlowe cried out. "Tae, do it to me."

Tatum thrust deep, pumping her hips with the motion. Harlowe had never seen anything sexier than Tatum grinding on her, riding Harlowe's thigh with every thrust into her. Their synched breaths filled the air, the wet sound of Tatum fingers driving into her got faster. Sparks flared into life and swam through Harlowe's vision. She didn't care how she looked, spread wide under Tatum, taking her over and over again. She was only heartbeats away from exploding.

"Close," Harlowe said. Her hands clamped down on Tatum's muscular shoulders. She bit off a whimper and canted her hips, demanding more.

"I need to hear you," Tatum said, low and urgent.

"God," Harlowe cried out. "Oh *fuck*, fuck me hard, Tae." She couldn't stop the moans that blossomed into a rhythmic string of *yes* and *Tae* and *please*. One last, powerful thrust and Harlowe lost herself. Her back arched, her head slammed into the pillow with the force of her release. Her thighs shook, her hips jerked. An explosion of pure release filled her. It was different from any other time. Her inner muscles clenched, spasms rippled through her like an earthquake. She hung onto Tatum as if she would spin into space if she didn't. She was viscerally aware of Tatum's rhythm crumbling, her fingers holding strong and hard within her, her regular thrusts on Harlowe's thigh becoming urgent and random. Harlowe greedily savored Tatum's grunt and shudder as she came as well.

Slowly, the grip of her climax faded. The receding waves left Harlowe trembling, breathing hard and looking up into Tatum's flushed face. The spray of hair that trailed into her eyes was sweat-damp. Wonderingly, Harlowe reached down to where Tatum was still sheathed within herself.

"Just a moment longer," Harlowe breathed. She closed her eyes, letting her fingers play over Tatum's hand, then her own aching hardness. A spark of pleasure flared. Harlowe wasn't finished yet.

"One more?" Tatum asked with a smirk and a knowing brow-raise. At Harlowe's nodded assent, Tatum shifted. She lowered her head to tease Harlowe's throbbing nipples with kisses and tonguing, slowly easing in and out of her below. Harlowe had never felt anything that good in her life. She let out a groan of pure decadence. Her breathing quickened. Desperate for something more, Harlowe's slick fingers circled her clit, gaining speed as her pleasure rocketed. Tatum matched her, pumping deep and hard. It wasn't going to take much. She was already hot and wet. Harlowe needed to come. She didn't care if Tatum saw how she pleasured herself, in fact she wanted her to.

"Coming," Harlowe cried out. She let her body move with the rhythm of Tatum's long, gorgeously talented fingers plunging into her, giving herself completely over. "God, so close, Tae—"

Tatum paused in giving attention to Harlowe's breasts. She spoke, her breath was hot on Harlowe's wet skin, "I'm here, God you're so fucking hot, let go, baby-girl."

That was all she needed. The second orgasm ripped through Harlowe, electrifying her. Tatum's strokes got slow and deep, in time to the rolling waves of Harlowe's release. Her cries slowly quieted to moans, then long, contented sighs. When the last tingling wave faded, Tatum softly withdrew from her. Harlowe felt the loss, but Tatum deliberately taking first one finger, then the other into her mouth and sucking on it with a decadent expression drove that thought from her mind. Harlowe shivered in anticipation.

"Gorgeous," Tatum said. "Are you all right?"

"Oh yeah," Harlowe said. She stretched out, luxuriating in the boneless relaxed state left in the wake of her explosive orgasms. Almost as an afterthought, Harlowe peeled her crumpled camisole off. Completely bare, she snuggled back into Tatum's arms, pressing their bodies together. Tatum chuckled into her ear, then kissed her softly on the side of her neck.

"Are *you* all right?" Harlowe asked.

"Absolutely, extremely perfect," Tatum said. "Nobody has ever—no, I'm sorry, that was tactless."

"It's all right," Harlowe said. She brushed back the stubborn ebony strands that were determined to get into Tatum's face. "Tell me. I want to know about you, and that includes the past. I'm not going to be immature about it or get jealous, okay?"

Tatum's drawn brows relaxed. "Okay," she said softly. "Harlowe, nobody has ever been so responsive to me before. I mean, I got the job done, but it was never like this."

Harlowe tilted her head. She asked, "Like, how exactly?"

"It's hard to explain." Brow furrowed in thought, Tatum pressed a hand to her chest. "Like something in me is connected to you that makes me feel good when you do. Which sounds crazy, right?"

"No, it doesn't," Harlowe said. "I guess it's natural to feel that way when you care deeply for your partner. And you're amazing at finding out what gets me going. I want to do that too for you. So basically, that means you're gonna be finding little old me in your bed a lot from here on in."

Tatum chuckled and nuzzled into Harlowe's hair, finishing with a light kiss. "I'll take that." She pulled away and sat up. Harlowe watched with interest as Tatum unselfconsciously stretched her arms over her head. She lowered them with a sigh and said, "Before I make you brunch, I'm going to offer you a shower, and apologies for getting my stuff on you." Somewhat sheepishly, Tatum brushed a hand over Harlowe's thigh.

"Yes, to the shower," Harlowe replied. "And no to the apology. I happen to like your stuff on me. If you didn't get me messy, then what's the point?"

Tatum cracked a crooked grin. "In that case, I've got a bunch of dirty tricks you might like."

"I can't wait," Harlowe said.

On the way to the bathroom, Harlowe pulled Tatum into the elevator. They ended up sloppily making out all the way to the hot tub and were *very* late for brunch.

****

Later on that day, the setting sunlight streamed into the sunroom, bathing Harlowe in crimson warmth. She pulled her feet up to sit cross-legged on the loveseat and studied the screen in front of herself. Instead of lending her a tablet, Tatum surprised her by presenting Harlowe with her very own, one that Tatum claimed she threw together from odds and ends she had lying around.

On the space-age tablet, she double-checked the captions to the photos from the Discovery Day interviews, using the permission forms to check she'd spelled everyone's name correctly. The booth photographed well, and

Harlowe was pleased with the results. Ellie's family photo was especially cute, with her bear in the seat of honor.

Triumphant, Harlowe scrolled through her article once more, excitement building at the sight of her first legitimate byline. Tatum had an appointment with her therapist which wouldn't be over for another half hour, so Harlowe savored the moment alone.

With a final look, Harlowe set aside her article and was just getting started on some editing when her phone chirped a reminder. She quickly propped the tablet in the holder and smoothed her hair back. It was getting to where she needed a trim, and she knew exactly who she had in mind to give it to her. Harlowe had a few ideas about how she would repay Tatum for the favour. But first she had her weekly one-on-one meeting with Bucky to get through.

"Hello there," Bucky said the moment he appeared on the screen. "You are looking quite cheerful this fine evening. Does that mean you have some good news for me?"

"Yes, I do," Harlowe said. She couldn't contain her bubbly happiness, for more than the reason Bucky thought. "I just finished the article. I'm ready for your final check."

"Wonderful," Bucky said. He beamed at her like an indulgent uncle for a moment, then sobered and held up a finger. "You know, you've been keeping a secret from me."

"Uh, I have?" Harlowe squeaked. "But all those parking tickets were waived in traffic court. How did you find out about them?" She nervously twirled a short strand of hair around her finger, mind whirling. "And I paid Mr. Brenner back for wrecking his mailbox, the donut fiasco was written off as a natural disaster, and I was only five when I made that underground newspaper—"

"Actually, none of those," Bucky said, cutting off Harlowe's stream of confessions. She closed her mouth and squirmed in her chair. His eyes twinkled at her. "And while I do think all those things you just told me are extremely fascinating, I found out that your town boasts of something interesting—or rather, someone interesting. Have a look-see and tell me if this rings any bells."

A video jumped onto the screen. Intrigued, Harlowe studied it and gasped. It was a short clip of the presentation Tatum did for Discovery Day. By the angle, one of the parents standing at the edge of the crowd took it. The clip showed Tatum revealing her string of paper snowflakes. It had been edited slightly to have a fuzzy, snowy border, but there was no mistaking who it was. Harlowe breathed again when the clip ended far before the trouble with Shelby began. She minimized the video and faced Bucky.

He said, "This little clip was brought to my attention by an eagle-eyed reader. If you happened to write an article about this mysterious individual, I can see it being very beneficial for both you and the Gazette. What do you say?"

"Yeah, I know her," Harlowe said. "But I can't write about her."

"Why not?" Bucky's bushy brows climbed toward his receding hairline.

"She's a very private person, plus, um..." Harlowe flushed with pride and pleasure. "She's also my girlfriend. It might be a conflict of interest."

"Oh! Well, congratulations," Bucky said. "Actually, as long as it's edited and fact-checked, you're very welcome to write about any person you please. Of course I would never ask you to compromise your personal life, but I just wanted to let you know it would mean a lot to all of us here to get the scoop on this person. You don't think you could? Even a little mention? A memo even?"

"No, I don't think so," Harlowe said with a shake of her head.

"You're off the hook for now, but if either of you changes your mind the offer stands," Bucky said with a hopeful twinkle in his eye. "By-the-by, how about I forward you a detailed explanation of our spousal and partner benefits? We have a very inclusive policy."

"It's a bit early for that," Harlowe said. Her ears and cheeks got warm. "But thanks."

She got though the rest of the meeting and signed

out. Harlowe stared at the blank screen, her thoughts in a tangle. As much as she wanted to stay in the isolated bubble of the bunker with just herself and Tatum, she couldn't deny the existence of the world outside. Would Tatum ever venture out into the community again? Would she be willing to meet Harlowe's parents?

Her thoughts were interrupted by Cartlyn trundling into the room with a large paper bag, a bottle of wine and two glasses. Her morose thoughts banished, Harlowe jumped up and quickly set out the Greek feast. She was just pouring the wine when Tatum poked her head in.

"I see you've got the party started," she said.

"Yup," Harlowe said. She scooted over to make room on the love seat, obligingly Tatum settled down next to her. Harlowe looked at her closely. She seemed at ease and comfortable. Harlowe ventured, "How was your session? Um, if it's okay to ask."

"It was good," Tatum said. She raised her glass and tapped it very lightly to Harlowe's before taking a slow sip. She swallowed and let out an appreciative hum. "Evelyn's been with me though a lot of stuff. She helped me process what's happened and figure a few things out."

"I'm glad to hear that," Harlowe said. She happily helped herself to feta and olive-topped salad. As she munched, her mind went back to the discussion she had with Bucky earlier.

"Someone posted a video of you from Discovery Day," Harlowe said.

"I know," Tatum said with a careless shrug. "I have alerts set up for that kind of thing."

"Was there only the one?" Harlowe's heart clenched.

"There were a couple, all pretty similar."

"It doesn't bother you?"

"It does a little," Tatum said. She set down her fork and turned to face Harlowe. "But I was expecting it. That's actually part of what I talked through with Evelyn. I want to live authentically, I want to be a good partner to you, and that means getting out there and being part of society again."

Tatum's fingers closed over Harlowe's.

"Wow, really?" Harlowe breathed.

"Yes, really," Tatum replied. She stole an olive from Harlowe's plate and popped it into her mouth. "So if your boss is looking for someone to do an expose on the Mysterious Stranger in the Bunker on the Hill, you are the only reporter who is ever going to get my exclusive."

Harlowe sputtered on her sip of wine. "How did you know? Bucky just asked me about you."

"That was fast," Tatum said, raising her eyebrows. "Honestly, I didn't know, I'm not monitoring you or anything creepy like that. I just figured with the video out there, it might eventually get back to him, and since you're in the area, it makes sense he'd ask you to look into it. It would be a really good addition to your body of work, too."

"Maybe so, but I don't know if I should do an article about you," Harlowe said. She pouted and crossed her arms over her chest. "If word got out how hot you are, there's going to be a line of eligible women lining up outside your door."

Tatum shook her head with a chuckle. "Sweet pea, you have nothing to worry about. The only one I want is you. My love for you isn't going to be swayed by anyone or anything. That's a promise I intend to keep for as long as I'm alive."

Harlowe was silent for a moment, pondering the weight of that statement. "So, where do we go from here?"

"Wherever we want," Tatum said.

"Tae," Harlowe said softly. "I promise I'll be with you, too."

Epilogue

"Why am I nervous?" Harlowe asked her reflection in the mirror, adjusting the yellow crown of roses that sat on her head, matching the filmy short-sleeved dress that just brushed her knees and made her look like a pixie made of pure sunlight. A small bouquet of the same yellow roses sat on the dresser. "I shouldn't be nervous. It's preposterous."

She gave her reflection one more look-over, satisfied she turned her attention to the window. Behind the cottage, the garden was the gayest it had ever been in its mid-summer glory. Rainbow streamers competed with the lush froth of flowers for Most Colorful Decoration. The bushes looked particularly spectacular that day, trimmed the previous weekend by Tatum, using her own specially-designed shears. Instead of the bladed battle-suit, she'd created an updated one that was both beautiful and functional, streamlined and most importantly, non-violent. She'd offered to make Harlowe one so they could fly in tandem, but Harlowe much preferred being the passenger in her lover's arms.

The mossy ground hosted a cluster of rented chairs, which held the very small number of guests who could attend in person, all in their very best clothing. Harlowe's mother and father were there, along with a few older relatives who lived close enough to make the jaunt to the cottage. A large screen and portable speakers were set up in front of a camera and laptop. The screen was full of squares of happy, expectant faces of the family and friends who were joining them online.

The white path between the chairs was pristine, and ended in a floral arch bedecked with even more rainbow streamers. The local pastor stood off to one side of the arch, looking far more serene than Harlowe felt. In just a few minutes, she'd be walking down that path with Tatum. At least she found flats that matched her dress. If she had to navigate the so-called Virgin Road in heels, well, it would be bad.

A light knock at the door heralded Danny, the wedding planner, into the room. Graceful and willowy, with close-cropped curly russet curls and fashionably un-fashionable glasses, he was in creatively embroidered jeans and a T-shirt bearing the logo of a classic Broadway hit. He had a tape measure around his neck and carried a digital tablet in his hands.

"Chop chop, sweetie, the ceremony's in five," he sang. He paused and looked Harlowe up and down. "Oh my, you do look like the most delicious little daffodil, don't you? Your Tatum is going to fall on her face when she sees you. Mm! Mm! Mm!"

"Stop," Harlowe said, slapping at him. She pressed her hands to her cheeks. "Where is she? Can I see her?"

"She's already in place and you'll see her soon enough," Danny said. "Don't worry about a thing. You've got your bouquet, your handsome Tatum is waiting for you, and you look fabulous, girlfriend. Now go out there and do your thing."

Harlowe swallowed and nodded. She checked her makeup, basically just lip gloss and mascara, then grabbed the bouquet from the table.

"Okay, I'm ready, let's go."

Harlowe allowed herself to be ushered from the master bedroom to the back door, which led to the garden. She stopped short at the sight of Tatum, elegant and knee-meltingly handsome in her grey morning suit. Her hair was pulled back into a low ponytail, but her ever-present swoop of bangs hung into her face, spilling over one eye. She had a single yellow rose in her boutonniere. Harlowe's heart felt like it would burst out of her chest. Tatum had a similarly besotted expression on her face. Danny looked from one to the other, sighed, dramatically checked his watch, and flitted off.

"Oh wow, you're gorgeous, that dress...wow," Tatum breathed. She leaned close to Harlowe and whispered in her ear, "It'll look even better on the bedroom floor tonight."

Harlowe gasped in pleasure and gave Tatum a playful punch to her shoulder. Tatum pretended to be mortally injured, which caused Harlowe to burst into giggles.

"Well, my dress is going to have company," Harlowe whispered back. "Those pants aren't going to stay on your fine ass for long."

Tatum's mouth hung open for a moment, and Harlowe gloated over the fact that she could still make Tatum flustered, even after eight months together. Pattering sounds from the second floor rang out and Danny popped into existence once more.

"Look sharp, folks. The music's starting in five, four..." he mouthed the last of the countdown and signaled "one" with two finger guns. Perfectly on time, the first strands of music from the DJ booth filled the air. Instead of the traditional wedding march, they played Culture Club's "Love is Love."

"Ready?" Tatum whispered.

"As ready as I'll ever be," Harlowe replied out of the corner of her mouth.

"Here we go," Tatum murmured and opened the door. She held out her arm and Harlowe took it. Just as they'd practiced at the previous day's rehearsal, they stepped forward in perfect sync. Tatum had to shorten her usual ground-devouring lope to accommodate Harlowe, and she did it with grace.

Harlowe forgot her nerves as she walked down the aisle, head held up in pride. She drew strength from Tatum's presence beside her. On either side, smiles and a few happy tears met them. Harlowe felt her own eyes grow misty. She gave Tatum's arm a quick squeeze.

They reached the altar and Harlowe reluctantly let go of Tatum and stepped away from her. The song faded out and an expectant silence fell. As one, the entire assembly held their breaths and looked over to the house once more.

The DJ raised his hand, then dropped the needle onto a new record. A cheer went up as the song "We Are Family" blasted through the speakers. Harlowe jumped up and down, clapping and whistling as the door opened and her great-uncle Florian danced out with Rockwell at his side. They were in matching pink tuxedos. Florian was small and plump, with a wreath of rainbow-colored flowers on his balding head and a large wicker basket in his hands. At his side, Rockwell looked even taller and ganglier than usual. Instead of a wreath, he was draped in several brightly colored leis. Together, they discoed down the aisle, stopping to give out high fives to various guests and sprinkle flower petals everywhere. Rockwell distributed leis and chuckled patiently at the jokes that came back about "getting lei'ed", mostly courtesy of Harlowe's dad.

When they reached the arch, Harlowe got an enthusiastic hug from her great-uncle and Tatum shook hands with Rockwell.

Silence fell once more and the pastor stepped forward.

"We are gathered here today, in the presence of family and friends to witness the renewal of vows that were taken in secret but now can be celebrated openly."

Harlowe's eyes filled with tears of joy as her great-uncle and Rockwell clasped hands. The look that passed between them was pure and timeless. Harlowe pressed a hand to her heart and met Tatum's gaze. She drew in a breath.

Someday, that will be us.

She felt the words as clearly as if Tatum had said them aloud. The ceremony renewing their vows was simple but heartfelt. Afterwards, everyone converged under the open tent at the end of the garden, overlooked by the dragon-shaped bush. Good smells had been wafting from it for some time now. The catering staff were waiting at the long grill to serve up juicy steaks and burgers, while a buffet of fancy breads, cold meats, and salads of every kind filled a long table leading up to the grill. An open bar completed the array. Already, several members of the wedding party were gathered around it with colorful cocktails in their hands.

Harlowe hung back with Tatum while the other guests were served. Beside her, Tatum was silent and tense.

"Are you okay?" Harlowe asked. She teased Tatum's hands from her pockets and clasped them in both of hers. "Is it meeting my family? Because they already love you."

"They do?" Tatum raised her eyebrows, then shook her head. "I'll be fine, it's just going to be different face-to-face."

Harlowe wrinkled her nose in sympathy. "I know how my family can be, and I really appreciate you being here with me today," she said. "Okay, how about this, the secret word is 'pineapple.' It's the signal for me to get us out of there by any means necessary."

Tatum replied with a single raised brow. "Pineapple, huh?" she squeezed Harlowe's hands. "At least I won't forget it. All right, let's go."

Under the tent, numerous small tables were set up for people to sit where they pleased, with the head table being only slightly larger with more decorations. Harlowe picked her way to the table where her parents sat. Immediately, both of them jumped up with delighted looks on their faces. Like Harlowe, her mother Jillian was petite and blonde, while her father Ben was average in every way, except for the handlebar mustache he'd grown especially for the day, citing wanting to keep the feeling of the original day. He enthusiastically shook Tatum's hand.

"Pleasure to finally meet you in person, Tatum," he said. "Tall drink of water, aren't you? How's the weather up there?"

"Daaaad!" Harlowe crossed her arms and tapped her foot.

"It was a lovely ceremony," Tatum said.

"Harlowe made me promise not to hug you," Jillian said, pouting a little. "So I won't, but I am glad you could join us today."

Tatum smiled in return, but Harlowe's sharp eyes detected a hint of tension in the expression.

"I'm starving," Harlowe said. She threaded her arm through Tatum's and leaned close to her. "Sorry Mom and Dad, but the buffet is calling."

"Go," Ben said, making a shooing motion. He cupped a hand over his mouth and said in a stage whisper to Tatum, "The secret to surviving the women of this family is make sure to feed them prompt and regular."

"I heard that," Harlowe puffed. She stuck her nose in

the air and swept off in a flurry of yellow chiffon.

Back from the buffet, she and Tatum found a table at the very edge of the group so they could avoid the head table where the grooms and a number of assorted members of Harlowe's family converged, all talking loudly with additions from the large screen that someone dragged over. Harlowe glanced up at them with a sudden sense of sadness. She'd never heard Rockwell talk about his family, and his side was completely absent from the party. She wondered if, like Tatum, he was alone, or if they'd separated for another reason.

The DJ kept up a steady stream of tunes, a mix of old and new. The atmosphere turned jovial and loud as the drinks flowed and the sun edged toward the horizon. Harlowe munched her cheeseburger and stole bits of Tatum's grilled lamb. Even after all that time, Tatum wasn't a very social person. She needed silence and peace and only ventured outside when it was absolutely necessary. Although she spent a lot of time in her workshop, she always made time for Harlowe, whether it was exchanging flirty text messages, working silently side-by-side, or enthusiastically showing off some new thing she'd made. Harlowe didn't mind the time apart either; her own work kept her busy enough. She'd put forward a proposal to Bucky for her own column where she interviewed a different person every week. At first he'd been hesitant, but the fact that Tatum had volunteered to be the first interviewee had swayed his position immediately.

Tatum couldn't do her robotics work at the cottage, so when they stayed at Harlowe's, which was about a third of the time, it was purely time for the two of them. Of course, they made good use of the bunker's facilities as well, particularly the hot tub. No matter where they were, in the same room or not, Harlowe's love for Tatum lived in her heart always. She stole a peek at Tatum, breathtakingly handsome in her tailored outfit. Harlowe couldn't help but remember how they'd woken up, with Tatum cuddling her from behind, fresh from her post-workout shower, pumped biceps hard against her. Harlowe idly wondered if she could tire Tatum out enough that night to actually make her sleep in past the crack of dawn.

The hazy daydream broke as Harlowe's great-aunt Florrie, short for Floridina, Florian's twin sister, came up to them with a colorful printout in her hands. Her wrinkled cheeks were flushed and her eyes sparkled.

"I was wondering if I could have this autographed," she said, and held out the paper. It was the article that Harlowe had written, introducing Tatum to the world. The title was: "The Face Behind the Robots, Tatum Edwyn AI Engineer." It had only been published for a week and already half the newspapers in the country had picked it up. Besides Harlowe's words, it also featured a number of photos of Tatum in various situations, all of which Harlowe thought were too hot to even exist.

Harlowe glowed with pride. "Sure thing, Great-Aunt Florrie, just let me get a pen."

"Not you, child," Florrie said. She flapped the article at Harlowe as if trying to shoo her off. "Your name's already on it. I'd like Tatum to do the honors."

While Harlowe sulked, Tatum took the proffered article with a genteel bow. "Where would you like me to sign it?"

"On that photo," Florrie said, pointing. "The one where you're lifting that heavy object and your arms are just so...ooh!" She fanned herself with a lace handkerchief she pulled from her sleeve.

Tatum raised a brow.

Harlowe couldn't resist. "Good choice, Florrie. That's my third favorite picture. The best one is the suspenders one where she's got her back to the camera and her sleeves are rolled up."

"Oh yes, the back view is just so tasty," Florrie gushed. She elbowed Tatum and fluttered her lashes. "If I were thirty years younger, your Harlowe might have some stiff competition."

"Excuse me?" Tatum said in an incredulous voice. She held her head in her hands and sighed. Recovering, she asked, "Anyway, so it's Florrie with an I-E at the end?"

"Yes, that's fine dear," Florrie said. Tatum signed the article with a flourish, rising to her feet and bowing her head once more to air kiss Florrie's knuckles. Cackling in delight, Harlowe's great-aunt escaped with her prize. Tatum resumed her seat with a wary look.

"Um, sorry about that," Harlowe said. "I just want you to know that not everyone in my family is a horny trouser-chaser, okay?"

Just at that moment, a cacophony of shouting and glass-clinking erupted from the head table where it appeared that Harlowe's parents were having a kissing contest against Florian and Rockwell.

"Ooh, I see tongue!" someone crowed out. "That's ten points to Jill and Ben."

"Tush-grabbing for another ten points," someone else shouted.

"Who's going to be the first to...oh! How many points is *that*?"

"At least thirty! Looks like someone's going for the record!"

All Tatum had to do was level Harlowe with a single look.

"Ignore that," Harlowe said. She waved her hand dismissively. "Ignore all of them."

Tatum chuckled and gently took Harlowe's hand, resting open on the table. "Sweet pea, I know all about you—how naughty and insatiable you can be." She scooted her chair closer and whispered in Harlowe's ear, "And that's one of the many things I love about you, which I will demonstrate tonight when we're finally alone."

Harlowe's entire body lit up at those soft words. She looked around wildly. "When is this thing over? What do you mean by demonstrate?"

Tatum gave her a mysterious look and drained the last of her wine. A very energized Harlowe was just about to jump up and offer to get refills when an older lady she'd never seen before sidled up to their table. She was in a stiff, navy blue dress that looked decades old. Her dark hair was streaked with gray and pulled back into a severe chignon. She was tall but stooped, and seemed extremely ill-at-ease.

"Excuse me," she said. "But is this the Creaver-

Meadows gathering?"

"Yes," Harlowe answered slowly. "And you are...?"

"Elvira McCurdie, formerly Meadows." She rooted around in an ancient beaded handbag and pulled out an invitation. "Rockwell is my younger brother. We've been...out of contact for quite some time. This came in the post and I—I wanted to come and wish him well on this joyous day."

"Oh wow," Harlowe said. Suddenly, she jumped to her feet. "Sorry, I forgot my manners. He's—they're over, hang on a moment..." She paused and studied the newcomer with suspicion. Weddings were drama-magnets and Harlowe didn't want to be the one to precipitate any.

Harlowe wasn't the only one with doubts. Tatum stood and slowly crossed her arms over her chest. She'd ditched her jacket long ago, and her rolled-up sleeves showed off her sculpted and tattooed forearms. She glowered down at Elvira. In a dangerously soft voice, Tatum said, "I trust you are here in good will."

Elvira gulped and retreated a step. "Y-yes."

Tatum didn't get a chance to reply before Rockwell loomed over the table. Harlowe felt extremely small and bright in the middle of the three tall, dark figures.

"Elvira?" he asked in a shocked voice.

Harlowe glanced at Tatum, who was steadily inching away. Suspicious rumblings stirred in the crowd. She peered between Rockwell and Elvira to see several people from Harlowe's family angrily stomping across the mossy turf. Florian was in the lead, waving what looked to be a samurai sword festooned with rainbow ribbons.

"Who invited that witch?" Florian hollered over the commotion.

Rockwell held out his hands. "I can explain. Please put the sword down."

"No, I will not!" Florian pushed into the gathering, face red and floral tiara askew. He brandished his sword in one hand, with his other hand planted sassily on one hip. The look he fixed Elvira with was full of haughty disdain. He said, "A lot of nerve you have coming here after all this time."

"I'm sorry," Elvira said. The invitation in her hands shook. "I shouldn't have come."

"Yeah, exactly," Florian huffed. "Now go run along to your precious white-bread suburban home and all your moral uprightness."

"Florian, just give her a chance," Rockwell said.

"A chance to ruin everything again? That's a no from me."

Meanwhile, the rest of the guests shouted accusations about some incident that apparently happened a very long time ago but was definitely not forgotten. People crowded around the table, all of them shouting over each other. Harlowe felt like she was standing in the path of a speeding locomotive. Reflexively, she clutched at Tatum's sleeve. Tatum jumped at the contact, then pressed a hand over Harlowe's.

"I need a drink," Tatum croaked. "Something sweet, like a pineapple Daiquiri."

"Coming right up," Harlowe chirped. She backed them away from the crowd until they got to a safe distance, then she pulled Tatum behind a large platypus-shaped bush.

The secluded corner was dark and private, only the smallest glimmer of the venue lights filtered through. Shouts and crashes echoed around the garden. The music cut off and someone started blowing on a whistle, apparently ineffectively as even more crashes and hollering ensued.

"Sorry about that," Tatum said. She pinched the bridge of her nose and closed her eyes. "I'm not good with that kind of thing. Family stuff."

"Me neither," Harlowe said. She slipped her arms around Tatum's waist and leaned her cheek against the tailored grey vest of her suit. "There's a reason why I jumped at the chance to live so far away from civilization. I think the wilds of the backwoods suits me more than life in the city, in the middle of a bunch of relatives."

"You really don't mind living all the way out here?"

"I love it here," Harlowe said. She tilted her head to meet Tatum's tender gaze. "Especially since you're with me."

Tatum chuckled and pulled her close. She pressed a kiss into Harlowe's hair. She held still for a moment while Harlowe snuggled into the embrace.

"What's going on out there?" Harlowe asked. "Do I want to know?"

"The shouting and fighting has stopped for the most part," Tatum said. "One of the caterers took the cake sword away from your great-uncle and a couple more are helping to pick up all those tables Florrie and your mom flipped. The bartender's got everyone sitting down, drinking water, and it looks like they've put out the fire at the reception desk. No need for a visit from the fire department tonight." Tatum shivered and Harlowe instinctively held her tight.

Harlowe sighed. "Okay, at least things are quieting down. My mom always goes overboard whenever she gets the chance to flip a table. She gets it from my grandma. Back when my mom was in high school, one thanksgiving Gramma single-handedly chucked the entire dining table end-over-end with the turkey and everything on it."

"Table flipping runs in your family, good to know." Even without looking, Harlowe could see, clear as day, the Tatum Edwyn brow raise.

"Do you think it's safe to go back?" Harlowe asked. "Or if you want, we can vanish into the night, fleeing on slippers of mist and darkness."

Tatum snorted. She ruffled Harlowe's hair, then let her go. "No vanishing without at least saying goodbye to the gentlemen of honor," Tatum said. "And we haven't had any cake yet. It looks like it survived mostly unscathed."

They resettled at their table, which had lost its tablecloth in the excitement. The chairs were still there with a few new dings and scratches. Elvira was now seated at the end of the head table with a teacup and saucer in front of herself, looking somewhat shell-shocked. Florian and Rockwell were drinking cocktails from elaborately decorated coconuts, red-faced and disheveled, but at least none of them were waving swords.

Harlowe's father came over to their table with

glasses filled with ice, a bottle of lime-flavored spirits of some kind, and a half-eaten bag of ketchup chips cradled in his arms, plus a mug of beer clutched in one hand.

"A peace offering," Ben declared unsteadily. His handlebar mustache was coated liberally with fake-ketchup powder, which rained down gently as he spoke. "Eat, drink and be merry! Who knows, the next wedding may be..." He waggled his eyebrows at them. "What d'you say, Tatum? Are you going to make an honest woman of my daughter?"

"Dad," Harlowe said, blushing furiously. She did not want to have that conversation with her parents. "That's private."

"I'm in no hurry," Tatum said with a quiet intensity that always made Harlowe's insides quiver. "But rest assured, I will treat Harlowe with the care and respect she deserves. When it's time to make a decision, we will certainly let you know."

"I know you'll take good care of my li'l punkin," Ben said. His eyes got bright as he pounded Tatum on the shoulder and pumped her hand. He swigged his beer and said, "Look, I want you to know, this all right here is your family. They took me in when I got with Jill, and now it's your turn. Before the, uh, kerfuffle, we had a meeting and took a vote. You're officially one of us." He gestured extravagantly, sending beer sloshing over the side of his glass. He quickly moved to slurp up as much as he could, lapping the foam off his shirt-sleeve. Harlowe held her head in her hands.

"Ben, there you are, honestly." Harlowe's mother came over to them with a bottle of whiskey in one hand and no sign of a glass anywhere. She grabbed her husband by his collar and tugged. "Come on, buckaroo, let's leave these two to enjoy their evening in peace."

She dragged a beer-stained and ketchup-encrusted Ben off, gulping from the bottle as she did so.

Harlowe wrinkled her nose. "Um, you can opt out of being an honorary member of this family if you want. I totally understand."

"It's all right," Tatum said. Her lips quirked up. "They're wonderful. I've never had a family, it might be nice to try it out."

"Okay, but feel free to trade them in for something more normal if you ever get the chance."

"Never," Tatum said.

"Hello lovelies," Danny popped up beside them. "How are you doing over here?"

"Just fine," Harlowe said. "Thanks for all this. The ceremony was beautiful. Sorry about the, um, brawling."

"All in a day's work," Danny said with a light flutter of his fingers. "I've seen much worse, believe me. Anyway, I'm not just here to hang out with you delightful people. I'm here with a quick reminder we're cutting the cake and then it's time for the first dance. Get ready, folks."

"Okay," Harlowe said. Danny elegantly exited stage left while she downed the rest of her drink for courage. In a small voice, Harlowe said, "I can do this. I won't fall on my ass in front of my entire family."

"You'll be fine," Tatum reached out and cupped Harlowe's cheek. "It's my honor to be your partner on the floor tonight, and every night."

"Only the floor?" Harlowe asked with a smirk. "How about the bed?"

"Definitely there too," Tatum replied. The look in her silver-blue eyes was far from chaste. "Make sure you get enough to eat. We still have a long night ahead of us. Hopefully."

Harlowe swallowed and licked her lips. "Oh yeah," she said.

The cake was cut with the ribbon-festooned sword, and served with appropriate ceremony. Once everyone had a generous piece, tapping on a wineglass silenced to the assembled guests. The soft background music faded. All eyes turned to Florian, who stood at the somewhat jumbled head table. He sheepishly rubbed a hand over his balding head and raised his cocktail-umbrella topped coconut. He bowed once to the in-person guests, then to the large screen.

"Thank you all for joining us today," Florian said. He held out a hand to Rockwell, who briefly grasped his fingers with a look of pure adoration that made Harlowe's heart squeeze. "We thought what passed between us was only our business, but it is not. I look at all of you, my precious family, and I know I have a duty to be open and honest. For my lovely great-niece, who has put me to shame with her openness." Here, Florian turned and looked directly at Harlowe. She squeaked and blushed under the sudden attention. He continued, "And for my newest great-nephew, Matthew, who is finally able to become the man he's always been. Congratulations on your new legal name. Nice peach-fuzz by the way, it looks grand on you, son." A warm wave of clapping and laughter met that remark. On the screen, a young man self-consciously rubbed the shadow of beard on his chin and grinned. Florian sobered and said, "For everyone who doesn't conform to the so-called normal, I realized that people from my generation paved the way for you by bravery and sacrifice. And so, even late, I decided it was time to do my part by setting an example for the future generations. Cheers!"

A great cheer went up and everybody guzzled their drinks. The lights dimmed and the empty dance floor was illuminated in a rainbow of spotlights that merged to white in the middle. Florian put down his empty coconut with a flourish and stood up with a twirl before taking his place on the dance floor with Rockwell.

Applause and cheering drowned the DJ's announcement out.

"Oh jeez oh jeez," Harlowe said, grabbing Tatum's hand and squeezing it. "I didn't think it would be so…spotlight-y. Is it too late to say pineapple?"

"Yes," Tatum said. She stood and offered her hand to Harlowe, which caused the entire assembly to break out into applause. The strains of some sappy melody filled the air, but Harlowe was only aware of Tatum's hand on her waist, her other hand guiding them in a slow spiral. Her mind went back to that day they first danced together in the middle of a snowstorm. How much had changed since then? How much had they grown and experienced together?

It hadn't been a smooth road, though. Especially that horrible night when Shelby shot Tatum and everything had gone to hell for a while. Harlowe felt like a lifetime had passed since that night. She was eager to put it behind her forever. At least Shelby was out of the way. The entire town was in the process of putting together a class-action lawsuit for the damage Shelby caused when the entire family up and vanished. Most people speculated they went down south or even as far as Mexico. Harlowe didn't care where they were, as long as it was far away from her and Tatum.

And what would their future hold? Harlowe wondered where their path would lead. All she knew was as long as Tatum was there with her, that was all she needed.

The romantic mood lasted until the end of the song, when the DJ put on a rocking selection of oldies that had even the most reticent of guests out on the dance floor. After a while, someone cued up a song on the karaoke machine and the party took a turn for the musical. Harlowe indulged her inner diva and took the stage a few times, not to be outdone by anyone.

After a particularly inspired duet with her Great-Aunt Florrie, Harlowe jumped off the stage and found Tatum, who was just tousled enough to be casually gorgeous. Tatum pulled Harlowe to her and said in her ear, "Are you ready to go home now?"

"Absolutely," Harlowe said.

On their way back to the cottage, Harlowe spotted a minivan pulling into the driveway. Soon, the second party would begin at McTavish's Pub, which had been reserved for them. The benefit of that venue was the pub was housed on the first floor of a roomy bed and breakfast, which was where the entire wedding party, *sans* Harlowe and Tatum, would be spending the night (and the next day recovering).

After seeing the other guests off, Harlowe made a bee-line for the master bedroom and skipped into the bathroom. She left the door wide open in invitation, not wanting to wait longer than absolutely necessary, and started brushing her teeth. Tatum slipped in behind her. Harlowe stuck her toothbrush into her mouth and offered the toothpaste. She rinsed her mouth just as Tatum was lathering up.

"Leave the dress on, and *only* the dress," Tatum said through her mouthful of toothpaste. She waggled her eyebrows in a silent promise of the good things to come that night.

"Okay," Harlowe said with an expectant thrill in her chest. While Tatum scrubbed up at the sink, Harlowe stripped off her stockings and panties and sat down on the toilet. When she was finished answering nature's call, she flushed, tossed her discarded underthings into the hamper, and stepped into the shower stall. Over her shoulder, Harlowe called, "Tae, can you help me with my skirt?"

"Of course," Tatum answered immediately. Harlowe turned around and grabbed the shower head while Tatum obligingly gathered up the fluffy layers of yellow chiffon. She wrapped her arms around Harlowe's waist, admirably holding the skirt up while enfolding Harlowe in a firm embrace. Harlowe soaped herself up while Tatum dropped a line of kisses down the side of her neck, causing Harlowe to moan.

"No fair, you're distracting me," Harlowe said. She tried to pout, but couldn't quite get there. The roughness of Tatum's trousers against her bare backside cranked up her arousal.

"You are so beautiful," Tatum whispered into her ear. "I can't wait to take you tonight. First, I want you on my lap, spread for me. Then I want you on your back. I'll take you deep and hard, I want to hear you lose control."

Harlowe whimpered. Unconsciously, her hips bucked. She wished it was Tatum's hand on her instead of the warm shower spray, teasing her tingling clit. As the months passed and they got more comfortable with each other, Tatum had started talking a lot more during intimacy, and Harlowe loved it. Although, when things got really hot, neither of them was very eloquent, which Harlowe also loved for the raw intimacy of it.

The last of the soapy suds spilled down her legs. Harlowe took the towel Tatum offered and quickly dried herself off.

"Do you need to go next?" Harlowe asked. She dropped her skirt over her nudity and turned around.

Already she was wet and throbbing, aching for Tatum's hand, and more, on her.

"No, I'm good," Tatum said. She held out a hand and steadied Harlowe as she stepped out of the shower. "I took a little side-trip while you and Florrie were serenading everyone from here to the moon."

"That was fun," Harlowe said with a giggle. She bit her lip and looked up at Tatum. "But not nearly as fun as the after party we'll have tonight." She stepped forward, lifting her chin in preparation for a kiss. Tatum met her, and the touch of her lips to Harlowe's was light, merely a brush across her skin. Harlowe gasped at the first meeting of their lips. The thrill of it electrified her, as if it really were the first. The unspoken promise of what was coming inflamed Harlowe. Her pulse thundered in her ears, her thighs grew sticky.

"Count to ten," Tatum whispered against her mouth. "Then you can come out."

Harlowe hadn't yet caught her breath to reply when Tatum turned and strode into the master bedroom. She counted out loud, shivering more with each one. Finally, she reached ten and slowly opened the door. Tatum had moved the chair to face her. She'd taken off her tie and unbuttoned her shirt enough for Harlowe to know she wasn't wearing anything underneath. The shadowed inner curves of her breasts half-hidden by the tailored menswear sent a shock of lust straight to Harlowe's clit. The bathroom door swung shut soundlessly behind her. Harlowe had the exquisite agony of walking across that room, unable to look away from the gorgeously sexy form of the woman who was the other half of her soul—the woman who was going to fuck her senseless in just a few minutes.

Each step brushed the filmy layers of her skirt over her naked skin, wetness streaking her thighs. Her inner muscles hummed with tension. Tatum's eyes focused on her, her breathing was deep but quick. When Harlowe was directly in front of her, Tatum lazily patted her hand on her thigh.

"I want you here, baby-girl," she said in a low husk. "Now."

A shiver gripped Harlowe. There was nowhere she'd rather be than slung open over those strong legs. Tatum wasn't going to be the only one tantalizing with a flash of skin, though. Harlowe got a naughty little smirk as she bent her knee and raised it, lifting her skirt slightly higher than necessary before she shimmied into place on Tatum's lap. The swoosh of cool air on her exposed lower region, coupled with Tatum's breathed, "Sweet God" told Harlowe she'd achieved her goal.

Tatum's hands stole under her skirt, stroking up and down Harlowe's legs, trailing enticingly up her inner thighs, only to dance away before they reached the apex. Harlowe arched her back, spreading her knees wider, offering herself completely. With a soft chuckle, Tatum didn't take the invitation. Instead, she leaned into Harlowe, dropping kisses onto the side of her neck. Each brush of Tatum's lips sent shivers of anticipation through Harlowe. Her breath came hard and fast. She bit down on her lower lip as a raw moan tumbled from her throat.

"God, Tatum, I need you," Harlowe gasped out. "Can't wait any more."

"Hold on to me," Tatum murmured into her ear.

Harlowe whimpered a *yes* and wrapped her arms around Tatum's broad shoulders. The first brush of Tatum's fingers to her jolted another moan from Harlowe. She ached to be filled. Her heart pounded. Tatum very gently parted her and ran her fingertips up and down Harlowe's length.

"There you are," Tatum said. "So wet for me. Good girl. My good girl."

"Please," Harlowe panted.

Tatum rose up against her, claiming Harlowe's lips with hers in a hard, raw kiss. Harlowe opened her mouth to Tatum, gleefully taking her tongue deep. At the same time, Tatum pushed into her. Harlowe held still for a moment, loving the feeling of Tatum within her. She was buried to the hilt. Her palm cupped Harlowe perfectly, putting just the right amount of pressure on her clit.

"Oh fuck," Tatum whispered. She broke the kiss, breathing hard. Under her tailored vest, her chest heaved. "Fuck, you're so good, so sweet."

A hand snaked around Harlowe's hip and slowly, smoothly, Harlowe moved. She pulled away, feeling the slick glide of Tatum's penetrating fingers before she thrust hard and took her deep once more. Their breaths merged, coming in rhythmic bursts. Like waves on the shore, Harlowe kept up the seductive pace. Her body hummed with pleasure. Her wetness covered them both. The smack of slick flesh filled the room. Tatum's eyes drifted half-closed. Under Harlowe's bare ass, Tatum's thighs clenched together, then spread slightly. The hand Harlowe rode lowered, nestling into Tatum's crotch.

"Keep going," Tatum gritted. "Fuck that's good."

Harlowe replied with a whimper that turned into an openmouthed moan as Tatum urged her faster, harder. The inevitable rise to climax started. Harlowe's inner muscles grew heavy and tight. She couldn't stop. Tatum's quickened breaths drove her. The peak rose within her. Harlowe didn't care if she wrecked her dress, or spilled on Tatum's suit trousers. She needed to come. She thrust hard one last time, clenched, then shuddered hard as the wave broke. Tatum bucked under her, arching back in her own release with a grunt. Harlowe panted into the air, shivering as the rapid jolts of her climax broke over her. Her sex throbbed, her inner muscles trembled. She slowly eased back and forward, impaled fully and not letting go. Her clit rubbed over Tatum's palm, sliding easily. This time, the feeling came from outside of her, the wondrous pleasure she wanted to savor. The intimacy of trusting Tatum with her most precious place. Harlowe hummed with renewed arousal.

"Not done yet, are you baby-girl?" Tatum asked. She licked her lips and parted her legs further, drawing Harlowe to her.

"Uh huh," was all Harlowe could get out. One sleeve slipped down over her shoulder and the bodice of her dress started to sag. Harlowe let it, she wanted to be bare before Tatum. She ground her clit against Tatum's hand, needing the friction. Her other sleeve went down, now Harlowe's breasts were exposed, the tight pink nipples just peeking over the neckline.

"I need this off you," Tatum said. She stroked her

free hand up from Harlowe's backside until she tugged at the zipper. Harlowe wriggled in pleasure as the dress fell, draped around her hips like a voluminous, fluffy wreath of daffodil-colored chiffon. She let her breasts swing with a shimmy of her hips. Tatum's eyes tracked her hungrily. She breathed, "Gorgeous. Now up and over to the bed."

Tatum withdrew from her softly, lingering to swirl one last wet pass over Harlowe's tingling clit. On weak legs, Harlowe rose. Her dress fell to the floor and she stepped out of it, free and ready for anything. Harlowe's belly grew warm and heavy with desire. She wanted Tatum to hold her down, spread her wide and take her over once more. Her thighs trembled. Her sex pulsed. Harlowe slowly went over to the bed and sat down on the fluffy comforter. It billowed out around her. She leaned back on her hands, extremely aware of Tatum's attention. She was focused on Harlowe as if her life depended on it. Harlowe felt powerful, loved, and treasured. Her breaths deepened. She slowly opened her legs and parted herself. Arousal fluttered into life when Tatum's piercing eyes travelled downwards.

Harlowe tilted her head and asked, "Do you want this?"

"Fuck yes," Tatum gritted.

"Come and take it, then." Harlowe said.

Tatum rose from the armchair, smooth and gentlemanly once more. She tugged down her sleeves and unbuttoned her shirt. The loose vest came off first, followed closely by the shirt. Her movements got rougher the closer she came to Harlowe, finishing by pulling her trousers and boxer briefs off all at once and kicking them away. This time Harlowe was the one enthralled. Tatum's body had always aroused her, and now that she knew each plane and crevice, the feelings were only amplified. Under her sculpted belly, framed by a dark, damp thatch, Tatum's sex was thick and flushed, visceral evidence that she'd just come. Harlowe wanted that body on her, she wanted Tatum's wet, spread lips pumping over her. She wanted to grip that tight ass and feel it clench and release. But first, there was something she wanted more.

Tatum eased one knee onto the bed and slowly came to lie down next to Harlowe. Her lips quirked up in a brief smile before she bowed her head and kissed a slow path down over Harlowe's throat, taking time to torment her nipples and buff her hands over the fullness of Harlowe's breasts.

"God, you're so beautiful," Tatum whispered. Her breath played over Harlowe's wet nipple, drawing a moan of longing from her. "What do you want, baby-girl?"

"Your mouth," Harlowe said impatiently. She pointed down. "There."

Tatum's chuckle tickled her sensitive skin. With one last lingering swipe of her tongue, Tatum raised herself on to her hands and eased her body down Harlowe's length. When she was in position, Harlowe bent her knees and spread her legs, welcoming Tatum to her. Tatum didn't waste any time before she went to work, cradling Harlowe's hips in her arms as her mouth plundered Harlowe's folds, then latched onto her clit with merciless attention before she took Harlowe. With a cry of ecstasy, Harlowe threw her head back and rolled her hips, greedily taking the plundering tongue. Tatum returned to her clit, working her tongue in tight circles, demanding Harlowe to submit.

"Oh God, oh *fuck*, yes Tae..." The gasped words trailed off into moans. Harlowe's breathing picked up, getting more ragged with each pass over her throbbing clit. Sparks started to swarm her vision. Her inner muscles squeezed. *Not yet, please, not yet*, she thought wildly to herself. Harlowe's hand closed over the base of Tatum's ponytail.

"Up," Harlowe managed to squeeze out. "Up here. Finish with me."

Tatum raised her head, her lips and chin were gloriously shiny with Harlowe's essence. She made a move to wipe it off, but Harlowe was having none of that. She shimmied down until they were eye-to-eye. Tatum's long body rested on hers, held between Harlowe's spread legs. Without another thought, Harlowe drew Tatum into a messy kiss, only breaking it after both of them were breathing hard.

"So sexy," Tatum said. Her eyes fluttered for a moment before she squared her shoulders and bore down, pressing her firm, hot sex to Harlowe's. "Here?"

"Uhn, yes, right there." Harlowe caught her lip between her teeth. She was doubly glad all the guests and staff had long gone, and her only neighbor was currently locked between her legs because Harlowe was about to get loud. "Ah!" she cried out at the next deep thrust. She couldn't help it, even if she didn't know Tatum loved hearing her. Harlowe pulled her knees back, opening herself fully to Tatum. They slid easily, slick with both of their arousal, Tatum's clit was firm on hers, pumping against her. Harlowe was primed to come, it wasn't going to take much. She wanted Tatum to come with her. Tatum's body was hard and taut. By the tension in her jaw and the heat of Tatum's sex, Harlowe was sure she was close too. She cried out with each thrust, welcoming Tatum home. She couldn't stop.

The rhythm broke. On her, Tatum shuddered and let go with a deep groan. That set Harlowe off. She was helpless to resist, and let the climax take her. Her throat rebelled at the volume of her moans. Unholy sounds came from her. Harlowe's hips jerked reflexively, her thighs tightened, holding Tatum's hips. With one hand under Harlowe's backside, Tatum thrust against her, long and slow, riding out the last fading swells of orgasm. Harlowe's moans faded to long sighs.

"So good, yes, my good girl," Tatum murmured. She sucked in a breath, gently rocking their bodies together. The urgency was gone, leaving pure love and a very satisfied feeling in its wake. Harlowe stretched lazily and folded herself into Tatum's arms.

"Are you all right?" Tatum asked. She always asked, and that made Harlowe feel cherished.

"Uh huh," she replied eloquently. Harlowe nuzzled into the crook of Tatum's neck, savoring her scent and warmth. "You?"

"Extremely all right," Tatum said. She lazily drew a hand up and down Harlowe's back. "I guess it's true what they say about people hooking up at weddings."

Harlowe giggled. "We need to go to more weddings,

then."

"I'll pass on the wedding part," Tatum said. She waggled her eyebrows. "But I'm down with hooking up."

Harlowe rolled her eyes in mock annoyance before she snuggled against Tatum once more.

****

"You've been quiet," Harlowe said. She turned down the volume of the Supergirl episode they were watching. "Does that mean I tired you out so much you're not even laughing at my witty commentary?"

"What?" Tatum straightened up. She shook her head. "Sorry, Sweet pea. I was...thinking."

"Okay, that's allowed." Harlowe snuggled deeper into her bunny robe before she pulled her sock feet up to sit cross-legged on the sofa. She glanced at Tatum one more time before she reached for the remote. Silent Tatum wasn't anything new; she was generally a quiet person, but something was different about her silence that night. If something was bothering her, she'd talk about it when she was ready. Harlowe settled back into the comfortable sofa, absorbed in the episode. She felt extremely relaxed and sated after their post-wedding private party, without much room for other emotions. Her eyes were drifting closed when Tatum suddenly stood up. Her jaw was set, her shoulders squared.

Without another word, Tatum strode out of the room, with her nightshirt hem flapping about her long legs. Alarmed, Harlowe paused the episode and looked around worriedly. Just as she was wondering if it was a good idea to go after her, Tatum reappeared. Her hands were cupped around something and her face was set. She crossed the small living room and sank to one knee before Harlowe.

"I have something for you," Tatum said. She shook back the stubborn fall of bangs that fell across her face. "Um, it's not what you think. I have an explanation."

"Go ahead," Harlowe said. "I'm here. I'm listening."

Tatum was silent for a moment, head bowed in the same way she had months ago the first time she revealed her past to Harlowe. It had been hard for her to speak then, and something equally weighty seemed to be on her mind that night. Then Tatum looked up, her silver-blue eyes sorrowful, but not drowned with the endless, hopeless sorrow she once had.

"Before I met you, I lived in the darkness," Tatum said. "I wasn't even living. I was afraid of the light. You, Harlowe, you brought light back to my life. You led me back to a place where I wasn't afraid to live. More than that, you showed me how to find the light inside myself."

With that, she opened her hands, revealing a small jewelry box.

"Oh my God," Harlowe breathed. Her heart pounded.

"I had it made for you, Sweet pea," Tatum said and opened the box. Inside was a shining gold ring, set with two gems, one sparkling white, one deep purple. They were cleverly cut and placed together to make a yin-yang symbol. It was exquisite in design and detail.

Inside, Harlowe was squealing with joy and wondering who she should tell first. But she couldn't jump to conclusions.

"It's beautiful," Harlowe said.

"It's a promise ring," Tatum said. "A promise that I will never go back to the darkness. A promise that I won't turn my back on you like I've done before. The future is ours, but I don't think the time is right for either of us to make any permanent decisions. I wanted you to have this, a concrete reminder of my promise to you." Tatum stopped and looked uncomfortable.

Harlowe couldn't stay still. She bypassed the ring box and threw herself into Tatum's arms. Tatum caught her with an *oof* and held her tightly.

"You have the most beautiful soul of anyone I've ever met," Harlowe said. She moved back, now on her knees as well, on the same level as Tatum. "I can't think of anything I'd rather do than wear your ring. Would you put it on me?"

Hesitantly, she looked down at her hands. Which finger should she go for? Tatum saved her by gently taking her right hand and slipping the ring onto her ring finger.

"For now," Tatum said with an intense look in her

eyes that froze Harlowe.

"Wow, it's really nice," Harlowe held up her hand and studied the sparkling gems. With a mischievous giggle, she said, "And to think, I only cleared out a drawer for you."

Tatum laughed low in her throat. "I am very appreciative of that."

Harlowe jumped up. She wanted to dance and sing. She wanted to take a hundred photos of her ring, the ring Tatum had given her, and send them to everyone she knew before she plastered it on the front page of the Maritime Gazette. Instead, she got comfy on the sofa and patted the empty cushion beside her.

"That's all very well and good, but we have the rest of the episode to watch."

Tatum rose with a smooth elegance and settled down beside Harlowe. She looked much more at ease than before. She put an arm around Harlowe and pulled her close, kissing her on the temple. Harlowe resumed the episode and basked in her newfound happiness. The ring on her finger seemed light, as if she'd been given the keys to the sky. She looked up. Tatum met her gaze with strength and confidence that didn't waver. The darkness was gone, replaced by the light of pure love.

THE END

About the Author

Mildred Gail Digby's favorite thing to do is add women-loving-women to any situation and make a novel about it. She will squeeze a happy ending out of anything and still blushes when she writes love scenes.

Bringing rainbow stories to life.

Flashpoint Publications welcomes submissions from writers of every color and books featuring characters of every color. In addition, Flashpoint Publications encourages job applicants of every color whenever a staff position becomes available. We believe that EVERYONE is entitled to a seat at our table.

www.flashpointpublications.com